THREEFOLD DEATH

THREEFOLD DEATH

E.R. DILLON

FIVE STAR
A part of Gale, Cengage Learning

GALE
CENGAGE Learning

Farmington Hills, Mich • San Francisco • New York • Waterville, Maine
Meriden, Conn • Mason, Ohio • Chicago

GALE
CENGAGE Learning·

LIBRARY OF CONGRESS CATALOGING-IN-PUBLICATION DATA

Names: Dillon, E. R., author.
Title: Threefold death / E.R. Dillon.
Description: First Edition. | Waterville, Maine : Five Star, a part of Cengage Learning, Inc. 2016. | Description based on print version record and CIP data provided by publisher; resource not viewed.
Identifiers: LCCN 2016006085 (print) | LCCN 2016001560 (ebook) | ISBN 9781432831974 (ebook) | ISBN 1432831976 (ebook) | ISBN 9781432832025 (hardback) | ISBN 1432832026 (hardcover)
Subjects: LCSH: Murder—Investigation—Fiction. | Scotland—History—1057–1603—Fiction. | BISAC: FICTION / Mystery & Detective / Historical. | FICTION / Mystery & Detective / Police Procedural. | GSAFD: Mystery fiction | Historical fiction
Classification: LCC PS3604.I462 (print) | LCC PS3604.I462 T58 2016 (ebook) | DDC 813/.6—dc23
LC record available at http://lccn.loc.gov/2016006085

First Edition. First Printing: July 2016
Find us on Facebook– https://www.facebook.com/FiveStarCengage
Visit our website– http://www.gale.cengage.com/fivestar/
Contact Five Star™ Publishing at FiveStar@cengage.com

Printed in the United States of America
1 2 3 4 5 6 7 20 19 18 17 16

To my son, Paul J. Tuger, whose vivid imagination and knowledge of the Middle Ages proved to be a valuable resource to me in writing the second story in this series.

ACKNOWLEDGMENTS

My thanks and appreciation to Frances Faber and Rebecca Lovingood, both of whom contributed their time and effort to the historical and grammatical accuracy of this story.

Special thanks to Steve Kleyle for his assistance with the graphics.

HISTORICAL NOTES

Prior Drumlay served at the religious house of St. John's Church in Ayrshire in thirteenth-century Scotland. He was a contemporary of William Wallace, the Scottish patriot who revolted against English oppression during the Scottish Wars.

John Langton, Canon of Lincoln and Lord High Chancellor to the King of England (died 1337). Langton was a clerk in the royal chancery who became chancellor in 1292. He resigned that office in 1302 and was consecrated as Bishop of Chichester in 1305. He again became chancellor shortly after the accession of Edward II in 1307. One of his accomplishments was building the chapterhouse at Chichester. He was also a benefactor of the University of Oxford. He died on July 19, 1337.

Sir Henry de Percy, Eighth Baron Percy (1273–1314). Sir Percy fought under King Edward I of England in Wales and Scotland and was granted extensive estates in Scotland, which were later retaken by the Scots under Robert Bruce. Edward I appointed Sir Percy as Castellan of Ayr and Warden of Galloway, circa 1296. Sir Percy died at the age of forty-one, of unknown causes.

ALL OTHER CHARACTERS in this novel are fictitious, as is Kilgate Manor, Cragston Castle, and Cragston Forest. Any similarity to actual persons or locations is entirely coincidental.

CHAPTER 1

July 1297

Ayrshire, Scotland

The slanting rays of the rising sun penetrated the gloom beneath the wharf on the south bank of the River Ayr. Light shimmered on the glassy surface of the water, broken only by eddies swirling around the timber piers supporting the long wooden dock.

The body of a dead man bobbed gently between two of those stout piers. He floated face down in the water, his arms splayed, his russet cloak snagged on a rope securing one of the fishing boats moored there.

Kyle Shaw, Deputy to the Sheriff of Ayrshire, swung down from the saddle and went over to join Vinewood and Hoprig on the wharf. He towered head and shoulders above both English soldiers, owing his lofty stature to his Viking forebears, who also endowed him with tawny hair and blue eyes as pale as a northern sky.

He leaned out over the edge to peer down at the body. "Fetch him ashore, will you?" he said.

Vinewood and Hoprig walked up the wharf until they came to the place where they could descend to the river that flowed into the Firth of Clyde a short distance away. They waded in waist-deep water to reach the dead man. Only the ebb of the firth's outgoing tide enabled them to gain access to the body trapped under the dock.

Hoprig disentangled the cloak from around the water-stiffened rope, while Vinewood hung onto the dead man's belt to keep him from being swept out to sea. When the body swung free, the pair of them towed it upriver for several yards to a sandy place where they could drag it onto the bank.

Water streamed from their clothing and that of the drowned man as they hoisted the dead weight of the body up the gentle slope. They laid it on the embankment just as they'd found it in the river, face downward.

Kyle descended the river bank to look at the body. He went down on one knee in the damp grass to draw aside the sodden cloak, which was cold to the touch and reeked with the smell of the river. There were no slashes or other indications of violence on the garment that he could readily see.

"Help me turn him over," he said to Vinewood.

He and the young soldier laid hands on the rigid limbs to roll the body onto its back.

Kyle gazed at the dead man lying in uneasy repose on the lush carpet of green clover. There was no sign of bloating on the lean features, nor had the crabs started in on him yet. That meant he went into the water late on Sunday, perhaps during the early hours on Monday.

The upturned face was clean-shaven in the Norman fashion. The high-bridged patrician nose and the stubborn chin laid claim to that same heritage. Thin lips tinged with blue framed the slack mouth, and sightless gray eyes stared up at the cloudless sky. His complexion, tanned deep gold by the summer sun, seemed unaffected by the pallor of death. His gray hair, now slick with water, put him at or near fifty years of age. He appeared to be a tall man, though with his body stretched out on the ground, it was difficult to gauge his actual height. He wore a jacket-like cotte of dark green velvet, with leggings to match. An oak-leaf-and-acorn pattern decorated the tooled leather belt around his waist. A polished carnelian adorned the hilt of the dagger in the silver sheath attached to the belt.

There was no doubt in Kyle's mind that this was a man of means, but the question of his identity remained unanswered. A cursory inspection of the front of the body presented no reason to suspect foul play. Perhaps the drowning was accidental, after all.

That conclusion only opened the door to still more unanswered questions. Did the man fall into the river? Did the undertow suck him down to his death? Was he pushed in? Why did he not cry for help? How did he fetch up here under the busiest wharf in the port town of Ayr? Where was the ever-present squire or servant who accompanied their lord on every outing?

As Kyle pondered these and other questions, a handful of fishermen from the harbor began to collect around the dead man sprawled on the riverbank. Their occupation was by nature perilous, and thus, drowning was a fate that might befall any one of them at any time. They shook their heads and murmured among themselves, yet not a single one came forward to name the victim.

Kyle closed the staring gray eyes with his thumb and forefinger. He unpinned the brooch that fastened the soggy folds of the russet cloak at the dead man's neck, after which he removed the cloak to cover the body with it.

He rose to his feet and brushed away the bits of sand and grass that clung to his brown leggings. The brooch in his hand was a simple affair in the form of a bronze ring and a pin. The flat part of the pin and the face of the ring were decorated with the same oak-leaf-and-acorn pattern that was imprinted on the leather belt. He tucked the piece into the pouch at his side for safekeeping.

The clop of hooves on the cobblestone street brought his head around.

The blacksmith approached the scene on a dappled gray horse. He was a great bear of a man, big-boned with broad shoulders and powerful arms suited to his craft. His sleeveless brown tunic, belted at the waist, reached to mid-thigh on his muscular legs.

"Macalister," Kyle said by way of greeting. "Where are you bound at this early hour?"

Macalister reined in and rested his forearms on the saddle bow. "The garrison stable," he said. "Sir Percy wants me to look over the horses." His brown eyes settled on the shrouded form on the ground. "Who have ye there?"

"I'm not sure," Kyle said. "We just pulled him from the river."

"A Southron?"

"More than likely."

Macalister grunted. "I'll take their trade, but I won't mourn their passing," he said, his bearded face grim. "I'll leave ye to it, my friend." He nudged the gray horse in the belly with his heels and continued down Harbour Street toward the garrison gates.

Kyle thought nothing of Macalister's remark. Most Scots hated the English, whose unwanted occupation of Scotland for the past ten years had brought hardship and oppression.

Early in that period of unrest, King Balliol of Scotland led a revolt against Edward of England. The uprising soon ended with Balliol's capture and imprisonment in the Tower of London. Without a king on the Scottish throne to oppose him, King Edward saw his way clear to claim feudal overlordship of Scotland. As such, he would receive a substantial portion of the taxes collected, in addition to utilizing Scotland's natural resources.

The Scots were willing to comply with the English king's material demands upon them, since they were already bound by law to pay their taxes. However, the King of England did not take into consideration the loyalty of the Scottish populace to the imprisoned king. When Edward demanded fealty from them as well, he only heaped fuel on the fires of rebellion.

A small crowd began to gather nearby to gawk at the body. Among them was a thin man of indeterminate age in dun-colored homespun, with dark eyes and a crooked nose in his long face. He kept glancing around, as though looking for someone in particular. He seemed relieved when a man in a brown tunic walked up to stand next to him.

The newcomer was a lean man in his thirties. Fine white mud smudged the front of his clothing. His coloring was like cast bronze, his nose curved like the blade of a scimitar. His hooded eyes were golden brown, like those of a hawk, with a gaze as direct and fearless as that bird of prey. His close-cropped black hair gleamed with blue highlights in the early morning light. He looked out of place among the fair-skinned Scottish folk around him.

Kyle singled out the thin man with the crooked nose for questioning, mostly because of the nervous sweat that slicked his brow. "What is your name?" he said.

"Simon," he said, fidgeting with the knot in the hemp rope that served as a belt around his narrow waist.

"Did you see anything out of the ordinary around here earlier?" Kyle said.

"Nay," Simon said, licking his lips. "I didn't see nothing."

"How about you?" Kyle said to the swarthy man in the brown tunic. "Did you notice any strangers hanging around the dock shortly before dawn?"

"Not that I recall," the man said. He spoke in a melodious voice with a hint of a foreign accent.

"What is your name?" Kyle said.

"Turval," he said, regarding him steadily.

"I know you," Kyle said. His eyes flicked briefly to the streaks of dried mud on the man's tunic. "You're the potter."

"So I am," Turval said with a slight smile. He waved a careless hand at the smudges on his clothing. "You must excuse my appearance. It is a hazard of my trade. I have a stall at the marketplace where I sell my wares. You might have seen me there."

"Maybe so," Kyle said. He let his gaze wander over the others looking on. Their expressions ranged from curiosity to puzzlement, which convinced him that none of them knew anything about either the dead man or how he ended up in the river. "Sergeant," he said, catching Vinewood's eye. "See if you can find a cart to transport the body, will you?"

"Aye," Vinewood said. He hurried off on foot to do as he was bidden, leaving behind a trail of water dripping from his black leather jerkin and gray woolen leggings.

Kyle liked the personable young man. Women liked Vinewood, too, because of his handsome face, engaging smile, and seductive brown eyes. By contrast, Hoprig was a dour fellow around his own age of thirty-three, slight of build, with reddish-blond hair, blue eyes, and sharp features in a lean face.

Kyle noticed Hoprig gazing down at the shrouded form, his fair brows locked in a pensive knot.

That was nothing unusual, for Hoprig's face was normally set in a habitual frown. This time, however, the frown seemed deeper and more thoughtful.

"Do you recognize him?" Kyle said, his pale blue eyes on Hoprig.

"Maybe," Hoprig said, as though unwilling to commit in the event he was wrong. He dropped to one knee and turned back the corner of the cloak to peer at the waxen features. "He puts me in mind of the Rylands. I don't know which one this is, though."

"How many are there?" Kyle said.

"Let me see," Hoprig said, ticking their number on his

fingers. "There is Sir Fulbert, the Master of Cragston Castle. There is his brother, Sir Humphrey. Then, there is his son, Sir Peter." He shook his head emphatically. "He's much too old for Sir Peter, so this must be Sir Fulbert." He dropped the corner of the cloak in place and climbed to his feet. "Or his brother," he added in a tone that indicated it was possible, but not probable.

"I don't know much about Sir Humphrey," Kyle said. "I did hear about Sir Fulbert and his heroic exploits in the Holy Land during the last crusade."

He also heard that Sir Fulbert Ryland was an English nobleman who held Scottish lands granted to him for services rendered to Edward of England. If the drowned man was indeed Sir Fulbert, he was rather far from home, for Cragston Castle was located four miles south of Ayr on the western coast of the lowlands. With the Scottish populace chafing under the harsh yoke of English domination and rebel activity on the rise, it was no surprise that an Englishman turned up dead. Yet, there was nothing here to suggest that a crime had actually been committed.

"That's what they say about him," Hoprig said.

"And you don't believe it?" Kyle said.

Hoprig turned on him, his expression harsh and bleak. "My father went on that crusade with Sir Fulbert and the others," he said. "The things he saw there haunted him for the rest of his days."

"What sort of things?" Kyle said, his interest piqued.

The rumble of wooden wheels on cobblestones effectively interrupted their conversation.

Vinewood and two local men in homespun tunics were coming up the street, pushing before them an empty flat-bed cart commonly used to haul sacks of milled grain. They came to a grinding halt close to where Kyle stood on the bank of the river.

"It was the best I could do on short notice," Vinewood said, dusting the flour residue from his hands. "I thought I could hitch my horse to it and pull it around to St. John's."

"That ought to work," Kyle said. He turned to Hoprig. "Ride over to John Logan's shop and have him meet us at the priory as soon as he can get there."

Hoprig nodded, rather than verbally acknowledging the direct order given to him by the Scots deputy to whom he had been assigned. Silence was evidently his way of defying the tall, tawny-haired Scotsman's authority without being overtly disrespectful. There was apparently nothing personal in his animosity. Being English, he treated everyone of Scottish descent the same way. In addition, the wet clothing flapping around his legs did little to improve his mood. He trudged up the embankment toward a chestnut mare with a cream-colored mane and tail. His waterlogged boots made a squishing sound with each step he took.

Vinewood and the townsmen with him descended the slope to pick up the body. They carried it back to the cart, where they laid it on the flat wooden bed. Vinewood then buckled his horse into the traces and gathered the reins in his hand, ready to move out at Kyle's signal.

Now that the excitement was over, Simon and Turval drifted away with the other on-lookers. The fishermen went back to their boats to mend torn nets or sharpen fishhooks in preparation for the next outing on the firth.

Kyle climbed into the saddle and urged his sorrel gelding to walk forward. He set out up Harbour Street ahead of the cart, bound for St. John's on the far side of the marketplace situated on the open stretch of sandy ground between the wall of the priory and the wall of the English garrison.

Good news was known to spread swiftly. Bad news, it seemed, traveled even faster. Customers at the marketplace early on

Monday morning apparently heard about the drowning, and for a brief moment, they turned their backs on the lure of colorful stalls and striped canopies. They lined up on either side of Harbour Street, standing shoulder to shoulder with merchants and vendors, peddlers and traders, to watch the horse-drawn cart jounce past them over the uneven cobbles. Even children paused at play to stare at the body swathed in russet fabric.

At first, only the two townsmen who helped Vinewood load the body trailed behind the cart. Soon, others joined them, so that the procession grew larger with each passing moment. When they reached the priory, Kyle led them through the open gates in the precinct wall. He reined in at the gatehouse and dismounted as the porter, a rotund monk clad in a long brown robe, came out into the bright morning sunshine to greet him.

"Good morrow, Master Deputy," the porter said with solemnity appropriate to the occasion. "It is a sad day, indeed, for the poor fellow. Ye may bring him to the mortuary chapel." He waved a hand in the direction of the large red sandstone edifice with the lofty bell tower that dominated the priory grounds. "Ye know the way."

Vinewood tugged on the reins, and his horse obliged by leaning against the harness. Those behind the cart pushed on the wagon bed until the solid wooden wheels, which were sunk to the hub in the deep gravel in the entryway, rolled forward.

"I'm glad you're back," Vinewood said to Kyle, who fell in step beside him with the gelding in tow.

Six weeks earlier, Kyle traveled to Aberdeen to visit Joneta, a lovely widow with whom he had fallen in love. He only meant to stay for a few days. While he was there, though, Joneta's mother-in-law died. The woman was quite elderly and suffered from a terminal illness, so her death was not wholly unexpected. He stayed for the burial, after which he brought Joneta and her five-month-old baby back to Ayr with him. Upon their arrival yesterday afternoon, he took her to her house a couple of miles down the coast. He went on to the sheriff's office, which was located within the walls of Ayr Garrison, and fell into bed, exhausted from the long journey. That was where he remained until roused from his sleep a little more than an hour ago.

"Did anything happen during my absence that I should know about?" he said.

"Sir Percy finally appointed a new Captain of Horse," Vinewood said.

"What is he like?"

"He's tough and demanding. Suspicious, too. He's the sort who sees a rebel around every corner."

"Unfortunately for the new Captain of Horse, there is a rebel around every corner these days. What is his name?"

"Anthony Morhouse."

An involuntary groan escaped from Kyle's lips.

"I take it you know him," Vinewood said, eyeing the pained expression on the deputy's face.

"That is putting it mildly," Kyle said. "While I was courting Ada Monroe, he pestered her with his attentions, unwelcome though they were to her. After we married, he never passed up an opportunity to corner her, just to talk, or so he claimed. She refused to let me 'persuade' him to leave her alone. She knew I would get into trouble if I laid a hand on an officer in the King's army. We ended up moving inland to get away from him."

A thoughtful expression crossed Vinewood's handsome face. "That explains his undue interest when Sir Percy mentioned your appointment here as deputy."

"Really?" Kyle said. "All of that happened over fifteen years ago. Besides, Ada has been dead for six years now."

"I'm sorry," Vinewood said.

"I am, too," Kyle said grimly.

The two of them walked in silence as they led the procession up the long driveway and around to the mortuary chapel built against the back of the church.

They stopped before the arched door barring entry to the chapel. The solid oaken panels below the pointed arch were stained green with lichens that blended into the verdant surroundings.

The chapel itself was made of quarried stone, with a thick layer of sod covering its sloping roof. It huddled in the shadows without windows or other apertures, which by design kept the interior cool, even on hot summer days.

Those in the procession broke ranks to form a half-circle around the cart. They all watched as two monks in long brown robes strode purposefully across the priory yard toward the chapel.

The younger monk kept pace with the older monk, who carried under his arm a folded cloth of unbleached linen and whose keys clanked with each step.

"Prior Drumlay," Kyle said as the older monk drew near. "I trust you are well."

Prior Drumlay ignored the greeting. "Master Shaw," he said with a downward turn of his narrow, implacable mouth. "So, ye came back, did ye?" He was a cantankerous Scotsman in his late forties. Despite the untidy gray tonsure and frayed robe draped around his compact body, there was an astute intelligence in the gray eyes staring out from under bristling brows. Even though his manner was brusque, he had a reputation for being a good administrator over the priory and a good shepherd to the fourteen monks in his care.

"Of course, I came back," Kyle said. "This is my home."

Prior Drumlay glanced over at the body on the cart. "Who do ye have there?"

"A nobleman, by the look of him," Kyle said.

"One of ours?" the prior said. He looked concerned.

"He's English," Kyle said.

The prior appeared relieved. "No sense in leaving him out in this heat," he said. He selected one of the keys on the iron ring at his waist and turned it in the latch to open the chapel door. He handed the bundle of linen to the young monk, who went over to the cart to unfold the cloth beside the body along its length.

Kyle stepped forward to lend a hand in shifting the dead man onto the long cloth. He and the young monk each took an end and lifted the body clear of the wooden bed. They carried it through the arched doorway and set it gently on the table-like slab of stone in the middle of the square chamber.

The chapel felt refreshingly cool after the warmth outside. The odor of stale incense masked the dank earthy smell within. There was an iron lamp stand in the corner, and a door on the far wall that provided access to the church vestry. A gray and white granite altar stood against a side wall, and a tiny vessel on its polished surface emitted a greenish glow that disappeared in the muted daylight coming through the open door. Sturdy timber beams supported the heavy sod roof above the slanted ceiling. The four stone walls were bare, except for the wooden crucifix that hung over the altar.

When Kyle and the young monk stepped back outside, the prior shut the chapel door behind them without locking it.

Since there was now nothing more to see, the onlookers lost interest and began to shuffle away. Vinewood departed with them to return the borrowed cart to its owner.

"It's too dark in there for Master John to examine the body," Kyle said to the prior. "He will need a proper light."

The prior scowled, as though he was about to disagree. After a moment, he jerked his head meaningfully at the young monk, who hastened away in obedience to the unspoken command.

The young monk returned before long with a lighted clay

cresset suspended from a thin chain.

A few minutes later, Vinewood and Hoprig rode up to the chapel and swung down from their saddles.

John Logan followed close behind the two English soldiers on an old brown mule. He was a good-looking man in his early fifties, with a full head of steel gray hair and shrewd green eyes. His tan linen tunic was bound at the waist with a leather belt. As he slid from the battered saddle, Prior Drumlay welcomed him with a smile.

It was obvious the prior liked the apothecary, who used his knowledge of herbs and medicines to help the poor in the shire as well as the rich.

After exchanging a polite greeting with the prior, John unhooked the strap of his leather medicament bag from around the saddle bow and slung it over his shoulder. "How was yer journey?" he said to Kyle.

"Long, but entirely agreeable," Kyle said. "Joneta and her wee bairn traveled back with me."

"What about her mother-in-law?"

"She passed away five weeks ago."

"Ah, well," John said with a nod of sympathy. "It's a wonder she lived as long as she did." He tilted his head toward the mortuary chapel. "Is it truly Sir Fulbert in there?" he said.

"Possibly," Kyle said. "Hoprig seems to think so."

"Lead the way, then" John said, with a sweep of his hand toward the arched door.

"Give the fire holder to me, brother," Prior Drumlay said to the young monk. "Then you may go."

The young monk handed over the clay cresset without a word and scurried away.

The prior opened the chapel door and went inside, with Kyle and John on his heels.

Kyle once again caught a glimpse of the elusive radiance that vanished before his eyes. He walked over to the altar to inspect the contents of the tiny vessel, which looked like fine powder. "I know I saw a light over here," he said, puzzled.

"You did," John said. "The monks call it cold fire. They use it in this chapel because it glows in the dark without heat."

"How clever," Kyle said with appreciation.

The prior hung the lighted cresset on the iron lamp stand, which he moved closer to the table. Yellow light from the burning wick illuminated not only the shrouded form, but every corner of the small chamber.

John removed the russet cloak from over the body, folded it, and set it aside. The rigor gripping the limbs made it difficult for him to undress the dead man, so after removing the belt, he slit the clothing from neck to groin with his dagger. He laid back the green velvet cotte to expose the vest-like garment beneath, which was woven from the coarse hair of goats. Red patches riddled the chest and stomach area where the prickly fibers irritated the skin. "What have we here?" he said.

"That is a hair shirt," the prior said, crossing himself. "This man was a true penitent, a Southron though he be." He crossed himself again. "God rest his soul."

It was common for a monk or a priest to repent of past sins by wearing under his robe a shirt made of scratchy fibers or bristly animal hair. A cleric so disposed might also fast at length to mortify the flesh, or flagellate his own back by using a whip with metal shards tied to the end of each leather strip. However, nothing in the dead man's possessions indicated that he had taken holy orders.

As Kyle looked on, he wondered at the nature of the sins that warranted such drastic measures for atonement. Did the man indulge in lustful behavior? Was he a glutton or a greedy person? Or was he guilty of something far more serious? Murder, perhaps?

With the prior's assistance, John stripped off the rest of the clothing, until the body lay naked before them.

Kyle watched with interest as John began his examination.

John inspected the front and sides of the body, looking for fresh cuts, grazes, or bruises among long-healed battle scars on the expanse of bare skin. Except for red prickles from the hair shirt, he found nothing worthy of notice. When he rolled the body over, the movement caused clear water to dribble forth from the dead man's mouth.

They all saw the large purple bruise at the same time. It lay between the shoulder blades on the broad back.

"That is about the size of a man's knee," John said, pointing at the affected area.

"What are you suggesting?" the prior said.

"That this drowning may not be accidental," John said. "The placement of the bruise that high on his back suggests someone knelt upon him, using their own weight to hold him under the water."

"He's a big fellow," the prior said. "Would he not be able to throw them off in a struggle?"

John felt around the back of the skull through the wavy gray hair, now dry and springy. "Not if he was unconscious," he said. "From the size of the lump here, it appears someone knocked him on the head before they forced him under."

Kyle's thoughts harkened back to the hair shirt. Did the man, indeed, reap what he sowed in that he killed someone, which in turn, brought about his own death? Or was there a simpler, more plausible explanation? "There was no coin purse on him when we found him," he said. "Maybe he was the target of a robbery gone awry." His gaze shifted to the dagger protruding from the silver sheath on top of the velvet garments. "Or maybe not," he added, touching the reddish-brown carnelian set in the hilt. "Any thief worth his salt would never forego such a prize as this."

John made no reply, for he was staring down at the body, as though lost in thought.

"Is there something more?" Kyle said.

"When I first rolled him over," John said, "water should have gushed from his mouth. If he was dead before he went into the river, there would be no water in him at all. A trickle like that might result from an obstruction in his throat." He turned the body face up on the table and pried the stiff jaws apart with his thumbs. He tilted the head toward the light to look into the cavity of the mouth. "Just as I thought," he said. "There's something down there." He glanced over at the prior. "I will need tongs to reach it."

"I shall get them for ye," Prior Drumlay said. He withdrew in a jingle of keys through the door to the church on the inside wall of the chapel.

"Can you make out what it is?" Kyle said, leaning over to peer into the gaping mouth.

"It's green, like some sort of frond," John said.

"Perhaps he drew in seaweed as he gasped for breath," Kyle said.

"Possibly, but only if he regained consciousness before he drowned," John said. "In any event, we'll soon find out."

"What about the time of death?" Kyle said.

"The rigidity of the limbs would not be an accurate gauge in this case," John said. "The cold water in the river cooled his body more rapidly than if he had been ashore. Nevertheless, considering the minimal shriveling of his skin and the lack of fish bites on his face and hands, I would say he died between three to four hours ago."

"That is as I thought," Kyle said.

John's clean-shaven face broke into a sudden grin that showed the dimple in his left cheek. "Ye haven't heard my news," he said. "Colina and I are married."

"Congratulation," Kyle said with a grin. "I wish both of you every happiness."

"I wanted to wait until ye got back," John said, "but Colina didn't like staying in that big house alone, with her mother so ill. She says she feels better about it now that I've moved in."

"She wasn't exactly alone with her brother there," Kyle said.

"Neyll rode out of town more than a month ago," John said. "Before he left for parts unknown, he bequeathed a considerable dowry to Colina, along with his permission for her to marry any man of her choosing. He also gave to her, in writing, the ownership of the house and the land, as well as the income from the tenant farmers. She thinks he's a saint for doing all that for her."

"A saint!" Kyle cried. He gritted his teeth at the notion, for the man had no qualms about profiting at the expense of his own countrymen or in treating his sister like a prisoner in her own home. The only reason Neyll abandoned his illegal activities and showed any generosity to his sister at all was because Kyle coerced him into doing so by threatening to publicly expose his illicit affair with another man. "He's an unscrupulous bastard," he said.

"I agree," John said.

"Good riddance to him, now that he's gone," Kyle said.

"I agree with that, too," John said. "However, there is no need to mention any of this to Colina. He is her brother, after all."

"My lips are sealed on the subject," Kyle said. An image then popped into his head of the horrid woman whom Neyll hired as a companion for his sister. In reality, the woman spied on Colina's every move and bullied her like a prison warden. "By the way," he added. "Is the Housekeeper from Hell still on the premises?"

"Nay," John said with a chuckle. "Berta left at the same time Neyll did, although I don't think they went off together, if ye know what I mean."

"Too bad," Kyle said. "They deserve each other."

The door on the church wall creaked open as Prior Drumlay stepped back into the chapel. "Will this do?" he said, holding out a narrow pincer-like instrument.

"That will do nicely," John said, taking possession of the flat metal tongs. He bent to the task of thrusting them down the dead man's throat, only to draw forth a bruised yellowish-green sprig trapped between the pincer ends. The small crease between his brows grew deeper at the sight of the tiny elongated leaves on the segmented stem.

"What is it?" Prior Drumlay said.

John brought the tongs close to his nose to give the sprig a tentative sniff. "Unless I am mistaken," he said, "this is mistletoe."

"*Lignum Sanctae Crucis,*" Prior Drumlay said, crossing himself.

"I've seen folks wearing amulets made from the 'wood of the holy cross,' as ye call it," John said. "They believe talismans like that will cure them of the falling sickness and diseases of the heart." He laid the sprig on the table and set the tongs beside it. "A dram of powdered mistletoe mixed with water is far more effective in treating those ailments."

"I thought mistletoe was poisonous," Kyle said.

"It is," John said, "which is why it must be measured with care before it is ingested."

"Was he poisoned, then, before he drowned?" Prior Drumlay said.

"Not with this," John said. He picked up the sprig and held it between his thumb and forefinger. "It would take a much bigger piece to kill a man his size."

Kyle frowned at the bruised frond. "Somebody shoved that down his throat," he said. "Yet, it was not done to harm him." He lifted his eyes to John. "So, why do it at all?"

John shrugged his shoulders. "To send a message, perhaps," he said.

"What kind of message?" Kyle said.

"The kind that would be recognized by someone who knew what it meant," John said.

"Go on," Kyle said. "I'm listening."

"Mistletoe has medicinal properties that are beneficial for patients with certain illnesses," John said. "However, it is also reputed to possess powers of an arcane nature."

"Arcane practices are forbidden by the Holy Kirk," Prior Drumlay interjected, his tone dogmatic.

"So they are," John said. "In spite of that, there are those who ascribe mystical properties to mistletoe and who harvest it solely for that purpose."

"Who does that?" Kyle said.

John glanced from Kyle to the prior and back again. "Druids, of course," he said, his expression grave.

CHAPTER 2

Prior Drumlay drew in a sharp breath, as though horrified by the mere mention of the dreaded sect.

Kyle laughed softly. "That's what I like about you, John," he said. "You have such an imagination."

"I'm deadly serious," John said.

"I don't doubt that at all," Kyle said, still grinning. "I might point out, though, that not a single druid has been seen in this vicinity for hundreds of years."

"How else do ye explain the mistletoe?" John said.

"I plan to find that out when I question Sir Fulbert's kinfolk," Kyle said.

"Druids are an abomination in the sight of God," the prior said. "They perform pagan rituals under the cover of darkness in sacred oak groves." He lowered his voice and added with evident revulsion: "Did you know they practice human sacrifice to their gods and drink the blood of their victims?"

"You seem to know a lot about druids," Kyle said.

"I do," the prior said with pride. "If there are any in this shire, I shall do everything in my power to drive them out." He turned to John. "Have you finished with your examination?"

"I have," John said. "The body may now be prepared for burial."

While John put the tools of his trade into his medicament bag, Kyle took another look at the dead man's leather belt.

The replication of oak leaves and acorns on it, as well as on the brooch, was indeed evocative of sacred oak groves. On the other hand, there was nothing about that motif that suggested bloodthirsty druids.

He rolled up the belt and placed it on top of the folded russet cloak. When he raised his eyes, he caught the I-told-you-so expression on John's face. He responded with a maybe-so-maybe-not shrug of his broad shoulders and the upturning of his palms.

He and John took their leave of Prior Drumlay and went out through the arched door of the mortuary chapel into the daylight beyond. Both of them were glad to fill their lungs with clean fresh air.

John approached the mule grazing near the chapel wall and captured the trailing reins. "Ye must bring Joneta over to the house for dinner soon," he said, mounting the docile beast. "Colina would love to see her and the bairn."

"I'll do that," Kyle said. He waved as John set out for the priory gates.

Behind the church, Vinewood and Hoprig lounged in the shade of a beech tree. The horses dozed nearby with their heads bowed to the ground.

The two men got to their feet as Kyle approached.

"I must break the news to Sir Fulbert's widow," Kyle said. "But first, I want to go back to the wharf."

The three of them mounted their horses and rode from the priory grounds. They turned down Harbour Street and threaded their way through pedestrian traffic until they reached the place where the body had been pulled from the river.

"Wait here," Kyle said, dismounting. He handed the reins to Vinewood before walking over to where Simon worked beside a couple of fishermen who were cleaning last night's catch.

"Simon," Kyle said. "Do you remember that fellow we pulled from the river this morning?"

"Of course," Simon said.

"That was no accidental drowning," Kyle said.

Simon froze in the middle of scaling a trout. "I don't know nothing about it," he said, his eyes wide.

"I'm not accusing you, Simon," Kyle said. "I just want to know if you saw anybody on the wharf in the early hours of the morning that didn't belong there."

Simon shook his head, his eyes fixed on the fish before him. His white knuckles stood out against the stained wooden handle of the scaling knife in his hand.

"If you do happen to recall anything, let me know," Kyle said.

Simon bobbed his head. It was a jerky movement that seemed more like a nervous twitch than a nod of assent.

Kyle mounted the gelding and set out at a walk up Harbour Street.

"He's lying," Vinewood said after a moment.

"He was, indeed," Kyle said. "I would certainly like to know why." He glanced over his shoulder in time to see Simon scurrying up the street toward the marketplace. He watched as the man turned onto the market grounds and vanished behind a stall.

They rode down winding streets to the edge of town. The lanes were wider there, lined with wooden houses set farther apart than those in the heart of town. The blacksmith's shop stood among them, set back from the road. Three well-fed horses tied to the rail out front dozed in the warm sunshine with their heads down.

A large tan dog lay in the side yard gnawing on a bone. A long chain on the beast's spiked collar secured it to a stout post, around which the ground was worn bare.

When Kyle saw Macalister leading a strawberry roan out from under the low porch of the shop, he turned into the yard and brought the gelding to a halt. "It looks like business is picking up for you, my friend," he said, tilting his head at the horses at the rail.

"I can't complain," Macalister said. "These came from the garrison at Sir Percy's behest. I'll be done with them by this afternoon." He squinted up at Kyle against the morning sun. "Did ye ever find out who it was that drowned?"

"He's likely one of the Rylands," Kyle said. "We're headed out to Cragston Castle now to confirm his identity."

"I did a bit of trade with that lot last month," Macalister said, rubbing the roan's velvety nose. "Their groom brought in a big white destrier that threw a shoe."

"Did he say anything about the Rylands?" Kyle said.

"He hardly spoke at all," Macalister said. "He dropped the horse off and came back later in the day to settle up."

"Ah, well," Kyle said, taking a deep breath. "I'd best be off. I've sad news to deliver to the family."

"I don't envy ye that task, even if they are Southrons," Macalister said. "By the way, I'm going fishing early on the morrow. I found a great spot. It's a little further south than I like, but I come back with a full string of fish every time. Do ye want to come along?"

"It sounds tempting," Kyle said. "However, I must attend to this drowning business at present."

"Maybe next time, then," Macalister said.

"I'll hold you to that," Kyle said. He turned the gelding's head toward the street, his hand raised in a parting wave.

He and the two English soldiers left the outskirts of town and headed south along the coastal road under a blue sky without a cloud in sight. A cool breeze from the firth somewhat tempered the heat of the mid-morning sun beating down upon them. To the right, the incoming tide rushed up onto a pristine beach that seemed to stretch out for miles in either direction.

Further along the southern road, bleached sand gave way to mossy boulders and sheer cliffs. The incessant pounding of waves against the rocks sent white spume high into the air. Seagulls wheeled and glided on updrafts over the churning water, screaming and shrieking all the while.

They rode past the ruins of an abandoned castle, a crumbling hulk that was now a mere shadow of the formidable stone structure that once overlooked the crashing surf far below.

Before long, they approached Cragston Castle, which loomed ahead of them on a precipice high above the surging water of the Firth of Clyde. Crenellated parapets jutted up over the thick stone wall surrounding the fortress. A deep ravine formed a natural barrier on the landward side, and the sea barred access from the rear.

As Kyle rode up the causeway leading to the castle, he noticed that the drawbridge was down, the portcullis was up, and the huge outer gates were wide open. The ring of shod hooves on stone should have alerted the gatekeeper of their approach, yet no one challenged them from the watchtower above the arched entryway.

"Looks like nobody's home," Hoprig said, stating the obvious.

Kyle halted to scan the parapet, searching for the guards at their post, but there were none to be seen. "We'll know for sure in a minute," he said. He shook the reins, and the gelding started forward.

They rode across the wooden drawbridge with the hollow drumming of hooves in their ears.

On reaching the far side, they passed under the pointed iron teeth of the portcullis and entered the bailey, where outbuildings and animal pens lined the inside of the curtain wall. The smell of death and decay in the air caused their mounts to mince and sidestep, with eyes rolling and nostrils distended.

Kyle reined in, as did Vinewood and Hoprig behind him. He patted the gelding's sleek neck and spoke in a soothing tone to calm the nervous creature. He let his gaze rove around the entire courtyard. There was no stock in the pens. Neither was there a chicken scratching for bugs in the fallen hay nor a dog sprawling in the shadows. Not a living soul moved about the courtyard.

The quiet was absolute, until the creak of rusted hinges shattered the eerie silence.

The sound brought Kyle's head around just as a middle-aged woman stepped through the doorway of the storeroom on the ground floor of the three-story keep.

She did not appear to be a servant or a charwoman, for her light blue linen gown with embroidery at the neck and cuffs was too fine. Her face was pale beneath the matching light blue cap that covered every strand of hair on her head. Her eyes were narrowed against the glare of the sun, making it difficult to discern their color. She stood near the open storeroom door with the poise of a noblewoman, her hands clasped demurely at her thick waist, as though waiting for him to introduce himself and state the reason for his presence there.

Kyle dismounted and signaled for Vinewood and Hoprig to do the same. "Mistress Ryland?" he said. Though it was merely a guess on his part, it was evidently a good one, for the wary expression on her face relaxed into curiosity.

"Aye," she said in a high child-like voice.

"Kyle Shaw, Deputy to the Sheriff of Ayrshire, at your service," he said with a slight bow.

"Welcome to Cragston Castle," she said.

"Is there some place where we may speak in private?" Kyle said.

The wary expression returned to her face. "What is it you wish to say?" she said.

"When was the last time you saw Sir Fulbert?" Kyle said.

"Only a moment ago," she said with a puzzled frown. "Why do you ask?"

Kyle cast a pointed glance at Hoprig, who, by a shrug of his shoulders, absolved himself from all blame for mistaking the dead man's identity.

"I would like to speak to Sir Fulbert, if I may," Kyle said.

"He is inside," she said. She stepped into the storeroom and beckoned for them to come with her. "This way."

Kyle and the two English soldiers followed her through the barrels and kegs to the hewn steps that led up to the main hall on the second floor.

Sir Fulbert, whose clean-shaven face closely resembled that of the drowned man, sat alone at a long trestle table, with both hands cupped around a pewter mug. A clay pitcher of ale stood within easy reach. Crusts of bread and bits of smoked fish left over from a meal for half a dozen people littered the wooden tabletop. His gray head turned at the tramp of boots advancing toward him on the timber-plank floor. "Who are you? What do you want?" he demanded. It was obvious he had been drinking heavily, for his speech was slurred and his movements slow and deliberate. His bloodshot eyes shifted to Mistress Ryland. "Why did you bring them here?"

Kyle introduced himself to Sir Fulbert. "I asked to see you because of the body pulled from the river early this morning," he said.

"How does that concern me?" Sir Fulbert said, immediately defensive.

"It may be Sir Humphrey," Kyle said.

Sir Fulbert did not even blink an eye at the news that his brother might be dead. Mistress Ryland, on the other hand, clapped both hands over her mouth to stifle the cry of anguish that came from deep in her throat.

Sir Fulbert glared at her. "Drowned, you say?" he said, focusing with difficulty on Kyle's face. "How did it happen?"

"I'm not sure yet," Kyle said. "When was the last time you saw him alive?"

"Early yesterday, I think," Sir Fulbert said. He gave Mistress Ryland a fierce scowl, as though daring her to contradict him.

"When was the last time you saw him?" Kyle said to Mistress Ryland, ignoring Sir Fulbert's silent threat.

"It is as my husband says," she said, her eyes downcast. "He went out riding yesterday morning, and that's the last I ever saw of him."

"Where is your groom?" Kyle said. That was an assumption on his part, for if there were horses in the stable, there must be someone to care for them.

"Gone to Maybole for supplies," she said. "He should be back any time now."

"What about your son?" Kyle said.

"He is out hunting," she said.

"When will he return?" Kyle said.

"Later today, I expect," she said.

"And your daughter?" Kyle said. That was another assumption, but he could tell he hit a nerve from the pure hatred that blazed in Mistress Ryland's hazel eyes as her gaze flicked to her husband.

"She is unwell just now," she said, nearly choking with anger as she spoke.

"Perhaps I can talk with her another time, then," Kyle said.

"Perhaps," she said. She turned her face away from her husband, as though she could not stand to look at him.

Kyle reached into the pouch at his side and withdrew the ring-and-pin brooch taken from the dead man's cloak.

Mistress Ryland's eyes widened at the sight of the brooch, which confirmed her recognition of it.

"What is the significance of the oak leaves and acorns on this?" he said to Sir Fulbert, holding up the brooch. "The pattern is repeated on Sir Humphrey's belt."

Sir Fulbert up-ended the pewter mug and swallowed its contents, as though stalling for time to think. "There are oak leaves and acorns on the Ryland family crest," he said after a moment. He spoke with difficulty around the thickness of his tongue.

Kyle laid the brooch on the table. "Why would anyone thrust mistletoe down Sir Humphrey's throat?" he said, watching Sir Fulbert closely.

The question had a sobering effect on Sir Fulbert. He sat up straight on the hard wooden bench. "Who did that?" he said, his eyes now bright with acute cognition.

"That's what I'd like to know," Kyle said, leveling a piercing gaze at him.

Sir Fulbert picked up the clay pitcher in front of him and filled his mug to the brim with ale. He brought the mug to his lips and took a long swig before setting it back on the table. "I have no idea," he said, avoiding the pale blue eyes boring into him.

"I understand you went on the last crusade to the Holy Land," Kyle said in an abrupt change of subject.

"I did," Sir Fulbert said with alacrity, as though eager to move on to another topic. "I fought beside young Edward before he was crowned as King of England. The ground ran red with Christian blood as city after city fell into the hands of a barbarian by the name of Baibars. I was lucky to survive the carnage, as did a scant handful of the men under my command." His countenance grew dark and forbidding. "Before we left the Holy Land to come home, we caught up with some of those heathen dogs who saw fit to desecrate holy ground." His eyes glittered with malicious satisfaction. "We saw to it that every one of them got what they deserved."

Kyle was about to take his leave of the Rylands when an attractive woman in her early twenties entered the main hall.

Large brown eyes looked out over elegant cheekbones in her oval face. Her skin was flawless, and the fawn color of her silk gown flattered her creamy complexion. She glided toward them with a light quick step, her head up and her shoulders back. Her skirts rustled across the timber-plank flooring as she approached the trestle table. Vinewood's appreciative gaze upon her brought a slight smile to her full lips, as though she expected his admiration and was gratified to receive it.

"This is Eleanora, my daughter by marriage," Mistress Ryland said to Kyle. "She is wife to my son, Peter." She then related to the young woman the reason for Kyle's visit.

On hearing the news, the coquettish flutter of Eleanora's slender hands ceased. Her entire body went utterly still. Only her eyes moved to search Kyle's chiseled features, taking in the white seam of a scar that ran from temple to jaw on his clean-shaven face. "Are you sure it is Sir Humphrey?" she said in a strained voice.

"I do not know him by sight," Kyle said. "For that reason, one of you must go to the mortuary chapel at St. John's Priory to identify his remains. If it is indeed Sir Humphrey, you must then make arrangements for his burial."

Eleanora shook her head, causing the frilly edges of her off-white bonnet to quiver. "Not me," she said. The air of soft femininity about her seemed to harden as her gaze settled on Sir Fulbert. "He's your brother. It's your duty to go."

Sir Fulbert paid no heed to her scolding tone. Instead, he reached for his mug of ale and buried his high-bridged patrician nose in it.

Mistress Ryland wrung her hands, looking sufficiently distraught for Kyle to offer a suggestion. "Perhaps your son can undertake the task," he said.

"Of course," Mistress Ryland said, clearly grateful. "It is settled, then. Peter shall call upon Prior Drumlay on the morrow."

Kyle turned to Eleanora. "When did you last see Sir Humphrey alive?" he said.

Her face brightened at receiving the handsome deputy's undivided attention. She reached up to touch her cap. Her restless fingers slid down to the back of her neck before moving around to caress her chest above the swell of her breasts under her gown. "Yesterday morning, I think," she said. "Is it important?" she added, her eyes wide.

"Perhaps," Kyle said.

He saw through her pretense of innocence. She was lying. All of the signs pointed to it. In his experience, there were many reasons why people lied, the foremost being fear or shame or guilt. He never even mentioned to the Rylands that Sir Humphrey had been murdered, except by innuendo when he asked Sir Fulbert about the mistletoe. Since she had not been present at that time, there was no reason for her to evade the truth— unless of course she was the one who killed Sir Humphrey, or if she did not do it herself, perhaps she knew who did. He would give her time to relax her guard before he questioned her about it again.

There was one more thing he wanted to know before he left.

"Mistress Ryland," he said, directing the question to the only person present who would give him an honest answer. "Were you aware that Sir Humphrey wore a hair shirt under his clothing?"

Before she could respond, Sir Fulbert flung up his head. "I knew he would do something like that," he said, pounding his fist on the table. "What a pathetic wretch!"

Mistress Ryland ignored the outburst. "If he did," she said, "I never saw it."

Kyle knew he would get nothing more from the Rylands, so he took his leave. He strode from the main hall with Vinewood and Hoprig a step behind him. They descended the hewn stairs to the storeroom and went out into the sunlit bailey beyond.

"Those Rylands are a kettle of cold fish," Hoprig said, with his usual flair of putting a finger on the pulse of the matter. He drew in a deep breath of malodorous air. "As bad as it smells, I'd rather be out here, than in there with them."

"I think Mistress Eleanora is rather fetching," Vinewood said with a crooked grin.

"She certainly knows more than she's letting on," Kyle said.

The grin faded from Vinewood's face. "What makes you say that?" he said.

"She couldn't keep her hands still," Kyle said. "Anybody that nervous surely must have something to hide."

"Now that you mention it," Vinewood said, "she did look a bit edgy."

They were about to mount their horses when Kyle noticed a wagon that had not been in the courtyard earlier. It was parked near a stone-built kitchen with a blackened chimney jutting up from its tiled roof.

A young man in tan leggings under a belted white shirt stepped through the open doorway of the kitchen. He went to the wagon and took a basket full of root vegetables and collard greens from among the supplies piled on the wooden bed.

Kyle walked over to the wagon and introduced himself. "Are you the groom here?" he said.

"Aye," the young man said. "Ye can call me Arnald." He was about twenty-five years old, with a lean build that made him look taller than his middle height. His sharp features were comely, and his dark blue eyes stood out against his ruddy complexion. His long face was shaved clean, except for a thin moustache on his upper lip. The straight brown hair that reached his shoulders glinted with reddish highlights in the noonday sun. His calm manner and low voice were well suited for the job of handling spirited horses. Because of his coloring and the clothes he wore, he could pass for an Englishman; that is, until he opened his mouth, for he spoke with the soft burr of a low-lander.

Kyle removed a sack of flour from the back of the wagon and heaved it onto his shoulder. "Where do you want this?" he said.

"Just put it on the table in here," Arnald said. He led the way into the kitchen and set the basket of vegetables on the stone floor beside the hearth.

Kyle deposited the heavy sack on the wooden table with a grunt. "What is the cause of the stench in the bailey?" he said.

"It's from dead stock," Arnald said, heading back out to the wagon. "The pigs and cows just kept keeling over during the past few weeks until there wasn't a single one left alive."

Kyle picked up one of the two slatted cages with half a dozen squawking chickens inside. The chickens quieted down when he started to walk. "What killed them?" he said.

"Rumor has it that the former occupants of this castle placed a curse upon it," Arnald said, lifting the other slatted cage with both hands.

"Do you believe that?" Kyle said.

"I don't," Arnald said with a shake of his head. "The Southrons assigned here to serve under Sir Fulbert must have done, though, because every one of them put in for a transfer back to the garrison."

"What do you think killed those animals?"

"Bad feed."

Kyle carried the chicken cage into the kitchen and set it on the floor against the wall. "How so?" he said.

Arnald set his cage next to the other one. "I fed the pigs and the cows with feed from the sacks newly purchased from the marketplace at Ayr," he said. "The horses ate oats from the sacks taken from our storeroom. Sir Peter wanted them used up before he bought any more. Since none of the horses died, I concluded that the new feed must have been tainted."

"Could it have been poisoned?" Kyle said.

A frown creased Arnald's smooth forehead. "That would mean someone did it on purpose," he said.

"Do the Rylands have any enemies that you know of?" Kyle said.

"Anyone who ever met them, I imagine," Arnald said. "They're a disagreeable lot, even to other Southrons."

"I'd like to get a sample of that tainted feed," Kyle said.

"There's still some on the ground over there," Arnald said. He started across the courtyard toward the empty animal pens. "I haven't had a chance to clean it up yet. I did burn the carcasses, though, just to get rid of them."

"Did Sir Humphrey go out early yesterday morning?" Kyle said, falling in step beside the young man.

"He did," Arnald said.

"Did you saddle his horse?"

"Aye, like I do most days."

"Where does he usually go?"

"Cragston Forest," Arnald said. "He likes to go hawking there. It is abundant with small game, so he says." His eyebrows drew together over his dark blue eyes. "I often wondered why he bothered to take the hawk with him at all."

"Why is that?"

"Because he never brought any game back with him."

"Maybe he went there for some other reason," Kyle said. He glanced over at the young man to watch his reaction. "To meet a woman, perhaps."

The pucker on Arnald's brow deepened. "Whatever Sir Humphrey does is no concern of mine," he said. "That goes for the other Rylands, too."

"I admire your loyalty," Kyle said. "However, Sir Humphrey's body was found early this morning—"

"He's dead?" Arnald cried, interrupting him.

"Aye," Kyle said. "We pulled him out of the River Ayr just after sunrise."

"I don't believe it," Arnald said.

"It's true," Kyle said.

"Sir Humphrey hated the water," Arnald said. "He couldn't swim, ye see."

"Sir Peter will make a proper identification on the morrow," Kyle said. "By the way, do you know why Sir Humphrey wore a hair shirt under his clothing?"

"I'm only a groom," Arnald said, "not a manservant." He opened the gate of the nearest pen and went inside. "Besides, ye don't even know that it is Sir Humphrey," he said, squatting to scoop up a handful of dry feed.

Kyle removed a scrap of cloth from the pouch at his side and held it out to receive the feed. He folded the cloth and tucked it into his pouch. "His resemblance to Sir Fulbert is remarkable enough to convince me that they are kinsmen," he said.

Arnald dusted his hands on his leggings and leaned his forearms on the top rail that encircled the pen. "I can't take it in that he's truly dead," he said.

"Didn't you suspect something was amiss when he failed to return last evening?" Kyle said.

Arnald shook his head. "It was not unusual for him to spend the odd night away now and again," he said.

Kyle looked over at the wagon parked outside the kitchen. "Who prepares the food here?"

"My mam comes in six days a week to cook and wash up," Arnald said. "She says God rested on the seventh day, and so must she. The Rylands are left to fend for themselves on Sundays." He chuckled, as though at some private joke. "She'll be along shortly to prepare dinner."

"What's so funny?" Kyle said.

"As contrary as the Rylands are," Arnald said, "they're afraid to say a wrong word to Mam for fear she'll leave, never to return. They would then have to eat Mistress Marjorie's cooking."

"Who is Mistress Marjorie?" Kyle said.

"Sir Fulbert's daughter."

"Ah," Kyle said. "I have not yet had the pleasure of making her acquaintance."

Arnald's comely face darkened into a scowl. "She's unable to receive anyone at the moment," he said.

"Is she ill?" Kyle said with concern.

Just then, the clash of hooves on the cobbled stones of the gateway echoed in the bailey. A white horse with a plaited mane entered the courtyard at a trot and clattered to a halt. A heavy-set man in a maroon velvet cotte swung down from the ornate saddle on its back.

"It is Sir Peter," Arnald said, his face still set in a scowl. "I must attend to his horse." He hastened from the animal pen toward the waiting man.

Kyle followed the groom across the courtyard at a more sedate pace.

Sir Peter appeared to be a year or two short of thirty. His full cheeks were brick red, as though burned from the wind. His clean-shaven face bore the stamp of the Rylands, with its high-bridged, arrogant nose and stubborn chin. His eyes were hazel, like his mother's, and his hair was light brown. A long white feather protruded from the maroon cap perched at a jaunty angle on his head.

He handed the reins to Arnald. "Who is that?" he said, his

gaze on Kyle.

"That is the sheriff's deputy," Arnald said. "He's come about Sir Humphrey."

"What about him?" Sir Peter said.

"He's dead," Arnald said.

Sir Peter's only reaction to the news was the stiffening of his body.

The movement was slight, but Kyle caught it as he drew near.

"What's this about my uncle?" Sir Peter said in a brusque tone, as though speaking to a servant. He professed interest, yet he seemed otherwise unaffected by the loss of a family member.

Kyle recounted what he knew thus far, short of mentioning murder and the sprig of mistletoe. "Identity must be confirmed," he said, "before the body can be released for burial."

"I suppose I must handle that," Sir Peter said in a petulant tone. "Just as I am expected to handle everything else around here."

"Your mother hoped you would see to it on the morrow," Kyle said.

"I'll wager she did," Sir Peter said. He turned away with a derisive snort and started toward the storeroom door on the ground floor of the keep.

Arnald set out for the stable set against the curtain wall with the white horse in tow.

"Just one more thing before I go," Kyle said.

Arnald paused to look over his shoulder, uncertain whether the deputy was addressing him or the scion of Cragston Castle.

Sir Peter kept walking, not even bothering to slow down.

"Do you know why anyone would push a sprig of mistletoe down Sir Humphrey's throat?" Kyle said in a voice loud enough to ensure that both men heard every word.

The uncertainty on Arnald's comely face gave way to bewilderment.

Sir Peter stopped abruptly. He turned slowly, his wind-burned cheeks now blanched white. The Adam's apple in his throat bobbed as he swallowed involuntarily. "Are you sure it was mistletoe?" he said, licking his lips.

CHAPTER 3

"The apothecary recognized it as such when he removed it," Kyle said. He noted that Sir Peter appeared more interested in the kind of plant found in his uncle's throat than in how it got there.

Sir Peter met Kyle's pale blue eyes with an unwavering stare. "I am afraid I cannot help you," he said, his tone curt and dismissive. He swung around and continued on to the storeroom doorway.

Kyle made his way over to where Vinewood and Hoprig stood in the shade with the horses. He would come back another time to question Sir Peter about his movements on the day before his uncle's drowning, although he would probably receive as little cooperation then as he did now. English nobility, like the Rylands, often considered themselves above the law, especially in a provincial country like Scotland.

They mounted their horses and set out in a clatter of hooves across the courtyard, through the entryway, and down the causeway, which circled around to the coastal road.

A steady wind blew in from the firth, and the rolling waves shimmered with reflected light from the sun at its zenith. On the landward side, Cragston Forest lay beyond the long bare ridges and hump-backed hills that opened into wooded valleys in the distance.

As they rode northward, Kyle pondered whether the trip to Cragston Castle had been worth the effort. As expected, the

Rylands closed ranks on him—a Scottish lawman nosing into their personal affairs. He found it interesting that none of them seemed especially grieved at Sir Humphrey's passing, except perhaps for Mistress Ryland. The mere mention of mistletoe elicited an unexpected reaction from both father and son, yet neither appeared willing to impart the significance to him.

Sir Fulbert's tale of the crusades brought to mind an unfinished conversation he recently had on that subject. "Hoprig," he said. "You mentioned that your father journeyed to the Holy Land."

"He did," Hoprig said. "It cost him a princely sum to board the ship headed for the port of Tyre. He saw himself as *Milites Christe*—a Knight of Christ—bound for glory and untold riches. They all did. With God on their side, they could not fail, or so they thought." His frowning countenance settled into a grimace. "In a matter of months, starvation and disease thinned their ranks. Saracen warriors trimmed their number even further, and no wonder, given that their goal was to take Saracen land by force. They never even got near Jerusalem, for the Saracens repelled them at every turn. My father came back a broken man. There was no rest for him at home, either. Creditors hounded him day and night until, in desperation, he sold everything he owned to pay off his debts. That, of course, left him a pauper."

"I didn't know that," Vinewood said quietly. "I'm sorry."

Vinewood's sympathy seemed to embitter Hoprig even further. "It is common knowledge where I come from," he said, his thin lips drawn tight. "My father squandered the family fortune and fell out of royal favor because of excessive debt." He lifted his head, his chin thrust out in anger. "There's more, in case you haven't heard. Upon my enlistment in the King's army, I was consigned to serve as a lowly man-at-arms. There was no money left, you see, for me to buy a commission as an officer, as did my father and his father before him. My mother was so embarrassed over my situation, she arranged to have me sent up here, where nobody would know that I was the only son of the late Lord Hoprig of Evesham and sole heir to nothing."

Vinewood, normally glib with a quick and ready wit, evidently had nothing to say, for he rode in sober silence. Kyle did the same, occupied with his own thoughts.

Before long, they approached a beaten track that crossed open land on an almost level course, climbing gently toward the east, only to disappear over a hill.

"Go on to the garrison," Kyle said to the two English soldiers. "I'll be along later." Without waiting for a reply, he turned onto the track and urged the gelding into a lope.

He followed the well-used pathway through the rising grass, up the hill, and down the other side. He rode into the woodland beyond, where sunlight filtered through the leafy branches overhead. In a short while, he left the trees behind to enter a wide meadow lush with summer growth. A three-room timber dwelling crouched beside the narrow creek that ran through the center of the field.

He dismounted in front of the house just as a slender woman in her mid-twenties appeared in the doorway.

She wiped her hands on the white apron over her black tunic. Her unbound hair hung about her shoulders, and when she stepped outside, the light auburn tresses blazed like a halo of fire around her head. Reddish freckles marched across her nose, and the hazel eyes in her lovely face changed to green in the glare of the sun.

His heart skipped a beat at the welcoming smile she gave him. "Good morrow, Mistress Joneta," he said. He hoped she could not hear the treble in his voice from a nervousness that gripped him only in her presence.

"Good morrow to ye, Master Kyle," she said. Her gaze swept

him from tawny head to booted toe. "Ye look like a man who could use a good meal."

"I surely can," he said. "I'm famished."

"Come in, then," she said, beckoning to him. "There's rabbit stew in the pot."

He loosened the girth strap on the saddle and dropped the reins to let the gelding graze at will. "Have you caught up on your rest?" he said, walking toward her.

"Not yet," she said as she led him into the house.

The front room was neat and tidy, the wood-plank floor swept clean. A cross draft from the open windows on either side helped to keep the interior cool. The smell of wood smoke from the hearth fire drifted in the air. Chunks of meat simmered in a soot-blackened iron pot suspended over the flames. A gray woolen blanket hung across the doorway that led to the back rooms.

"How is Bruce?" he said.

"He's fast asleep," she said.

"I envy him," he said, stifling a yawn.

"Me, too," she said.

She cut a round loaf of brown bread in half and scooped out the center. She ladled a generous portion of thick stew into the hollow crust and set it in a wooden bowl, which she placed on the trestle table near the window.

He slid onto the bench at the table and started in on the stew.

She sat across from him, her fingers laced before her on the scuffed wooden surface.

While he ate, he told her about finding the drowned man earlier that morning and the subsequent visit to Cragston Castle.

"Over the past year or so," she said, "I have become well acquainted with Sir Humphrey's niece, Marjorie. She comes by nearly every Thursday to visit. I gathered from what she told me about her family that she is desperately unhappy, despite the advantages of wealth and position."

"I didn't get to meet her while I was there," he said. "According to her mother, she was unwell."

"That's putting it mildly," she said with a snort of disdain. "She's more than likely laid up with a bloody nose or a black eye."

He stopped chewing to stare at her. "Why do you say that?" he said.

"Because it's happened before," she said.

"Who would do that to her?" he said.

"Her father," she said. "He has a terrible temper. It's mostly harsh words and idle threats on his part. On occasion, though, he's so violent that Marjorie and her mother are afraid to sit in the same room with him. Anything can set him off, even when he isn't deep in his cups."

He lost his appetite over the mental image of Sir Fulbert venting his anger upon a defenseless woman. "I should have guessed he was a bully," he said, "from the shabby way he treated Mistress Ryland." He pushed away the wooden bowl, his meal unfinished.

"She nearly died a while back because of him," she said.

"His wife?" he said. "Why?"

"Marjorie saw the whole thing," she said. "Sir Fulbert accused her of engaging in a tryst with his brother. She denied it, but he didn't believe her. He beat her within an inch of her life and left her where she fell on the floor, battered and bleeding. Then, he went outside to horsewhip his brother in front of the guards. Sir Humphrey pulled the whip from his hand and struck him with it, calling him a drunken fool and a lout. Normally, Sir Fulbert would challenge anyone who insulted and humiliated him like that, but he was so drunk at the time, he could hardly stand up."

"When was that?" he said.

"Three or four years ago, as I recall," she said. "It was when Sir Humphrey first went to live at Cragston Castle."

He sat in silence, reflecting on what she revealed to him. "It appears," he said after a moment, "that Sir Fulbert has a very good reason for wanting his brother dead."

"If he did indeed kill Sir Humphrey," she said, "why wait so long to do it?"

"Perhaps the opportunity did not present itself before yesterday evening," he said.

"Ye may be right," she said. "On the other hand, Sir Peter has as good a reason as his father for wanting Sir Humphrey out of the way."

"Really?" he said, listening with candid curiosity.

She nodded her head. "Marjorie told me she overheard her uncle and her brother arguing over the repayment of a loan," she said. "It seems Sir Peter borrowed heavily from Sir Humphrey and has yet to come up with the funds to settle the debt."

"Do you know how much money was involved?" he said.

"Nay," she said. "It must have been a lot, though, judging from the heat of the dispute."

She caught her breath sharply, as though something just occurred to her. "Ye must think me a frightful gossiper," she said as a pinkish flush bloomed on her cheeks.

He covered her clasped hands with his own. "On the contrary," he said. "I learned more from you in ten minutes than I did from the Rylands in over an hour."

"I was merely trying to be helpful," she said, her gaze on his handsome face.

"You were extremely so," he said. He withdrew his hand, for feel of her smooth skin beneath his fingers scorched him like fire, though from her expression, not all of the shock of contact was his alone. "There is something I must tell you," he added

53

gravely. "I trust you won't take it amiss."

"What is it?" she said. She waited with bated breath for him to speak, her lips parted slightly, her eyes wide and hopeful.

"I cannot act on the information you imparted to me, despite the truth of it," he said. "It is hearsay, unless Marjorie herself states that it is so. I shall give her every opportunity to relate those things to me. I doubt she will, though, seeing as how doing so will expose her family's secrets."

She got up from the bench, her face averted, her shoulders slumped, as though in disappointment.

He was perceptive enough to realize that he let her down somehow. Was she perhaps expecting him to declare his love for her? There was really no reason why he should fail to do so. He did care deeply for her. He loved her, in fact. Each night in his dreams, he saw her face, heard her voice, felt her touch. Each waking moment, she dominated his thoughts. Even so, something held him back from committing both body and soul to her in holy matrimony. The excuse that she would be widowed for a second time if he was killed in the line of duty was just that: an excuse. Although unsure why, he was just not ready yet to pledge his troth. It was as simple as that.

She went to the sideboard, where she poured warm ale from a clay pitcher into a mug. She came back to the table, her countenance now composed and serene. She placed the mug before him and resumed her seat on the bench across from him.

"Thank you," he said. He took a sip from the mug and set it on the table. He spread his elbows on the wooden surface and leaned forward. "It worries me that you are out here on your own. Should illness strike you or the bairn, how would you get the help you need?"

"My niece and her husband live with me now," she said. "They came out here to keep an eye on the house while I was in Aberdeen. When I got back yesterday, I invited them to stay on with me. Meg helps with the cooking and the washing. Drew does the hunting and lends a hand with the heavier chores."

"I'm relieved to hear it," he said. "I would still like to visit you from time to time, if that's all right."

"Ye are always welcome here," she said.

He stood up and stretched. "Many thanks for the stew," he said, hitching up the sword belt that slipped down his narrow hips. "I hate to impose on your hospitality without returning the favor. Is there any chore that needs doing before I go?"

"Not really," she said. "Drew took care of the milking early this morning. He also cut enough firewood to last out the week."

"Do you mind if I look in on the bairn?" he said.

"I don't mind at all," she said. She walked over to the woolen blanket and held it aside for him to pass into the darkened chamber beyond.

A five-month-old infant lay on a straw pallet in the corner under an open window. A strip of cloth encircled his loins. His pudgy arms and legs were bare, as was his rounded belly.

From where Kyle stood, it looked like the baby's eyes were open. He bent close to make sure and was rewarded with a toothless grin. "So, you are awake, you wee bugger," he said in a crooning tone.

He gently lifted the baby from the pallet and settled him in the crook of his arm, nestling the little body against the leather scale armor on his chest. The chubby pink cheek rested against the sleeve of his tan linen shirt that protruded from beneath the leather shoulder guards.

The baby nuzzled his arm in search of a nipple. The tiny fists closed over a fold in his sleeve and attempted to stuff the soft fabric into the open rosebud mouth.

He gazed down at the intelligent blue eyes regarding him steadily. "I think somebody is hungry," he said. He sought to extricate the fabric of his sleeve from the infant's grasp, but the diminutive features crumpled in warning. He immediately let the little one have his way to forestall the howl of protest sure to follow.

"He's always hungry," she said. "Like his father," she added with a wistful expression on her face. "He never even got to see his only child."

He smoothed the wispy dark hair on the baby's head with his calloused hand. "He would have been proud that he sired a fine healthy son like Bruce," he said. He swept aside the blanket hanging over the doorway and walked from the sleeping chamber with the baby in his arms.

She followed him into the front room, which was filled with reflected radiance from the early afternoon sun.

"Tell me," he said. "Has Marjorie ever spoken to you about her sister-in-law?"

"Quite a bit, and none of it complimentary," she said.

"I take it those two don't get along," he said.

"Not at all," she said.

"Did Marjorie at any time mention that she suspected Eleanora of carrying on with Sir Humphrey?" he said.

"Funny ye should ask," she said. "There was no proof of anything going on between them, mind ye, but Marjorie thought it mighty curious that Eleanora only rode out on the mornings that Sir Humphrey did, and she always left a quarter of an hour after him. Marjorie followed her on several occasions, but never managed to catch them together."

"If Eleanora was having an affair with Sir Humphrey," he said, "that gives Sir Peter another reason for wanting him dead."

"Maybe it was Eleanora who killed Sir Humphrey," she said. "She might have grown tired of him. When she told him it was over between them, he may have forced himself on her, which is why she struck him dead."

"That's possible," he said, "but not entirely plausible."

"Why not?" she said.

"For one thing, how did she get his body into the boat?" he said. "He was too heavy a man for her to lift by herself. For another thing, how did she get him out of the boat to dump him into the river?"

The baby started to squirm and fuss. He shifted him to his shoulder and patted his swaddled bottom to keep him quiet. He strolled across the front room to the side window. On glancing outside, he noticed a small patch of ground over by the creek that looked like an overgrown vegetable garden.

"I've glimpsed Eleanora from a distance," she said. "She is a very beautiful woman. It would hardly be difficult for someone like her to find a man to help her dispose of the body."

"She struck me as being a rather clever woman," he said, ambling back to where she stood. "In light of that, I cannot believe she would place herself in the power of the man who rendered such a service to her."

"What do ye mean?" she said, frowning.

"That man would be in a position to extricate a fortune from her in return for his silence," he said.

"Oh, I see," she said.

The baby's muted whimpering abruptly escalated into an ear-splitting shriek.

"You can have him back now," he said, transferring the baby to her arms.

The wailing subsided for a moment.

"While you attend to him," he said in the ensuing lull, "I'll be outside turning the soil in your garden."

She hurried to the back room to nurse the baby before the howling started up again.

He took off his leather scale armor and his sword belt and laid them on the bench. He went out the front door and walked around to the rear, where he entered the lean-to shed attached to the back of the house.

A black and white cow chewing its cud stood in the shade of the open-sided shelter. The docile creature watched with large brown eyes while he rummaged around for a spade. The one he found was old and rusted, but it was adequate for the job he had in mind.

He walked over to the far corner of the garden plot and began to dig, overturning clods of tangled weeds to expose the rich fertile loam beneath.

The ground was hard from a lack of rain, and the day was warm. His shirt soon became wet with perspiration. He stripped it off and spread it out on a bush to dry. The bulging muscles of his shoulders and back glistened with sweat as he continued to work.

After digging up more than a third of the garden, he took a short break to rest. He was leaning on the handle of the spade when a cart drawn by a brown and white pony rumbled into the front yard. He recognized the thin man in the driver's seat. It was Simon, whom he questioned after pulling Sir Humphrey's body from the river.

A young woman in a long brown garment, with a frilly white cap on her head and a covered wicker basket in her hand, climbed down from the seat beside Simon. She waved good-bye as the man turned the pony cart in a sweeping arc and drove up the track that led to the woods. She made her way to the house, staring openly at the thick mat of tawny curls on Kyle's bare chest.

Joneta came outside a short time later. She walked down to the creek to fill a clay pitcher with cool water, which she carried over to him.

"Meg's back, as I am sure ye are aware," she said, handing the pitcher to him. "Drew will be along later. I'd like ye to stay for supper to get acquainted with them. Except for Bruce,

58

they're the only family I have left here."

He drank some of the water and dumped the rest over his head. "I would like that," he said, returning the empty pitcher to her. "By the way, wasn't that Simon who dropped Meg off?"

"It was," she said.

"How well do you know him?"

"Not especially well, now that you mention it. I do know he's kind enough to take Meg to the market whenever he goes into town."

"Does he live somewhere nearby?"

"He has a house down the coast a ways," she said. "Has he done something wrong?"

"Not that I'm aware of," he said. "When I questioned him earlier about the drowning, he seemed afraid to answer me. It's probably nothing."

"Shall I get Meg to pry the information out of him?" she said. "She's good at it."

"That won't be necessary," he said. "I'll speak to him again later in the week."

"Very well," she said.

She went inside, after which he resumed the job of digging out tough, deep-rooted weeds and preparing the earth for planting.

By the time he finished his self-appointed task, his long shadow stretched out on the ground behind him. The azure sky above melted into streaks of gold and pink as the sun dipped toward the tops of the trees to the west.

He went down to the creek to wash the dirt from his face and arms. He was drying himself with his shirt when he saw someone break from the cover of the woods to the east.

It was a young man, whose sparse beard darkened the lower half of his lean face. The cropped hair on his head was as black as his eyes. His forest green shirt and brown leggings were like those worn by a hunter, meant to blend into his surroundings. The only weapons he carried were a dagger at his narrow waist and a bow over his shoulder. He swung along with a spring in his step and a brace of grouse in his hand.

Kyle put on his shirt. He was lacing the ties at his neck when the young man splashed across the creek and walked toward him. "You must be Drew," he said. "I'm—"

"I know who ye are," Drew said, cutting in sharply. He took Kyle's measure in a single glance, his youthful face closed and wary. "Are ye here on the sheriff's business?"

"This is a social visit," Kyle said.

Drew appeared to relax. "I see ye have been busy," he said, his gaze on the tilled soil in the garden plot.

"So have you," Kyle said, eyeing the two gutted birds dangling from the leather thong in his hand.

Drew laid his bow and the half-empty quiver on the ground. He freed the grouse from the thong and squatted at the water's edge to pluck feathers.

Kyle walked around to the rear of the house to put the spade in the shed, after which he headed back to the creek.

When the birds were plucked clean, Drew cut off the heads and the feet and flung them into the grass across the shallow creek for disposal by wild critters. He rinsed the blade, wiped it on his leggings and slid it into the sheath on his belt. "Meg!" he shouted as he climbed to his feet.

The young woman with the frilly white cap came out of the front door and hastened over to where Drew waited for her. She took the plump game birds from him and hurried back into the house.

Drew searched through the feathers scattered among the rocks. Whenever he found a well-shaped pinion, he would pick it up and tuck it into his pouch.

"Do you fletch your own arrows?" Kyle said.

"Aye," Drew said. He retrieved his bow and quiver and started toward the house.

"Where do you get the glue?" Kyle said, falling in step beside him.

"From the tannery in town," Drew said. "They sell it cheap enough."

"It's not all that hard to make, you know," Kyle said.

"I've never needed to do it myself," Drew said.

"The stuff from the tannery," Kyle said, "likely comes from hooves and tendons rendered to a sticky paste."

"Have ye ever made glue?" Drew said.

"I have," Kyle said. "It takes time and patience—lots of patience." He chuckled. "I once made glue from the skin of a codfish. First, I scaled it. Then, I peeled off the skin, which I put in water and boiled down to a gooey mass. The smell was terrible, but it did the job."

"How did ye know it would work?" Drew said.

"An old soldier told me how to do it," Kyle said. "He was a mite spare on the details, so it took some trial and error before I got it right."

"Are ye any good with a bow?" Drew said.

"Fair to middling," Kyle said. "That means I usually hit what I aim at. Bows and arrows have their uses, but it wouldn't do to rely solely upon them in battle."

"Why not?" Drew said.

"They are no good at close range," Kyle said.

"Which weapon do ye prefer?" Drew said.

"The battle axe," Kyle said.

"That's pretty deadly," Drew said.

"It is," Kyle said. "Although there's nothing pretty about the damage it can inflict."

"I've never fought in a battle," Drew said wistfully.

"Consider yourself fortunate," Kyle said. He fingered the scar that ran down the side of his face from temple to jaw—a wound inflicted by a Flemish halberdier who met his Maker a moment later.

By that time, they reached the house. Drew opened the door and walked inside. Kyle followed him into the front room. The tantalizing aroma in the air came from the two birds on a spit roasting over the hearth fire.

"Meg," Joneta said to the young woman who stood beside her peeling turnips. "That is Kyle Shaw, Deputy to the Sheriff of Ayrshire."

Meg bobbed a curtsey. She no longer wore the frilly white cap, thus exposing a wealth of curly red hair on her head. She glanced at Drew, as though to gauge his reaction to having a lawman in their midst. His calm demeanor and friendly attitude toward Kyle seemed to reassure her, for she went back to peeling the turnips without a word.

Drew loosened the string on the bow and hung it and the quiver on a peg in the corner of the front room. He sat at the table and beckoned for Kyle to join him. "I gather that ye are staying for supper," he said.

"Joneta invited me earlier," Kyle said, sliding onto the bench across from him.

"Good," Drew said. "There's always more to eat when we have company." He removed the feathers from his pouch and lined them up on the wooden surface before him. He inspected each feather and laid the good ones in one pile and the bent and broken ones in another pile. When he finished sorting them, he rose to his feet and walked over to the hearth to toss the discarded feathers into the fire.

"You must roam all around these woods during your hunting forays," Kyle said. "Have you ever seen anything unusual?"

"Like a doe with antlers?" Drew said, resuming his seat on the bench at the table.

"Not exactly," Kyle said, grinning. "More like robed figures prancing among the oaks in the dead of night."

It was Drew's turn to grin. "Nay," he said. "But then, I don't go into the forest after dark anymore."

"Why not?" Kyle said.

The grin ebbed from Drew's youthful face. "Because it's haunted," he declared with solemnity.

CHAPTER 4

"Haunted?" Kyle said.

"Aye," Drew said with an emphatic nod. "By wraiths. They float above the ground, their faces as white as death."

"Who told you that?" Kyle said.

"Nobody," Drew said. "I saw them with my own eyes."

"When?" Kyle said.

"About three years ago," Drew said. "It was during the summer. The moon came up late that evening. I was crouched in the underbrush, waiting for a stag to come down the deer trail. All of a sudden, these pale unearthly figures glided past me through the trees. They didn't make a sound." He suppressed a shiver. "Ye won't catch me out there at night ever again."

"I thought you lived in Ayr back then," Kyle said.

"I did," Drew said. "Meg and I used to come out here every so often. I would go hunting, while she visited with her kinfolk. We usually stayed two or three days before we went on home."

"How often have you seen phantoms roving the woods at night?" Kyle said.

"Only once," Drew said. "That was enough for me."

"Which part of the forest were you in when you saw them?" Kyle said.

"To the east," Drew said. "Where the ground begins to rise to the hills beyond."

"Interesting," Kyle said, reflecting on Drew's tale of ghostly apparitions. Could the young man instead have glimpsed mortal men clad in flowing white robes on their way to some ritualistic ceremony deep in the forest, away from prying eyes? To him, that was a more realistic explanation for what Drew saw. Yet, he wasn't even sure of that, for there was so much more to learn about that elusive mystic brotherhood known as druids.

Kyle and Drew watched with appreciation as Joneta and Meg brought to the table a pot of turnips and greens simmered in meat broth, a platter of roasted grouse, a bowl of well-seasoned stuffing made from stale bread and chopped onions, hot barley flatbreads with mounds of salted butter, and a pitcher of fresh milk to wash it all down.

The food smelled delicious and tasted even better, which Kyle discovered after helping himself to it, as did the others.

During the meal, Joneta brought up Sir Humphrey's death and Kyle's meeting with the Ryland family.

Drew paid close attention while Kyle related the information that he imparted to Joneta earlier.

"I think he was done away with on purpose," Drew said at the end of Kyle's account.

Kyle gave Drew a sharp look. He marveled at the young man's discernment, for not once had he even hinted that Sir Humphrey had been murdered. "What leads you to that conclusion?" he said.

"He's a Southron," Drew said. "Besides that, his kinfolk ousted a noble Scottish family from their ancestral home. Either one could get him killed in these troublous times."

"You might be on to something," Kyle said. It was a simple concept, yet entirely logical and worthy of consideration. Hatred for the English was pervasive throughout the entire country because of the starvation and rapine that they—the English— inflicted upon the Scottish people. It was no surprise that the downtrodden Scots had had enough and that they were more than ready to fight back. "What do you know about the curse on Cragston Castle?" he said.

Drew wiped his mouth with the back of his hand. "So ye heard about that, did ye?" he said, pushing away his empty bowl.

"The Rylands' groom mentioned it," Kyle said. "It seems the former occupants—presumably that displaced noble Scottish family—placed a curse upon their ancestral home after Edward of England took it from them and gave it to the Rylands."

"It wasn't the castle that was cursed," Drew said. "It was the Rylands themselves. As long as they remain in residence there, ill luck will plague their every step."

"The former owner may have started that rumor in the hope of frightening the Rylands into leaving," Kyle said.

"Maybe," Drew said. "Although I don't think Sir Humphrey would agree that it was a rumor, if he could speak, that is."

The conversation then turned to hunting and fishing, and the best way to lay a snare for small game. While they talked, the long summer day drew to a close, and the front room began to darken.

Joneta, who had been listening with interest, got up from the bench to take a burning twig from the hearth fire. She touched the tiny blaze to the lip of an oil lamp. After the wick flared to life, she set the lamp in the middle of the table. She closed the shutters on both windows in the front room to keep out flying insects drawn to the light.

"If ye don't wish to ride back to the garrison in the dark," she said to Kyle, "ye are welcome to stay the night."

"Your offer is very kind," Kyle said, rising from the table. "However, I have already trespassed too long on your hospitality."

He put on his leather scale armor and buckled the sword belt around his waist. "I am grateful for the tasty meal," he said. "The poor fare served at the Bull and Bear Tavern cannot hold a candle to your cooking." He turned to Meg. "Nor to yours, little mistress," he added, with a slight inclination of his head.

Meg, evidently pleased at receiving such high praise, ducked her head to hide a blush.

Joneta bestowed a smile upon him that made his heart beat faster. "It is ye who are deserving of thanks," she said. "Because of yer hard work, the garden is now ready for the fall planting."

"I did it for you," Kyle said. He took her hand and gave the back of it a quick peck with his lips. He was reluctant to make a showy display of his affection for her in front of Drew and Meg, although he suspected they already knew about it.

The four of them went outside, where the enormous yellow ball of the rising moon overtopped the trees to the east. Myriads of stars filled the sky above with pinpricks of light. A westerly breeze cooled the warm night air, and a thin mist blanketed the open ground.

Kyle pursed his lips and whistled. The long shrill sound brought an abrupt end, albeit temporarily, to the chirping of crickets nearby. A moment later, an amorphous shape loomed out of the darkness. As it approached, it took the form of a horse trotting toward him with a translucent miasma swirling in its wake.

He tightened the cinch and climbed into the saddle. With a wave of his hand, he set out up the track at a lope. Before he reached the trees, it occurred to him that he might as well take a look around, since he was out in this part of the shire anyway.

He turned the gelding toward the east and headed into the forest, where he followed one of many deer trails that cut through the undergrowth. The going was slow, for the mist grew thicker with each passing moment. Moonlight filtered through the branches above him, barely illuminating the way. The only sound he heard was the jingle of harness and the muffled clop of hooves on the soft rot of leaves along the narrow path.

After a while, he noticed the rising slope of the ground beneath him. That meant he was now in Cragston Forest, which encompassed a great swathe of wooded upland. Yet, some of it consisted of barren rock that dropped abruptly into yawning ravines and deep gullies, to the peril of the unwise as well as the unwary. He relaxed his hold on the reins and gave the gelding its head, trusting the acute senses of his horse more than he trusted his own to safely negotiate the trail in the darkness.

He rode at a plodding pace, creeping through dense shrubbery that closed immediately behind him, as though he never passed that way at all. Brambles tore at his clothing. A wolf howled in the distance, a forlorn sound that raised the hair on the back of his neck.

He was now deep in the woods, where the network of vines and boughs overhead shut out the light from the moon. The gloom closed in on him, and the crowding trees cast a sudden chill and shadow all around. He brought the gelding to a halt, his eyes and ears strained to the limit. The forest was silent and still, shrouded in a vaporous mist that reached as high as his stirrups.

This, he surmised, must be near where Drew had encountered the wraith-like images. There was something about the place that made him want to look over his shoulder. It was only when he gave in to the urge to do so that he saw them.

They stood without moving, several yards away, their pale forms visible against the darker trees around them. Their spectral appearance gave him pause, but only for an instant. There was nothing to fear from the dead, he reflected. It was only the living who presented the threat of danger.

He turned the gelding's head toward the pallid figures, his eyes fixed upon them in the gloom. He got the impression that they were watching him just as closely as he was watching them. As he threaded his way through the trees, they vanished, only to reappear and vanish again. He was afraid to blink, lest he lose sight of them completely.

When he drew near enough to touch them, he laughed out loud at his own foolishness. He was at once relieved and disappointed that the phantoms of the forest turned out to be a stand of silver birch trees, their smooth white bark conspicuous against the dark gnarled trunks of the ancient oaks around them.

Although he resolved that particular conundrum without difficulty, Drew's tale was not so easy to dismiss. The young man claimed that he crouched in the underbrush while the ghost-like figures filed past him. Since trees do not move, there must be some other explanation for the perceived apparitions. He preferred to believe it was the conclusion he already reached about men in white robes. He would discuss the matter with John, who may be able to shed more light on the subject.

He turned back the way he came and managed to locate a deer trail, which he followed downhill and which eventually led him out of the forest. Upon emerging from the cover of the trees, he made his way to the coastal road, where he turned north, bound for the garrison. A stiff breeze blew in from the firth, and the receding tide exposed an expanse of sand that looked white and pure in the moonlight.

He was riding at a lope, with the steady beat of hooves drumming in his ears, when he saw a light flash for an instant over the inky waters of the firth. It was some distance away and appeared to hover close to the surface before it disappeared. He slowed the gelding to a walk, keeping an eye on the seaward skyline in case the light reappeared.

It did.

It winked on and off one more time. He stared into darkness for several minutes in expectation of another flash, but it never came.

It was a signal, of course, but from whom? And to whom was

it directed? His first thought was of freebooters—sea-roving mercenaries who pillaged and plundered wherever they went. The crusades had spawned such bands of lawless men who returned from foreign lands, dismissed from the King's service without pay, with no recourse except to take what they needed by force.

That freebooters could turn up on the shores of the lowlands was not as farfetched as it seemed, considering such an incident occurred fifty years earlier. That was before his time, but stories of the invasion were told and retold, lest anyone forget the looting and burning that brought the townsfolk of Ayr to their knees. The prosperous burghers living there now had much to lose if seafaring marauders again broke through their defenses at the mouth of the river and sailed upstream to raid inland towns and villages.

On the other hand, it just might be the master of a merchant vessel signaling to his contact man on shore to off-load the contraband aboard his ship. With the price of trade goods on the rise and the threat of impending war with England, smuggling became a common undertaking. Even honest folk never gave a second thought to the fact that it was illegal in the eyes of the law.

He continued along the coastal road until he reached the outskirts of town. The windows on every house he passed were dark, and no one moved about the streets at that time of night. He turned up Harbour Street and headed for the garrison. When he rode across the drawbridge, the clop of the gelding's hooves sounded hollow on the wooden planking. After identifying himself to the guard in the watchtower over the gates, he waited for admittance.

"I need to speak with the officer of the watch as soon as possible," he said, his voice raised for the guard to hear him.

"I'll send him down," the guard yelled back.

A moment later, another guard opened one of the huge wooden gates wide enough to admit both horse and rider.

Kyle rode into the empty courtyard just as the officer of the watch descended the wooden stairs that led up to the guard walk on the stone curtain wall.

"You wanted to see me?" the officer said as he approached. He was a stout man dressed in light armor, with plump cheeks that looked like a tight fit under his nasal helmet.

"I do," Kyle said. He told the man about seeing a light flash twice over the firth. "It might be smugglers."

"Or it could be something more serious," the officer said. "I'll double the seaward watch for a while. Thanks for the warning. Perhaps you should let Sir Percy know what you saw."

"There's nothing to be done about it at this hour," Kyle said. "I'll inform him in the morning."

After stabling the gelding and seeing to its needs, he trudged over to the sheriff's office. Once inside, he took a moment to remove his boots, his sword belt, and his leather scale armor before crawling fully clothed onto the straw pallet that served as a bed. He fell asleep the instant he laid down his head.

Light poured in through the unshuttered window of the sleeping chamber, waking Kyle on Tuesday morning. He rose from his pallet and padded on bare feet to the laver bowl to splash cold water on his face. A moment later, the bells of St. John's rang in the hour of terce, which satisfied his curiosity as to the time of day.

Since it was mid-morning, which was too late to eat with the soldiery in the main hall, he decided to walk around to the marketplace to break his fast. But first, he would let Sir Percy know about the signal light he saw last night. Although he found it easier to deal with the Castellan of Ayr and Warden of Galloway on a full stomach, he would see the man straight away

71

just to get that obligation out of the way.

He laced up his leather scale armor and buckled the sword belt around his waist before he opened the door of the sheriff's office. On stepping out into the warm sunshine, he spied Simon driving a pony-drawn cart across the garrison courtyard. Turval the potter sat in the high seat beside him. A square of sailcloth covered the goods stacked in the wooden bed behind them.

Simon hauled back on the reins to bring the brown and white pony to a halt in front of the main hall. He and Turval jumped to the ground and drew aside a corner of the heavy cloth. Each of them removed a large round wineskin from the back of the cart and proceeded to carry it inside.

Kyle thought nothing of it as he crossed the courtyard. The ninety-odd soldiers and officers billeted at the garrison ate two meals a day, so there was nothing unusual about merchants delivering milled flour, fresh meat, and other foodstuff to the kitchen every day.

Wine, on the other hand, was an expensive luxury that had to be imported. Because Simon and Turval took the wineskins into the main hall, he assumed that Sir Percy was the recipient.

He entered the main hall, which was empty but for a handful of street urchins pressed into willing service to clear away the scraps of food from the tables and to collect clay mugs sticky with ale.

Although an overseer with a willow switch kept a watchful eye on his youthful charges, he turned his back often enough to allow them to consume pieces of buttered bread or bits of cheese when he wasn't looking. For most of the boys, those leftovers were all they would get to eat that day.

Kyle cut across the large room and mounted the wooden stairway against the back wall to the second floor. With the clump of boots echoing in his ears, he walked down the long corridor on his way to Sir Percy's office at the far end.

Simon and Turval, no longer bearing the wineskins, stepped from the open doorway of the anteroom that led to Sir Percy's office. They started up the corridor, headed for the stairway that would take them down to the main hall. Simon kept his gaze averted, while Turval met and held Kyle's pale blue eyes until they passed each other.

Kyle heard the two men behind him quicken their pace toward the stairway as he turned into the anteroom at the end of the corridor.

Sir Percy's new clerk looked up from writing on a parchment scroll spread out on the desk before him. "Ah, Master Deputy," he said with an English accent. "I see you made it safely back from your journey." He was about seventy years old, with a black skullcap over wispy gray hair and a long face scored with wrinkles. His hand, with its tracery of blue veins and knobby arthritic knuckles, shook as he put the quill pen into the holder beside the inkwell. Though his black robe showed signs of wear around the neck and at the cuff, the garment was neat and clean. Shrewd blue eyes, which appeared to miss nothing, took the deputy's measure in a single glance.

"You have me at a disadvantage, Master Clerk," Kyle said. "I do not know your name."

"It is Walter," he said. "A moment, if you please." He rose stiffly from his stool and went around the corner of the desk to enter the larger chamber beyond the anteroom. After a moment, he returned. "Sir Percy will see you now."

Kyle nodded cordially to the clerk, the top of whose head barely reached the middle of his chest, before going into Sir Percy's office.

A large oak desk with a marble top dominated the room. Light flared along the curved shape of a polished silver decanter sitting on the reddish-brown stone surface. A pair of high-backed carved chairs faced the desk. A wash stand with an

ornate pewter bowl and matching pitcher stood near an unshuttered window that overlooked the courtyard below. A huge storage trunk took up an entire corner of the room. A table with
two wineskins perched on it occupied another corner.

Sir Henry de Percy, a twenty-four-year-old man with brown
eyes and boyish features, sat on a cushioned chair, holding a
silver goblet in his hand. The midnight blue color of his velvet
garment flattered his ruddy complexion. He turned his head
from staring out of the window as Kyle walked into the room.

"Good morrow, m'lord," Kyle said with a slight bow. He
looked with mixed feelings upon the English nobleman seated
at the desk before him. Sir Percy could at times be quite personable. Yet, there were occasions on which the man failed to give
important matters the due consideration they deserved, likely
because of his youth and inexperience.

The prestigious position of castellan—an appointment
granted by Edward of England himself—gave Sir Percy absolute
power over all the inhabitants of Ayrshire and Galloway, including the entire English soldiery garrisoned throughout both
shires. The fact that he answered only to his king for his actions
meant that if a Scotsman or Scotswoman sought justice in an
English court over which he presided, the outcome might
depend more on his mood that day, rather than on the weight
of the evidence presented.

Sir Percy returned Kyle's greeting with an impatient wave of
his hand. "Is it true?" he said.

"Is what true?" Kyle said.

"That we will shortly suffer invasion from the sea."

"I doubt it, m'lord."

"How can you be certain? You yourself witnessed the
exchange of signals last night. At least, that is what the officer of
the watch claimed this morning."

"It is true that a light flashed twice over the water. To my

74

knowledge, no one received or returned the signal, so there is no cause for alarm just yet."

"Just yet?" Sir Percy said, sitting upright on his cushioned chair.

"The guards on the garrison wall have been instructed to report any suspicious activity on the firth," Kyle said. "If they see something, you will be the first to hear about it."

Sir Percy looked unconvinced. "This wine is excellent," he said, after taking a sip from the goblet in his hand.

"From whence did it come?" Kyle said, feigning disinterest. There was no doubt in his mind that the wineskins on the table in the corner were the ones Simon and Turval brought in moments ago.

Sir Percy peered at Kyle over the rim of his goblet, his eyes narrowed. "Why do you ask?" he said.

"No reason," Kyle said. An evasive response, like the one he just received, implied the need to conceal information. Rather than discourage him, it only made him more curious as to the source of the wine. He dropped the matter for the present, but the guards on the wall would not be the only ones looking out to sea for the next few weeks.

"Prior Drumlay sent word to me that Sir Humphrey has been murdered," Sir Percy said. "Sir Humphrey is, or rather was, a peer of the realm. Thus, finding his killer requires your undivided attention. So, how goes your investigation into his death?"

"Slowly, but surely, m'lord."

"I want the brigand who did it brought to justice as soon as may be."

"As do I," Kyle said.

He took his leave and withdrew from Sir Percy's office. As he walked into the anteroom, a burly man stepped from the corridor into the open doorway.

The man was around Kyle's age of thirty-three years, with
dark wavy hair and brown eyes. His bearded face was plain,
with deep vertical lines between his dark eyebrows. He wore a
black leather jerkin over a gray linen shirt, the tail of which
reached down to the middle of his thighs. His black leggings fitted him well, showing off his muscular limbs. The hilt of his
sword was as unadorned as the leather belt around the considerable girth of his waist.

The two men stopped to stare at each other, oblivious to the
clerk's presence.

Kyle was the first to break the strained silence that fell
between them. "Well, well," he said. "If it isn't Captain Morhouse."

"Kyle Shaw, as I live and breathe."

"How nice of you to remember me."

"A face like yours is hard to forget."

"You flatter me," Kyle said.

"I didn't mean to," Morhouse said.

"You haven't changed a bit."

"Neither have you."

"You must excuse me," Kyle said with a tight smile. "I was
just on my way out."

Morhouse's large frame blocked the open doorway. "How
fares Mistress Ada these days?" he said, making no effort to
move out of the way.

"She died a few years ago," Kyle said.

Morhouse seemed stunned at the news, although he recovered
instantly. "I would have taken better care of her," he said with a
flash of anger in his brown eyes.

At that moment, Walter cleared his throat. His gaze shifted
from Morhouse to Kyle and back again. He had obviously been
following every word of their conversation.

Morhouse opened his mouth to speak, but he apparently

changed his mind. He stepped aside without a word to let Kyle
pass.

"I reckon I'll see you around," Kyle said as he started for the
doorway.

"You can count on that," Morhouse said, barely concealing
the menace in his voice.

CHAPTER 5

Kyle left the main hall and strode across the garrison courtyard, headed for the stable with the warm morning sun on his back. He wondered at the resentment that flooded through him at the sight of Anthony Morhouse. Ada lay in her grave, buried years ago in Scottish soil, so there was no longer any reason for hostility toward Morhouse. Yet, even after fifteen years, the old animosity between them still lingered.

He saddled the gelding and rode from the garrison. When he turned onto Harbour Street, he recognized the white destrier approaching the priory gates a short distance away. The man in the saddle was Sir Peter Ryland, dressed in a black velvet cotte with silver trim, in town no doubt to identify the body pulled from the river. He nudged the gelding in the belly to quicken the pace, for he wanted to be present during the viewing.

A Scots girl about sixteen years of age stood on the river side of the street, holding the hand of the five-year-old boy beside her. The similarity of their features marked them as kin. Both wore leather sandals and linen tunics the color of oatmeal, belted with beaded cords. The tangle of brown hair on her head half-covered her youthful face. The large brown eyes in her pale countenance stared keenly at Kyle as he rode past.

He only noticed the girl because she stood without moving amid the bustle of townsfolk coming from and going to the busy marketplace. Once he turned into the priory gates, he forgot about her, for more pressing matters now commanded his attention. He followed the long driveway around to the back of the church, where Sir Peter had already climbed down from his ornate saddle in front of the mortuary chapel.

Kyle reined in and dismounted just as Prior Drumlay walked up to join them in the shady solitude behind the church.

After the exchange of formal greetings, keys jingled as the prior unlocked the chapel door. He stepped aside to let Sir Peter and Kyle enter before him.

A lighted clay cresset on the iron lamp stand in the corner barely illuminated the cool interior of the small chamber. The body, which was naked but for a strip of linen draped across the loins, lay on a stone table in the center of the floor.

The sudden influx of air from the open door caused the tiny flame in the clay cresset to waver. Shifting light and shadow across the bare limbs made the corpse appear to stir.

Sir Peter's step faltered at the sight of it. He crossed himself with one hand and clung to the hilt of his sword with the other. In the next instant, he regained his composure, for he continued on as though nothing happened to give him pause.

Kyle kept an eye on Sir Peter's face as they walked up to the granite slab that served as a bier.

Sir Peter looked down at the waxen features of the dead man in the muted light, his expression impassive. "It is my uncle," he said after a moment, without a note of sadness or regret in his voice. "Drowned, did he?"

"Only after he was struck on the head and forcibly held under the water," Kyle said evenly.

Sir Peter swung around to confront Kyle. "Why did you not tell me this sooner?" he demanded, his face flushed and frowning.

"As an officer of the law," Kyle said, "I am constrained from broadcasting information to just anyone during a murder investigation. Because you identified the victim as a member of your family, you may now be informed of certain pertinent facts."

"I see," Sir Peter said, still frowning. "Do you have any idea who did it?"

"Not yet, m'lord," Kyle said. He met and held Sir Peter's gaze. "Tell me about the mistletoe."

A shadow flickered across Sir Peter's face. "Mistletoe?" he said. He twisted the ring on his middle finger with the thumb and forefinger of his other hand. "What mistletoe?"

"The mistletoe found in your uncle's throat," Kyle said. "What connection does it have with his death?"

"How should I know?" Sir Percy said, his voice a notch higher than before.

While not expecting to get a straight answer, Kyle gleaned quite a bit from Sir Peter's reaction to his query. Repeating a word to stall for time usually preceded a lie. Fiddling with clothing or jewelry indicated uneasiness or anxiety. A rise in pitch often signified deception.

The sprig of mistletoe, although not the cause of Sir Humphrey's death, clearly played an important part in it. Sir Peter looked frightened at the mention of it, but his fear appeared to be more for his own safety than for the possibility of being accused of murder.

"Were you aware that your uncle wore a hair shirt under his clothing?" Kyle said. "We discovered it during the examination of his body."

"My uncle was a queer duck who kept to himself," Sir Peter said. "There's no telling what he got up to or why."

"You didn't answer the question," Kyle said.

"If you must know," Sir Peter said with impatience, "I had no idea that he wore it."

"My condolence on your loss, Sir Peter," Kyle said in an abrupt change of subject.

"My deepest sympathy to ye and yer family," Prior Drumlay interjected with haste, as though unwilling to let a lawman show more compassion than a priest.

Their commiseration evidently reminded Sir Peter of his familial obligations, for he walked over to the granite altar and knelt down on the cold flagstone floor. After bowing his head for a brief moment, he clambered to his feet, placing both hands on the altar to haul his stocky body upright. In the process of rising, he knocked over the tiny vessel with the phosphorescent substance in it, spilling some of the finely powdered substance across the back of his hand. He righted the vessel before wiping his fingers on the breast of his cotte. He then turned to face the prior. "This place oppresses me," he said, glancing around the dank chamber. "If there is nothing more . . ." He took a tentative step toward the chapel door, letting the unfinished phrase hang in the air.

"But there is, m'lord," the prior said, effectively curtailing the man's flight.

Sir Peter paused with a heavy sigh. "What, for instance?" he said.

"The burial," the prior said. "Will it be here in the kirk yard or do ye plan to take the body with ye?"

"Bury him in the church yard," Sir Peter said. "Is that all?"

"Nay, m'lord. There is the matter of procuring a headstone and hiring a stonemason to carve the name and date upon it—"

"I give you leave to handle all the arrangements, whatever they may be," Sir Peter said, interrupting him. "How long will it take?"

"Three days."

"Then I and my family shall return on Thursday to attend the funeral."

"Very well, m'lord," the prior said. He did not exactly hold out his hand, but he assumed a petitioner's stance that made it clear he expected to receive some sort of monetary remuneration for the impending memorial service.

Sir Percy dug three silver pennies from the purse at his waist and dropped the coins into the prior's open hand. He turned on his heel and strode from the chapel.

"Bless ye, m'lord, for yer generosity," the prior called after the retreating nobleman.

Kyle followed Sir Peter out into the bright sunshine. He watched the man mount the white horse and ride up the driveway without a backward glance.

Prior Drumlay stepped through the chapel door to stand beside Kyle. "He was in some hurry," he said, his thin lips drawn tight in disapproval.

"He certainly was," Kyle said. He passed a hand over the stubble on his jaw, his brow furrowed in thought. Perhaps he should tag along behind Sir Peter, not all the way to Cragston Castle, but at least as far as the edge of town in case the man planned to meet up with someone in particular whom he—Kyle—should know about.

He took a hasty leave of the prior and swung up into the saddle. At his urging, the gelding broke into a lope. He rode at an angle across the glassy lawn, cutting the distance to the front gates in half. Along the way, he ignored the censorious glances cast in his direction by brown-robed monks going about their daily chores.

When he caught sight of Sir Peter riding at a trot through the priory gates, he slowed the gelding to a walk. It would not do to overtake his quarry, for that would surely give away his presence and defeat the purpose of the undertaking. With that in mind, he waited behind the stone fence surrounding the priory for a full minute before exiting the grounds.

As he turned onto Harbour Street, Hoprig and four other English soldiers in light armor approached at a brisk pace, undoubtedly on their way to the garrison. People in the street ahead of them scrambled to get out of their path.

With the exception of Hoprig, the soldiers appeared a little worse for wear. Their bull-hide armor was scored with gouges. Their nasal helmets, which hung from their saddle bows, were dented and bent out of shape. Three of them bore open wounds bright with fresh blood on their faces and hands, while one wore a bandage around his head.

Hoprig seemed untouched by what had plainly taken a toll on the others, for there was not a nick or a scratch on him or the helmet hanging from his saddle.

The sixteen-year-old girl on the far side of Harbour Street had evidently been watching for Kyle, for the moment he rode from the priory, she ran into the street, pulling the child along with her. So intent was she to catch up with him that she failed to heed the clatter of hooves on cobblestone growing louder as the horsemen drew closer.

Across the way, a man in a homespun tunic shouted a warning to the girl. A corpulent woman with a covered basket on her arm stared in open dismay. Those nearby looked on, some in horror, some passively, but none in surprise, for it was common for English soldiers stationed at the garrison to do as they pleased, with no thought as to the consequence for Scottish folk.

The urgency of the man's shout brought Kyle's head around. On seeing the mounted soldiers bearing down on the girl, he abandoned his pursuit of Sir Peter to turn back the way he came.

The girl made it to the middle of the street before she grasped the danger of her situation. Since it was too late to get out of harm's way, she thrust the child behind her and flung up her arms in a reflexive but useless gesture to ward off the inevitable.

★ ★ ★ ★ ★

Hoprig expected Blackwell, who rode the rawboned bay beside him, to swerve around the girl, as he himself started to do. By the time he realized the man meant to trample her down, there was little he could do but snatch at the bay's bridle. He yanked its head sideways in a desperate effort to bring the horse to a stop, even as he hauled back on the reins of his own mount.

To his relief, both horses came to a mincing halt mere inches away from the girl. She whirled to flee, reaching for the boy's hand.

At that same instant, the bay swung around against Hoprig's grip on its bridle. Its muscular haunches slammed into the girl from behind.

The jarring blow tore a shrill scream from her throat. The force of the impact flung her into skidding contact with the rough cobblestones. She came to rest on her left side, as limp and still as a discarded rag doll.

The girl's cry practically under the bay's nose startled it so that it reared up, dragging Hoprig from his chestnut mare.

Blackwell, taken by surprise, tumbled backward over the bay's rump.

The three soldiers behind Blackwell reined in to laugh at his plight.

Hoprig released his hold on the bay's bridle to hasten over to the girl's crumpled form, stricken with horror that she might be dead.

The boy, unhurt but frightened, tugged on her hand, as though trying to wake her up.

Hoprig slipped one arm under her shoulders and the other under her knees. He lifted her, light as a featherweight, and carried her to the verge on the river side of the street, where there were fewer people walking about. He knelt in the grass and gently put her down.

She lay unmoving in the flowering clover, her hands and forearms abraded from scraping along the cobblestones. Her face was as white as death, except for the purple bruise forming on her left cheekbone. Sunlight glinted on the long brown hair spread out around her head like a halo. The only sign of life about her was the shallow rise and fall of her chest.

"God have mercy," Hoprig said, choking on the knotted anguish in his throat. "What have I done?" The depth of his own distress astonished him. The girl meant nothing to him. She was a stranger, without a name, yet an inordinate concern over her fate threatened to overwhelm him.

The boy tried to push Hoprig aside. "Get away from my sister," he cried. "Haven't ye caused her enough harm?"

"I'm so sorry," Hoprig said. He got up slowly and stood there looking down at the girl, pierced to the heart at her plight and fretting at his own helplessness to do anything about it.

Blackwell sprang to his feet with a roar of anger. He tackled Hoprig from behind, which sent them both rolling in the grass. They scrambled to their feet to grapple with one another on the verge. Each pushed against the other with all his might, their heads lowered like a pair of bulls, while their three comrades-in-arms urged them on.

Hoprig was shorter than Blackwell, but his frayed temper and raw emotional state lent him the strength he needed to throw the bigger man to the ground and pin him down by sitting on his chest. "What is wrong with you?" he snarled. "You could have killed them."

"They should have gotten out of my way," Blackwell said, struggling to free his arms.

"They are but children," Hoprig said between his teeth.

"Who cares?" Blackwell retorted. "They are but Scots."

Incensed beyond reason by Blackwell's callous remark, Hoprig began to pummel the man's face with his fists until two of the other soldiers swung down from their horses to pull him off.

The two soldiers held Hoprig's arms while Blackwell clambered to his feet, his hand cupped to his nose to catch the blood that trickled from it. "You bastard!" he cried. "You broke my nose."

Kyle advanced on the scene just as Blackwell landed a solid punch to Hoprig's jaw.

The blow stunned Hoprig for a brief moment. Pain radiated from the side of his face and down his neck. He braced himself for the second blow, but it never came.

"Back off," Kyle commanded as he nudged the gelding forward to come between Blackwell and Hoprig.

"Mind your own business," Blackwell said, although he did take a step back to avoid the gelding's massive hooves. He daubed at the blood on his upper lip with the back of his hand.

"Let him go," Kyle said to the two who held Hoprig captive. When neither of them made a move to comply, he reached for his sword.

The steel hiss of the emerging blade clearly carried more weight than mere words, for the men turned Hoprig loose at once. They hurried for their horses without a glance behind them.

Blackwell and his cohorts mounted up and continued on their way to the garrison, this time at a slower pace.

Kyle sheathed his sword and swung down from the saddle to follow Hoprig over to the girl's side.

The corpulent woman sat on the ground beside her, patting her hand and clucking over her like a broody hen. The boy hovered nearby, a worried frown on his childish face.

"How is she?" Kyle said to the woman.

"How do ye think, after being struck down without cause?" the woman said. "What is the world coming to when an innocent child cannot cross the street without risk to life and limb?"

The townsfolk who gathered around them nodded their heads and murmured among themselves.

"Is she going to die?" the boy said to no one in particular, his brow puckered in concern.

"She'll be fine," Hoprig said, fervently hoping he spoke the truth. "What is your name?"

"Owen," he said. "Me and Isabel came to town to talk to the sheriff's deputy. She told me so."

The boy's words drew Kyle's attention. "Do you know what she wanted to talk to me about?" he said.

Owen shook his head, his gaze on his sister, whose eyelids started to twitch and flutter.

Isabel opened her eyes. "What happened?" she said, wincing at the sound of her own voice. Her questing fingers found the knot on her forehead.

"Those brigands practically trampled ye to death," the woman said, her tone indignant. She cast a scathing glance at Kyle. "There ought to be a law against it."

Isabel sat up without assistance and glanced at those around her. Her gaze settled on Hoprig, as though her eyes were drawn to him.

Hoprig looked down at her, so young and vulnerable huddled there in the grass. Her skin was as smooth as ivory, and the eyes that met his were light brown, fringed with long dark lashes. Drawn by her youthful beauty, he was at once entranced and afraid, for she must surely hate him for causing her injuries.

"My dear girl," the corpulent woman said. "Ye really should rest a while. It will help ye mend."

Isabel glanced down at the raw abrasions on her palms. "I'm all right," she said. "I shall be myself in a moment." She examined the tear in her linen tunic, as though to assess how it could best be repaired.

"Isabel, he was with the men who hurt ye," Owen said, pointing an accusatory finger at Hoprig.

"To my shame, mistress, that is true," Hoprig said to the girl. "To my credit, I did divert the horses, although I should have done it sooner."

"My brother and I would have fared much worse, had ye not intervened," Isabel said. She gathered her legs under her to rise. In order to steady herself, she reached for Hoprig's hand.

He offered it readily and helped her to stand. Her simple gesture made his heart rejoice, for it meant she forgave him.

At the corpulent woman's request, Kyle and the man nearest to him hauled her to her feet. She twitched her tent-like garment into place and accepted the basket that Owen handed back to her.

"I thank ye for yer kind attentions," Isabel said to the woman.

"It was the least I could do," the woman said. Her eyes shifted to Hoprig, then back to Isabel. "Have a care, my lamb," she added. "Beware of the wolf disguised as a sheep." She took her leave and waddled across the street with the covered basket on her arm, only to vanish behind the stalls in the marketplace.

Now that the excitement was over, the people around them lost interest and began to wander away.

"Mistress Isabel," Hoprig said. "Shall I fetch water from the river so that you may bathe your injuries?"

"I can take care of my sister by myself," Owen said, claiming her hand in a possessive manner.

"Of course, you can," Hoprig said. He produced a scrap of linen from the pouch at his side and held it out to the boy. "That is why you shall be the one to dampen this for her."

The boy took the proffered cloth and escorted his sister down the sloping bank, though it seemed more like she was the one conducting him to the river. Sunlight glistened on the ripples as he dipped the soft fabric in the water. He handed the sodden cloth to her, which she pressed with care against the large red lump on her forehead.

After a moment, she rolled her elbow-length sleeves back to her shoulders and squatted at the water's edge to wash the dirt from the cuts and scrapes on her hands and forearms.

Hoprig stiffened at the sight of the yellowish-purple marks on her upper right arm. The pattern was the kind that large fingers would leave on delicate skin. He exchanged a glance with Kyle. "Those bruises didn't come from any fall," he said with a scowl.

"They surely did not," Kyle said.

The girl rolled down her sleeves and rose to her feet. She trudged back up the gentle slope with the boy beside her. Behind her, the surface of the river reflected the cerulean sky dappled with wisps of cloud drifting overhead.

Hoprig gazed at her, thoroughly enchanted. In his heart of hearts, he longed for someone like her to protect and cherish for the rest of his days. But alas, that could never be. Not only was he twice her age, but he was English as well. He turned away, unaccountably saddened at the loss of that which he did not even possess.

Just then, a warm breeze carried with it the tantalizing scent of roasted chicken and fried funnel cakes from the marketplace.

Kyle's stomach growled, a reminder that he had not yet broken his fast that day. "The noon hour is nearly upon us, mistress," he said. "Shall we all walk to the marketplace for a bite to eat?"

Isabel looked down at Owen, who nodded his head. "Aye, m'lord," she said, glancing up at Kyle. Her eyes then settled on Hoprig, as though waiting for him to speak.

Hoprig avoided her gaze and went to gather the reins of the horses grazing several yards away.

"Come along," Kyle said. He took a step toward the street,

but the girl made no effort to move. "It's all right. I shall pay for the food."

"You are very generous, m'lord," she said, although she remained where she stood.

Kyle peered into the depths of her troubled brown eyes. "What is it, then?" he said.

At that moment, Hoprig walked up leading the horses. His gaze flicked from one to the other of them as he listened with open interest.

"There is a grave matter I must speak to ye about," she said.

"And that is?" Kyle said.

"It concerns a valuable jewel that went missing," she said. "I did not take it, but I fear I shall be accused of its theft."

"Why is that?"

"I help my mistress dress her hair every morning. After she goes downstairs, it is my duty to tidy her chamber."

"So, you are left alone in the chamber every morning with her possessions?"

"Aye," she said.

"I can see why that would give you cause for concern," Kyle said. "Does anyone else have reason to enter her chamber during the day?"

"Not that I know of."

"When did this jewel go missing?" Kyle said.

"Three days ago."

"What kind of jewel is it?" Kyle said.

"A great white stone that shimmers with many colors," she said. "My mistress told me it came from the sea."

"Is it a pearl?"

"That's what my mistress calls it," she said. "It is shaped like a teardrop and hangs from a gold chain."

"Why did she not send word to me sooner?"

"She said there was no need for a man of law to get involved since she probably misplaced the pearl herself. It was a gift from her husband, and she did not want him to know it was missing. I convinced her that if he ever did learn of it, he would wonder why the matter was never officially investigated."

"Well done," Kyle said with admiration.

"I also find its disappearance quite odd."

"How so?"

"In that the pearl was there on her vanity table one day and gone the next. My mistress rarely wore it, so how could she misplace it?"

Kyle considered her words for a moment. His eyes then strayed to her upper right arm. "Has your mistress ever struck you or treated you harshly?" he said.

"Never," she said, her tone emphatic. "She is very kind to me and Owen. She gave us food and shelter when no one else would. I am grateful to her for that, which is why I would never steal from her."

"Who is your mistress?" Kyle said.

"Lady Catherine de Salamanca, wife to Sir Anthony Morhouse, Captain of Horse at Ayr Garrison."

CHAPTER 6

Kyle received the news without batting an eye. He never met Lady Catherine, but in his opinion, she must be a saint to put up with Anthony Morhouse. From what he knew of the man's character, it was inconceivable that their union could have been a love match. More than likely, Morhouse wed her to gain wealth and position, a custom all too prevalent among nobles of that day.

"I shall interview Lady Catherine as soon as may be," he said. "But first, let us put something in our bellies."

He led the way across the street toward the marketplace, with Isabel and Owen following close behind. Hoprig brought up the rear, leading the horses.

On entering the marketplace, they passed row upon row of merchant stalls displaying wooden furniture, silver jewelry, leather goods, dyed wool fabric, bolts of linen cloth, pottery, and other items. A troubadour strolled around the grounds, strumming a rebeck while he sang a ballad. A juggler deftly kept brightly colored balls moving in the air above him. Peddlers steered wheeled barrows about, their raised voices extolling the freshness of their produce or the size of their fish.

The four of them made their way over to a cluster of vendors with pushcarts selling cooked foodstuff. Owen wanted a sweet cake from the baxter, so Hoprig bought one for the boy and one for himself.

Isabel appeared fascinated with the hot fried pasties laid out on a wooden rack to cool. The crimped edges of the folded brown crusts kept in the spiced mutton filling.

Kyle purchased four pasties from the pie man and gave two to her. He promptly consumed one pasty and started in on the second. "Where does your mistress live?" he said, between bites.

"At Kilgate Manor," Isabel said around a mouthful of food.

"I know where that is," Kyle said. "Have you been with her long?"

"Since before winter set in," she said. "Me and Owen were living rough in the woods outside of Paisley when my mistress found us and took us in." She consumed the last morsel and wiped her oily fingers on the front of her fine linen tunic. "She already had a cook and a gardener, so she engaged me to attend to her clothing and arrange her hair."

Kyle eyed the grease stain on her tunic and the unruly mass of curls on her head. "I see," he said. "Where are your parents?"

"The fever took them last summer," she said. "Me and Owen have been on our own ever since."

Owen seemed quite taken with Kyle's sorrel gelding. While he ate, he nipped off tiny pieces of his sweet cake to feed the tall warhorse.

The gelding seemed taken with the boy after that, nudging him with its long nose, evidently looking for more cake.

"Would you like to ride him?" Kyle said.

Owen responded with a wide grin and the vigorous nodding of his head.

Kyle lifted the boy and perched him on the saddle. He mounted the gelding and sat in the saddle behind him.

Hoprig swung up into the saddle and held out his hand to Isabel. Since she was too short to put a foot into the stirrup, he raised her high enough for her to scramble onto the horse behind him. He looked pleased when she slipped her arms around his waist and clung to him, rather than to the cantle.

They rode from the marketplace and turned up a narrow street with cramped weathered houses on either side. They soon left the older part of town to enter the outskirts, where the lanes were broader and the trees more plentiful. The homes there were larger and set further apart, with space enough between each one for a garden plot.

About a mile beyond the edge of town, Kilgate Manor came into view around a bend in the road. The early afternoon sun shone down on the three-story red sandstone house built like a stronghold within an enclosing wall. A single guard tower on one side of the imposing edifice extended beyond the pitched slate roof. Mullioned windows peered out at the rolling hills and forested dales that surrounded it outside the stone barrier. The road ended at a high wooden gate that barred entry to the grounds within.

A large black bird sat on top of the gate, preening its oily feathers. It paused to peer at them from its lofty perch, its head cocked, its beady eyes assessing whether they posed a threat.

"A crow," Isabel said in a whisper. "It is an evil omen."

"Do you truly believe that?" Hoprig said, looking over his shoulder at her.

"I do," she said.

"I've seen flocks of crows," he said. "Except for the family fortune going down the castle midden, nothing bad ever happened to me."

"It is the lone crow that bodes ill for the one who sees it," she said.

He patted her hands clasped around his waist. "I'll look out for you," he said.

"It's not me I'm worried about," she said with a slight frown.

Kyle leaned forward to tug on the bell rope hanging alongside the gate to announce their presence.

The loud clanging proved to be too much for the crow. It

fluttered into the air and flapped away toward the manor house.

After a long moment, a tiny portal in the gate opened an inch. "Who goes there?" a man barked in a gruff voice.

Kyle identified himself. "Lady Catherine sent for me," he said.

The portal shut with an abrupt snap. Wood scraped against wood as the man inside lifted the bar. The gate creaked open just wide enough for the horses to enter one at a time.

A bearded man of middle years in a loose brown tunic held the gate ajar while Kyle rode through the gap.

Hoprig's chestnut mare followed on the gelding's heels.

The porter's countenance darkened at the sight of Isabel's arms wrapped about the English soldier's waist.

Kyle and Hoprig let their horses amble down the shady lane that led to the house. Along the way, they passed storehouses and other outbuildings set against the inside of the surrounding wall. When they reached the stable across from the house, they halted to wait for a groom to come out and take their horses.

It took a couple of minutes for the porter, who walked with a slight limp, to catch up with them. "Isabel will take ye in to m'lady," he said. His manner was barely civil, although he did hold the stirrup while Kyle dismounted.

Kyle held out his hands to take Owen from the saddle.

"Can I stay here a little longer?" the boy said, his tone pleading.

"Of course, you can," Kyle said.

Isabel slid from the mare's rump to the ground. "Come this way, m'lord," she said to Kyle. She started toward the hewn stairs on the outside of the manor that led up to the entryway on the second level.

"Pay no heed to Edgar," she said, pausing at the bottom step. "He don't like Southrons much."

"I'm not English," Kyle said.

"But he is," she said, indicating Hoprig.

Edgar turned his back on Hoprig to lead the gelding into the stable with Owen still astride. The boy seemed to be enjoying himself immensely now that he had the entire saddle to himself.

Left on his own, Hoprig dismounted and led his horse into the stable. He emerged a moment later wearing a scowl. He walked across the yard to where Kyle and Isabel stood at the foot of the stairs.

"I won't be long," Kyle said to Hoprig. "In the meantime, take a look around."

Isabel mounted the stone steps ahead of Kyle. On reaching the landing on the second floor, she opened the solid oak outer door and entered the main hall.

Their footsteps echoed in the vaulted chamber as they walked across the timber-planked floor. A long wooden table stood in the middle of the room, with benches enough around it to seat up to fifty people. Half a dozen tall windows along the front wall let in sufficient light to see the undisturbed layer of dust on the unused portion of the table at the lower end.

She went through one of the archways leading out from the main hall and continued down a dimly lit corridor. At the far end, she stopped before a recessed door and knocked lightly.

"The sheriff's deputy is come to see ye, m'lady," she said. She listened at the door for a moment before standing aside to let him enter.

Kyle opened the door and stepped into a pool of bright sunlight streaming in through a large window. Reflected brilliance against the white plaster of the walls dazzled him after the gloom of the corridor. It took a few seconds for his eyes to adjust, which is when he noticed the woman there in the small chamber.

She sat on a cushioned bench facing a multicolored tapestry stretched across a wooden frame. With the needle in her hand,

96

she deftly stitched at the spiral horn of some mythical creature. Her olive skin with its rosy undertone marked her as a foreigner. A tight bun at the nape of her neck confined a wealth of shiny black hair. Ebony eyes peered out from deep sockets with mild curiosity. Her face was too angular, her nose too long and her mouth too wide, yet together, those features only added to her exotic beauty.

A silver pendant studded with cut diamonds hung from a delicate silver chain around her slim neck. The polished stones flashed and sparkled with each move she made. Her purple velvet gown seemed too heavy a garment to wear on such a warm summer day, but the sleeves were loose and she appeared content in it.

"I beg your pardon, m'lady," he said. "I didn't see you for the glare."

"Not to worry, Master Deputy," she said in a husky voice with a thick Spanish accent. "I am used to being overlooked. Make yourself comfortable." She indicated the chair across from her with a sweep of her hand.

Sunlight gilded the sewing basket on the floor at her feet. The statue of the Madonna on a pedestal in the corner and the translucent alabaster bowl on the wrought-iron table beside her gave the chamber a decidedly feminine air.

As he approached, he saw that her face looked pinched and drawn, as though from strain. There were dark circles under her eyes, like those caused by sleepless nights. Although it was none of his business, he could not help but think that Morhouse had something to do with her stressed condition.

After they exchanged a formal greeting, Kyle settled onto the hard-backed chair as bidden, repositioning the sword at his hip with a metallic clank.

She paused in mid-stitch to look him over, like a doting mother sizing up a prospective suitor for a favorite daughter.

She must have liked what she saw, for her lips moved in a faint smile before she turned back to the tapestry. "Do you mind if I continue to sew?" she said, plying the needle to the spiral horn. "I find it soothes my nerves."

"Carry on, by all means," he said. He cleared his throat. "As you know, m'lady, I am here to look into the theft of your pearl."

"Theft is such a vulgar word," she said. "Let us say 'misplaced' for now."

"Very well," he said. "I understand from Isabel that it has been three days since the pearl went missing."

"That is correct," she said.

"Who else has access to your jewels, besides you and Isabel?" he said.

"My husband," she said. "But he rarely comes into my chamber anymore."

"I met Edgar on the way in," he said. "He serves as porter, as well as groom and gardener?"

"He does," she said.

"Is he satisfied with his lot here?"

"What are you suggesting?" she said.

"Has he ever complained about too much work for the wage he receives?"

"I pay him well," she said. "I offered to take on another worker to help him, but he would not hear of it."

"And the cook?" he said. "Is she satisfied with what she is paid?"

"Apparently so," she said. "She has been with me for a year."

"When was the last time you wore the pearl?" he said.

"It has been so long, I do not recall," she said. She pivoted the frame on its metal pins to tie off the thread at the back of the tapestry.

"How did you come to notice the pearl was missing?" he said.

98

"I did not notice at all," she said, cutting the thread with a straight razor that she took from the sewing basket. "It was Isabel who brought it to my attention."

"Did you search for it?"

She deposited the razor on the wrought-iron table and laced her fingers in her lap. "Isabel made a thorough search of my chamber," she said, meeting his eyes without blinking. "The poor child was worried sick about being accused of taking it. I assured her that such a thing would never happen." She indulged in a rueful smile. "Do not trouble yourself too much over the loss of my pearl, Master Deputy. It was a mere trifle that can easily be replaced."

Kyle caught the subtle dismissal in her tone and rose to his booted feet. "Thank you for your time, Lady Catherine," he said with a slight bow. "We'll talk again another day."

He started for the door. As he walked across the chamber, he felt those alien black eyes boring into his back. Her pearl must have cost a great deal of money, yet she called it a trifle. Perhaps it was, compared to her diamond pendant, which was possibly worth a king's ransom. But the pearl still had value, and the fact that it was missing, whether stolen or misplaced, hardly seemed to bother her at all. She might not be lying about what she knew of the matter, but she certainly wasn't telling the truth. Not all of it, anyway. Before he gave up the hunt for the pearl as she suggested, he meant to find out what she was hiding from him and why.

CHAPTER 7

Hoprig walked around to the rear of the manor house to see what was there.

A small flock of sheep and a handful of milk cows grazed within a fenced enclosure that took up most of the open area at the back of the house. A dozen chickens scratched in the dirt inside the pen.

A storage shed occupied a corner of the yard. Years of rot and decay gnawed ragged gaps in the weathered boards, which hardly looked sturdy enough to withstand a strong gust of wind. Spindly stalks of corn and wilted greens struggled for survival among tall weeds in the garden plot beside the animal pen. A dilapidated wagon with a broken tongue and a missing wheel only added to the air of laxity and neglect.

Hoprig shook his head at the appalling sight. His father might have run off to the crusades and spent the family fortune in so doing, but the man never let his properties fall into ruin and disrepair.

The sun beat down on his bare head as he continued on around to the front of the house and made for the well under an open-sided structure that shaded the water from direct sunlight.

Isabel walked over to join him just as he let the wooden bucket down into the water. Her clothing was different from that torn in the accident, for she now wore a yellow linen tunic with a belted waist and white embroidery around the neck.

"Are you thirsty?" he said.

"Aye," she said. "It's so hot out."

He drew up the bucket and set it on the circular stone rim. He took the horn cup from the peg on one of the supporting posts and dipped it into the cool water. When it was full, he handed it to her.

She took the cup and drank most of the contents. "Ye saved my life," she said, wiping her mouth with the back of her hand. "And I don't even know yer name."

"It's Hoprig," he said. "Brian Hoprig."

"Brian," she said, passing the cup back to him. Her light brown eyes swept him from head to toe. "The name suits you."

"It was my father's name," he said. He filled the cup and tilted his head back to drain it. While he drank, a tiny stream of water leaked from around the lip of the cup and dribbled onto the bull-hide vest over his long-sleeved shirt.

She reached out to wipe the moisture from the side of his mouth with the tips of her fingers. Her touch was gentle, more intimate than a kiss.

It caught him off guard. He held perfectly still, painfully aware of the stubble of whiskers on his chin and the sweat stains on his shirt. His blue eyes searched hers for any hint of brazenness, but he saw only innocence reflected back at him. She appeared unaware of the effect that simple act had on him.

He turned away to hang the horn cup back on the peg, unsure of what to say to her.

"Have ye ever traveled anywhere?" she said.

He turned toward her, relieved that she took no notice of his momentary discomfiture. "I lived in London for a while before I came here," he said. "I didn't much care for it there."

"Do ye ever long to go home?"

"I have no home," he said with a hard edge to his voice.

"What about yer father and yer mother?" she said. "Do ye

not miss them?"

"My father is dead," he said. "My mother's only concern is for her own comfort. Ever since Father died, she has been on the hunt for another husband. I suspect any man with a title will do."

"I didn't mean to distress ye," she said with a worried frown.

"It hasn't bothered me for a long time," he said with a dismissive wave of his hand. "What about you and Owen? Caring for a motherless child can be a mighty burden for someone your age."

"I don't mind," she said. "He's my brother."

Her words pleased him for some reason, perhaps because it showed a tenacious loyalty to those she loved. At that moment, he heartily wished to be one of them.

She glanced over at the manor, which looked reddish-gold in the afternoon sun. "My mistress told me she lived here when she was younger, long before she married the master. This property belongs to her parents, ye know."

"Where are they now?" he said.

"In Spain," she said. "My mistress says they went back home because the winters there are more tolerable than the winters here."

"I'm sure they are," he said. "I wouldn't mind going to Spain someday. I've heard it's beautiful."

"It is," she said. "At least, my mistress says so. I've never been there myself." She looked down at her fine linen tunic. "This fabric came from Spain. My mistress gave me a length of it to make a garment. She even helped me sew it."

"It's very nice," he said. "Your mistress likes you, I think. She treats you more like a daughter than a servant."

"She does," she said. "I am in her debt for the kindness she has shown to me and Owen." She lifted her eyes to his face, her expression earnest. "I am no thief, Master Brian. I did not take that pearl."

"I never for one moment thought you did, Mistress Isabel," he said with equal gravity.

The warmth of the smile she bestowed upon him made him flush with pleasure. Then, a cloud passed between him and the sunshine of his happiness, for he recalled the futility of their situation. They had as much hope for a future together as a fish had with a bird. Should a fish and a bird ever marry, where would they live? So it went with the two of them. The English would never accept her as one of their own, nor would the Scots tolerate his intrusion into their way of life.

Kyle descended the hewn stairs to the yard below. On his way to the stable, he passed the rectangular stone kitchen set apart from the other outbuildings located against the inner wall.

It would do no good to question Edgar or the cook about the pearl's disappearance, for the slightest hint of accusation would put them on the defensive. Instead of making a formal inquiry, it might be more prudent to chat with the cook about some trivial matter. That would give him the opportunity to take her measure, which he had already done with Edgar.

Edgar appeared to be the kind of fellow who did what he must to get by. He showed no guilt or fear in the presence of a man of law, as would someone with something to hide. He also seemed clever enough to realize that steady work at the manor kept food on his table and a roof over his head, as opposed to reaping a questionable profit from stolen goods that came with the high risk of hanging. He might be tempted to hold back a tender cut of meat for himself whenever he slaughtered an animal for his master's table, but that appeared to be the extent of his thievery.

Kyle turned aside into the kitchen doorway. A blast of heat

met him head-on. In a matter of seconds, beads of sweat broke out on his forehead and ran down the sides of his face. He began to have second thoughts about meeting the cook in her own domain.

The place reeked of old grease. An oily brownish residue covered the stone walls. Soot blackened the stout beams supporting the sod roof. A bucket of cut wood stood close to the huge fireplace, and a black pot hung from an iron arm over the flames.

A stout woman in a stained white apron jabbed at the burning logs with a metal poker. Light from the renewed blaze glinted on the dark hair twisted into a loose knot at the back of her head. Stray tresses that escaped confinement stuck out around her plump heat-reddened face.

Across the room, a dark-haired boy about ten years of age sat under a table in the corner teasing a tan and black puppy.

The woman straightened her back and hung the poker on a hook by the chimney. "Where is that lazy boy?" she said in the melodious dialect of the Welsh.

The child under the table ignored her and continued to annoy the puppy.

"Tippy," she said, walking over to the table. "Go fetch some water. You can play with that mangy cur later." She picked up a basket of mud-crusted parsnips from the earthen floor and placed it on the table. "That lazy old coot should have washed these before he gave them to me."

The boy released the puppy, which scampered over to the wood bucket to hide behind it. He crawled halfway out from under the table, but stopped when he saw Kyle looming in the doorway.

"Hurry it up," the woman said. She prodded the boy with the toe of her felt shoe. "I need that water now."

When Tippy refused to budge, she looked down at him. On

seeing the wary expression on his face, she followed his gaze to Kyle. "Who are you?" she demanded.

Only then did she notice the fine linen shirt under his scale-armor vest and the high polish on his leather boots, for she added in a more genial tone: "M'lord."

"I am Deputy to the Sheriff of Ayrshire," Kyle said.

"Of course," she said, giving him a knowing look. "You are here about Lady Catherine's pearl." She shoved the basket of parsnips aside to clear a space on the scarred wooden surface. "Come in, come in. Set yourself at the table while I pour you a tiny nip."

Although Kyle preferred to remain in the doorway where the air was cooler, he complied with her invitation so as not to spurn her hospitality.

"Tippy!" she said in the no-nonsense tone of the mother-voice. "Get the fan!"

The boy scuttled out from under the table to take something from one of the shelves against the wall. He spread open a fan made of long black feathers sewn together and waved it in Kyle's general direction.

The moving air dispelled the heat somewhat, which made him more comfortable. He sat on the hard bench and stretched out his long legs under the table. "What is your name, mistress?" he said.

"Glynis," she said. She reached behind a crock of oat groats to retrieve a glazed jug with a cork stopper in the mouth.

"You're a long way from Wales, Mistress Glynis," he said.

"I am so," she said. Her expression reflected uncertainty, as though she wondered how he knew that about her.

"What brought you this far north?" he said, his pale blue eyes on her.

She fiddled with the cork stopper, thus avoiding his gaze. "Jobs are scarce back home," she said. "I must take work where

I can find it."

She spoke in an off-handed manner, but he could tell she chose her words with care. She evidently mistook him for an Englishman, perhaps because of his clothing. As a Welshwoman, she would not know that most lowlanders these days chose to dress after the English fashion of fitted leggings under a short coat-like garment, rather than the traditional tunic and cloak common among Scottish folk.

A more compelling reason for traveling so far to the north, one that she would never divulge if she thought he was English, was to escape the brutal subjugation of her homeland by Edward of England and his army. If she did indeed flee under those circumstances, he found it odd that she'd chosen to work for an Englishman like Morhouse.

She tugged on the stopper until it popped out with a hollow sound. "I think I know what happened to that pearl," she said.

Kyle spread his elbows out on the table. "Do you, now?" he said with interest.

"Aye, m'lord," she said. She placed a couple of leather jacks on the table and poured a generous measure of golden liquid into each tar-stiffened cup. She then joined him on the bench.

Kyle chose the leather jack nearest to him and lifted it to his lips. He filled his mouth, which he regretted at once. The instant the fiery liquor came into contact with his tongue, his eyes began to water. He swallowed it to be polite, only to regret that, too, for it burned all the way down to his stomach. After he caught his breath, he attempted to speak. "What is this?" he croaked, peering into the tarred cup.

"Grog," she said with pride. "I made it myself." She picked up her cup and drank every drop in it. The only visible effect it seemed to have on her was the heightened color of her full cheeks. She held the jug out to him. "More?"

"I'll pass," he said, putting a hand over the top of his cup.

The fire in his belly eased into a warmth that suffused his entire body.

She refilled her cup and sipped at the contents.

"Now, Mistress Glynis," he said, setting his cup firmly away from him. "What were you saying about the pearl?"

She took another mouthful of grog before she spoke. "I have an idea who took it," she said.

"Go on," he said.

"It was a crow," she said, looking him in the eye.

"Indeed," he said. Her suggestion was not as farfetched as it sounded. Crows were notorious thieves, especially when it came to small shiny objects. And there were crows in the vicinity, for he saw one on the gate when he first arrived. "Did you actually see a crow take it?"

"Nay," she said. "But one could have." She took another sip, her eyes on his cup. "Are you going to finish that?"

"I think not," he said.

"It's a shame to waste it," she said. She poured his grog into her cup without spilling any of it. "I came to the conclusion that a crow took the pearl because none of us did."

"By 'us,' do you mean you, Edgar, and Isabel?"

"Aye," she said. She cocked a thumb at herself. "I know I didn't take it."

"What makes you think that Edgar and Isabel are innocent?"

"If either of them stole that jewel," she said, "do you think they would stick around here? I wouldn't. That's a sure way to get caught."

"Good point," he said. Even in her tipsy state, her logic made sense. However, those three were not the only inhabitants of the manor. "What about Captain Morhouse, or even Lady Catherine?"

She burst into laughter, a raucous bray that startled the puppy out from behind the wood bucket. "What a notion," she said after a moment, daubing at her tearing eyes with the corner of her apron.

"As you say, what a notion," he said.

It occurred to him, though, that such a notion should be considered. Many a lord and lady judiciously sold their possessions, without their servants knowing about it, to stay afloat financially in this uncertain economy. Maybe that was why Lady Catherine did not want him to inquire too deeply into the matter, for it would expose her dire financial situation, which of course would greatly embarrass her.

"I will look into the possibility that a crow is the culprit, Mistress Glynis," he said. He rose from the table and straightened his sword belt. "Thank you for your time."

She made no reply, for her eyelids drooped and her head sagged toward her ample bosom.

Hoprig saw Kyle step through the kitchen doorway and head for the stable. "I must go now," he said to Isabel.

"Before ye leave, Master Brian, tell me this," she said. "Do ye attend vespers at the priory?"

"I've never been much of a church-going man," he said, glad for an excuse to stay with her a while longer. "I hope that doesn't disappoint you."

"It does not," she said. "I wouldn't go either, except for my mistress."

"Does she attend vespers?"

"Quite often," she said. "She takes me with her whenever she goes."

"Does she, now?"

"She does."

"Perhaps I, too, should go to vespers," he said. "It may do me some good."

"It can't hurt," she said.

"I might even see you there."

"Perhaps ye will," she said. She picked at a loose thread on her sleeve, betraying her nervousness in his presence.

"When will your mistress next attend vespers?" he said.

"Tomorrow," she said. "Is that too soon for ye to start going?" she added, a hopeful expression on her face.

"Not at all," he said, absurdly elated at the prospect of seeing her again. "Until the morrow, then."

He took his leave of her and started toward the stable. His long shadow stretched out on the ground before him. His spirits soared as he walked across the open yard, for he never looked forward to going to church as much as he did at that moment.

CHAPTER 8

Kyle awoke early on Wednesday morning. The air was still cool in the sleeping chamber of the sheriff's office, so he rolled onto his back on the straw pallet and tucked his hands behind his head to mull over the issues at hand.

Although mistletoe did not kill Sir Humphrey Ryland, it played a key role in his death. The dead man's brother, Sir Fulbert, and his nephew, Sir Peter, clearly understood the implications behind the use of mistletoe, whereas Sir Peter's wife, Eleanora, appeared oblivious to its significance.

Sir Fulbert hated his brother enough to kill him, yet according to his own wife, he never left Cragston Castle on the night in question. Mistress Ryland, however, appeared to be a timid woman, easily cowed with threats of violence. That, of course, cast a shadow over her credibility, which in turn weakened Sir Fulbert's only defense.

On the other hand, Sir Peter, whether by accident or design, thus far had failed to divulge his whereabouts at the time of the murder. Mounting debt gave him a motive to kill his uncle, whereas the ability to come and go unnoticed afforded him the means to do it. Having either motive or means was enough to place Sir Peter under suspicion. Both together put him at the top of the list of suspects.

Yesterday, he'd lost track of Sir Peter. Today, he planned to retrace the man's route. Surely somebody would recall seeing an English nobleman riding down the street on a big white horse with a plaited mane.

With regard to the pearl, the cook's suggestion that a crow made off with it sounded less plausible now than it did earlier. Did Glynis, in fact, employ the old trick of misdirection in order to point the finger of accusation away from herself? That hardly seemed likely, for she showed none of the classic signs of guilt during their conversation, like the subtle lift of a shoulder, folding the arms with curling fingers, or a nervous flutter of the eyelids. She maintained a calm demeanor the whole time, even prior to consuming copious amounts of grog.

Despite Edgar's unpleasant nature, neither his facial expressions nor his body movements gave the impression of a man with something to hide. The cook was right about a guilty person fleeing from the scene of a crime. Rarely did a villain linger after committing a felonious act. Edgar's mere presence there at the manor went a long way to substantiating his innocence.

By contrast, Isabel displayed definitive signs of fear, but only for being wrongfully accused of a crime she claimed she did not commit.

A less probable but still possible avenue to consider was that Lady Catherine took her own pearl. That would explain why she did not want him to look too closely into its disappearance. It did, however, raise the question of why she refused to admit it, for the pearl was hers to dispose of as she pleased. Did she in fact sell it for cash to sustain her household? Or was there a more sinister reason for her to part with it? Was she perhaps hiding a dark secret? Did she use the pearl to pay off someone who threatened to expose her secret? In either case, why make a mystery of it? Such a course only called undue attention to her plight, whatever that was.

Since both options involved marketing the pearl, it followed that he must track down those engaged in such trafficking, whether inside or outside the law. He was aware that such a hunt might well be a waste of time, for only a fool peddled such recognizable merchandise so near to where it was stolen. Nevertheless, he must start somewhere, and the local goldsmith was as good a place as any.

Now ready to start his day, he rose from his pallet to wash, shave, and dress. After donning his leather scale armor and buckling on his sword belt, he opened the front door and stepped outside.

The weather was fair and sunny, with barely a cloud in the sky. A faint westerly breeze brought with it the stench from the castle midden on the sea side of the garrison wall. The smell, though unpleasant year round, was especially offensive during the summer months due to the heat.

Ten heavily armed soldiers on horseback gathered in the open courtyard to form two columns. Captain Morhouse, his countenance stern and forbidding as usual, sat on a black warhorse at the head of the formation. When the last man fell in line, he gave the signal to move out.

The small troop started for the garrison gates with the jingle of harness and the squeak of leather. Blackwell and his three comrades rode among them, their faces grim and intent.

The clop of hooves on the wooden drawbridge soon faded, leaving the courtyard empty and silent once again.

Kyle headed for the main hall to break his fast, after which he walked over to the stable to saddle his horse.

He rode from the garrison and turned up Harbour Street. As he passed the market grounds, merchants and vendors there were busy opening their booths and uncovering their stalls in preparation for the day's commerce.

He rode through town to Tradesmen's Row, where craftsmen plied their skills in cramped shops along the crooked street. On reaching a whitewashed stone building with a wide alleyway beside it, he halted the gelding and climbed down from the saddle. He draped the reins over the rail out front and entered the apothecary shop.

Inside, the clean scent of dried herbs and aromatic spices filled the air. Light from an unshuttered window shone on a brazier in the far corner and a wooden table in the middle of the swept floor. Pottery jars and clay pots lined the shelves built against the side walls. A brown and beige striped curtain separated the large front room from the sleeping chamber at the rear.

John Logan looked up from placing a polished metal mirror before a thin middle-aged woman seated at the table with a jar of balm in her hand.

Her cobalt blue silk gown and bejeweled fingers spoke of wealth and privilege. Her demeanor was such that she appeared to be enjoying the personal attentions of the handsome apothecary.

"Good morrow," Kyle said with a slight bow to the woman. "Pardon the interruption, but I must confer with Master John for a moment."

"Of course, Master Deputy," the woman said with a gracious nod.

John excused himself to her and walked over to greet Kyle. "What can I do for ye at this early hour?" he said with a grin that caused a dimple to flash in his left cheek.

"There's bad business afoot, I'm afraid," Kyle said. He took a folded piece of cloth from the pouch at his side and handed it to John. "Can you test the feed in here for poison?"

"I can," John said. He laid back the corners of the tiny parcel and sniffed at the yellowish-brown kernels of grain. "I might even be able to determine what kind of poison it is." He frowned, clearly troubled. "Whose feed is this?"

Kyle told him about the dead stock at Cragston Castle.

"No one should eat those animals," John said. "The meat is most likely tainted."

"The carcasses have already been burned," Kyle said.

"Good," John said. He glanced over at the woman who was testing the balm on the back of her hand. "I've something to tell ye, but this is not a good time. Come to the house at noon. We can talk over lunch. Joneta will be there, too. I invited her yesterday when I made a call out that way. Colina is eager to see the baby."

"I look forward to it," Kyle said. "I have a few inquiries to make just now, but I can fetch Joneta and the babe after that and be back well before noon."

"There is no need to do so," John said. "Simon has business in town today, so she made arrangements to ride in with him."

"Simon?" Kyle said, frowning. He wondered at Simon's sudden interest in Joneta. Or was it perhaps the other way around? He indulged in a moment's jealousy, mostly because in his experience, women tended to feel sorry for those timid helpless fellows. They did not want to marry them, as much as they wanted to mother them, which was just as bad. Besides that, no one did a favor without expecting something in return. Simon was no exception to that rule.

"Are ye all right?" John said.

"I'm fine," Kyle said, emerging from his reverie. He was being ridiculous, of course, for he had no claim on Joneta. He drew in a deep breath and let it out in a long sigh. Perhaps it was time to change that. "I'll let you get back to your customer."

With a parting nod to the woman at the table, he walked out of John's shop and into the warm sunshine. The goldsmith's shop was on the other side of the street, so he left the gelding dozing at the rail to walk there.

He was crossing the street when a wagon rumbled by with fresh baked goods in a dozen wicker baskets on the wooden bed. A teenage boy, no doubt on his way to market, coaxed an ox forward with a willow switch. An adolescent girl sat among the baskets with a leafy branch in her hand to wave away the flies.

Kyle passed under the wooden sign suspended over the open door and entered the goldsmith's shop.

The front room was long and narrow, with uneven timber planks on the floor. Cracks riddled the plastered walls and cobwebs hung from the ceiling. Stacks of lidded boxes, some carved and some plain, filled the dusty corners. A workbench stood at right angles to the side wall, cutting the elongated room in half. Pliers, hammers, and other small tools littered the wooden surface.

A young apprentice stood at a small table several feet behind the workbench, tapping a dent out of a copper bowl laid over a wooden form. The black dog sprawled on the floor at his feet raised its head and pricked its ears when Kyle came into the shop.

A man with a prominent nose and dark hair graying at the temples sat on the far side of the workbench, facing the doorway. He hunched over a gold filigree brooch with foreign symbols adorning the front of it, examining the piece with an expert eye.

A lean man in a brown tunic sat on the near side of the workbench with his back to the entryway. His cropped black hair glinted with blue highlights in the light coming through the open door. He looked over his shoulder as Kyle walked up behind him. "Master Deputy," he said by way of greeting.

Kyle recognized the potter. "Master Turval," he said. His gaze shifted to the older man behind the workbench. "Master David," he added with a cordial nod. "I see you're busy. Take your time. I'm in no hurry."

Turval turned back to David the goldsmith.

"The work on this brooch is very delicate and quite intricate,"

115

David said to the potter. "It was certainly fashioned by skilled hands. I will give you two groats for it."

"Is that all?" Turval said, disappointment evident in his tone.

"That is a good price," David said.

"It belonged to my grandmother in the old country," Turval said. "It is worth twice what you offer."

"Of course, it is," David said. "If I paid you what it is worth, how can I hope to turn a profit from the sale of it? I have a wife and six children to feed." He handed the brooch back to the potter. "You are welcome to see if you can get more for it elsewhere."

Turval scowled down at the brooch for a moment. "I will take the two groats," he said at last, nudging the piece of jewelry toward the goldsmith. "You are a thief and you know it."

David lifted his shoulders in a shrug. He produced a handful of coins from the purse at his waist and counted out eight silver pennies.

Turval gathered up the money and left the shop without a backward glance.

David set the brooch aside. "What can I do for you?" he said, his dark eyes on Kyle. "Something for your lady, perhaps?" He reached for a tiny box near at hand and opened the lid to show off a gold ring of a size to fit a woman's finger, set with a single raised emerald. The polished facets of the flawless gem caught the light as he held it out to be admired. "The price is very reasonable."

"Nothing for me, thanks," Kyle said, his hand up to discourage further offers. "I just stopped by to see if anybody brought in a pearl for evaluation or sale during the last week or so."

"Not that I recall," David said with a thoughtful frown. "Are you interested in pearls? I have quite a selection to show you."

"I seek one pearl in particular."

"For yourself?"

"For a client."

"Since you are a man of law on the hunt for a client's pearl, may I assume it was stolen?"

"You may," Kyle said.

"Well, then," David said, lacing his fingers on the wooden surface before him. "Can you tell me about the setting or even the size of it?"

"I am afraid I cannot," Kyle said. "I've never seen it."

"That is regrettable," David said. "Pearls are as individual as people, you know. They come in all shapes and sizes. Even the colors vary. I can send word to you, if you like, should a pearl come my way."

"I'd appreciate that," Kyle said. "Thanks for your time." He started to turn away, but the image of the emerald ring emerged in his mind's eye. The clear green stone reminded him of Joneta's eyes in the sunlight. If he bought the ring now, he could give it to her when the time was right. Not right away, of course, for it was too soon to propose marriage to her.

Or was it? With men like Simon lurking in the wings, perhaps it would be better to declare his intentions now, rather than wait until it was too late.

He stood there, lost in thought for so long that the goldsmith began to fidget.

"Is something amiss?" David said, his brow furrowed with concern.

"What will you take for that emerald ring?" Kyle said. He tried to sound blasé. Otherwise, the man might smell a sale and demand the highest possible price for the item in question.

"For you, five groats," David said.

"I'll give you three groats for it," Kyle said.

"Four groats," the goldsmith said.

"Three groats."

The young apprentice at the back of the shop paused at his

work to watch his master and the customer, clearly entertained by their bartering.

"Have a heart, Master Deputy," David said. "I have a wife and eight children to feed."

"Eight children, is it?" Kyle said. He smiled as he removed three groats from his coin purse. "A minute ago, you had six children."

"Eight? Six? What does it matter?" David said, his hands lifted in a plea to the heavens. "They shall all starve because of you."

"Nonsense," Kyle said. He jingled the silver money in his hand. "What say you, Master David?"

"You are a hard man," David said, exasperation evident on his bearded face.

"And you shall be a wealthier one, should you accept my offer," Kyle said. He stacked the coins on the workbench and slid them to within easy reach of the goldsmith's fingers. "Well?"

After scowling in silence for a moment, the goldsmith picked up the tiny box with the emerald ring in it and placed it in front of Kyle. "It is yours for three groats," he said with a heavy sigh.

Kyle took the ring box and tucked it into the pouch at his side. "Thank you, Master David," he said, quite pleased with his purchase.

"I made that ring myself, you know," David said with pride. "Do you really like it?"

"I do," Kyle said. "The lady will, too." He took his leave and headed for the door with the goldsmith beaming after him.

As he walked from the shop, he made a mental note to do something he should have already done, which was to obtain a description of the missing pearl the next time he spoke to Lady Catherine. Since there was only one goldsmith in town, he must now turn to less conventional means to obtain information. Tapping those would likely cost him every coin remaining in his purse. It would be money well spent, though, if it gave him a solid lead to follow, even if it came from a source on the shady side of the law. He was certain that Lady Catherine would reimburse him for the expenditure if it produced results.

He was about to step into the street when the potter called out to him.

"Master Deputy," Turval said. "A word, if you please."

Kyle waited for the potter to join him. "What is it?" he said.

"I could not help but overhear that you are looking for a certain pearl," Turval said. "I know a fellow who may be of assistance to you."

"What sort of assistance?"

"If what you seek is anywhere in town, he will surely know about it."

It sounded to Kyle as though the fellow about whom Turval spoke was a purveyor of stolen goods. "What makes you think he will risk his neck to speak to a sheriff's deputy?" he said.

"Hul is friend of mine," Turval said. "He will do as I ask."

"What makes you think I won't arrest you, too?"

"Neither Hul nor I have dealings with criminals."

"Then how does Hul come by such knowledge?" Kyle said.

"He keeps his eyes and ears open. By doing so, he often comes across things that are of use to others."

"I see," Kyle said. So Hul was an informant. Those who followed that dubious vocation tended to vanish rather suddenly, never to be heard from again, or their body might turn up in some dark alley with their throat slit from ear to ear. "Selling information is a risky trade."

"It is a job, like any other," Turval said.

"I'd like to meet Hul," Kyle said. "I have a question or two to put to him."

"I can take you there now, if you wish," Turval said. "That is, if you have the time."

Kyle glanced down at the position of his shadow on the ground, which showed it was barely mid-morning yet. "I can spare an hour," he said. "Lead the way."

Turval started to walk up the street.

"Hold on, Master Turval," Kyle said. "We will get there faster if we take my horse." He crossed the street to the gelding and swung up into the saddle. He held out his hand to pull the potter up behind him.

At Turval's direction, Kyle headed west. As they approached the older section of town, the streets became narrower, winding through cramped houses separated by alleys barely wide enough for a dog cart to pass through. Weeds sprouted from cracks in the cobblestone paving. Children with grubby faces and ragged clothing stopped to stare as they rode by.

Kyle navigated a network of lanes and alleyways until he came upon a street that ended abruptly against the back wall of a two-story stone building somewhere in the heart of town. He glanced around to get his bearings, but the surrounding houses crowded in too close for him to catch a glimpse of a familiar landmark beyond the rooftops, like St. John's bell tower or the English flag jutting up above Ayr Castle.

The dwellings on either side of that dead-end street were little more than shacks fashioned from upright timber planks. Nearly all had roofs of thatch, but only a few had a window to let in the light.

The inhabitants there shared a village-like atmosphere. A young woman lounged on a bench near the open door of her house, singing a lullaby while she nursed a baby.

At the next house, a teenage girl knelt at a hand mill, grinding barley seeds with a small flat millstone.

Farther on, a woman of advanced age stirred the contents of a three-legged iron pot positioned over an open fire on the cobblestones in front of her house.

Across the street, five tough-looking men with an air of villainy about them crowded around a makeshift table, playing a game of chance with painted pebbles.

A heavyset man in an off-white tunic sat on a low stool in the middle of the open courtyard-like area between the houses that faced the street. He scratched on the cobbles with a lump of charcoal, while a small group of adolescent boys crouched in a semi-circle around him, looking on.

The clop of hooves into their private quarter drew every eye. The sound also brought forth from the alleys between the houses half a dozen mongrel dogs.

The fierce barking and menacing growls caused the gelding to snort and dance sideways. Kyle tightened the reins to steady the great warhorse.

The leader of the dog pack began to circle around to the rear, as though intent on nipping at the horse's legs.

The heavyset man rose from the low stool to bellow at the dogs. The sharp edge of his voice brought the scruffy creatures to an abrupt halt. They milled around for several seconds, only to skulk away with their tails between their legs.

The ruffians around the makeshift table stared at Kyle, their faces closed and wary. They abandoned their game to drift in his direction, their hands straying to the cudgel or the dagger thrust under their belt.

The adolescent boys needed no encouragement to scurry away.

One boy was slower than the rest, for he hobbled along on a foot wrapped in a dirty cloth bandage stained pink with a purulent discharge. When he reached the house where the woman sat nursing the baby, she got up from the bench to hustle him inside.

Turval slid from the gelding's rump. "That is Hul," he said to Kyle, indicating the heavyset man.

Hul's gaze rested on Turval. "What is it ye want?" he said.

"You cut me to the heart, my friend," Turval said. "How do you know I did not come here just to see your face?"

Hul grunted skeptically. "I suppose he came to see my face, too," he said, tilting his head at Kyle.

"In a manner of speaking," Turval said. "Hul, this is Kyle Shaw, Deputy to the—"

"I've heard of him," Hul said, cutting him off.

"You see?" Turval said, turning to Kyle. "Hul knows everything."

Kyle climbed down from the saddle, but he held onto the reins, since things, whether large or small, animate or inanimate, had a way of disappearing under sticky fingers in that part of town.

"What brings ye to our humble corner of town, Master Deputy?" Hull said.

"I am in search of a client's pearl that recently went missing," Kyle said.

"What has that to do with me?"

"I understand you might know how to find it."

"I'm afraid ye have the wrong man," Hul said.

"That's too bad," Kyle said. "I am sure the owner of the pearl will be most generous to the person who recovers it."

Hul shrugged his beefy shoulders. "How is that of interest to me?" he said.

"I just thought you should know," Kyle said.

"So now I know," Hul said. "I suppose ye will be on yer way, then."

"I suppose I will," Kyle said. "By the way, how did that boy yonder come by his injury?"

"What's it to ye?" Hul said.

"Nothing," Kyle said. "I only ask because if he does not soak that foot in hot salty water every day for the next week, he may lose it to gangrene."

"Are ye an apothecary, too?" Hul said, his tone skeptical.

"Nay," Kyle said. "But I do know the signs of infection."

"How can ye be sure?"

"I saw the discharge on his bandage," Kyle said. "Does it have a foul smell?"

"It does, now that ye mention it," Hul said. "But why salt? What does that do?"

"It hastens the healing process," Kyle said. "The water cleans only the outside, though, so after each soaking, you must squeeze out any infectious matter inside the wound. The bandages should be boiled if you use them again to wrap the foot."

"How do ye know any of that?"

"I picked up a thing or two from chirurgeons on the field of battle when I served as a mercenary," Kyle said.

"For the Southron King?" Hul said with lowered brows. Being a Scotsman, he naturally disapproved of a fellow Scot who sold himself to Edward of England to fight against his own countrymen.

"For Philip the Fourth of France," Kyle said.

"Ah, well," Hul said. "That's different." His whole attitude changed, and so did that of the five ruffians behind him.

Hul laid a friendly hand on Kyle's shoulder. "Come have a bite of Mam's stew. While we eat, ye can tell me about yer wealthy client."

The tough-looking men drew closer, as though interested in the deputy's response to Hul's invitation.

Kyle hesitated for only an instant. "I'd love to," he said.

After he explained to John Logan that he was not hungry for lunch because of his reluctance to offend a possible ally in his hunt for Lady Catherine's pearl, he knew the older man would understand. Hospitality was a serious obligation that was not to be taken lightly. To reject an offer like the one extended to him would be an unforgivable insult both to Hul and to Hul's mother.

He let Hul steer him over to where the elderly woman stirred the boiling contents of the three-legged pot. He peered into the black iron vessel and spied among the chunks of cooked turnips and wilted greens the headless body of a skinned animal that closely resembled a cat.

CHAPTER 9

Kyle spied a puny shrub clinging to life at the edge of the street. The tenacious plant grew close enough for him to keep an eye on his horse without appearing to do so.

As he bent down to tie the gelding's reins around the tough fibrous stalk, he got a good look at the charcoal marks that Hul made on the cobblestones when he first rode up. It appeared to be a crude map of the town, with an "X" here and there to define certain locations.

He straightened up after securing the reins, now enlightened as to how Hul kept a finger on the pulse of all the goings-on in town. The man sent out those adolescent boys to loiter at designated places, specifically to eavesdrop on certain individuals who would never suspect a child of listening to their idle chatter.

"Mam," Hul said in a loud voice to the elderly woman tending the pot. "This is Master Kyle."

Kyle gave her a courtly bow. "At your service, mistress," he said in an equally loud voice on the assumption that she was hard of hearing.

She flashed a toothless grin at him, evidently pleased at his courteous treatment of her. "Call me Abigail," she said in the quavering voice of the aged.

"He's hungry," Hul said. "Like the rest of us."

Several wooden bowls lay on a bench near the cooking pot. There was also a wicker basket with stale bread in it. Abigail chose the cleanest bowl from the stack and used the iron ladle to dredge forth the choicest portion of mystery meat from the pot.

"Eat," she said, handing the filled bowl to Kyle, together with a hunk of hard bread to sop up the gravy.

Kyle accepted the offering with a word of thanks and withdrew several paces to blow on the steaming contents before taking a tentative sip. To his surprise, it was quite flavorful, for Abigail clearly knew how to cover the strong taste of game with lots of onions and parsley, along with thyme, sage, and other savory spices.

Hul picked up an empty bowl and held it out to his mother.

"Get it yerself," she said, thrusting the ladle at him. She went into the house and shut the door behind her.

Hul dismissed her odd behavior with a shrug and helped himself to the stew. He snapped off a piece of stiff bread and settled on the bench to eat.

Turval and the other men there served themselves, after which they sought a place to sit while they ate their meal.

Hul beckoned for Kyle to join him on the bench. "Tell me about that missing pearl," he said.

"It disappeared about four days ago," Kyle said, settling beside the heavyset man. "I cannot tell you much more, except that it belongs to the Mistress of Kilgate Manor."

"Does it now?" Hul said with obvious interest. "How much do ye think she will pay to see it again?"

"Enough to make it worth your while to restore it to her," Kyle said. He knew full well that when the value of an item far exceeded the reward for its return, there was a good chance it would never be seen again.

"Then ye can count on me to look into the matter," Hul said.

"My client will appreciate it," Kyle said. He fished a groat from his coin purse and handed it to Hul. "Here's a small token to seal the bargain."

Hul's eyes lit up at the sight of the coin. He slipped it into his shoe, evidently planning to transfer it to a more secure hiding place later when he was alone.

Kyle used his dirk to spear a scrap of meat in his bowl. "By the way," he said, bringing the tender morsel to his lips, "you never did say how the boy hurt his foot."

"I must confess that I don't really know," Hul said. "He'll be here in a minute. Ye can ask him yerself."

"You might want to do the talking," Kyle said. "He may not be as forthcoming to a stranger as he would to you. What is his name, anyway?"

"Gilbert," Hul said.

True to Hul's prediction, the women and children who lived on that dead-end street soon ventured forth from their houses, carrying with them their own bowls as they walked over to the community pot.

Abigail came outside long enough to ladle a portion of stew into each of their bowls. "Do ye want some more?" she said to Kyle, pointedly ignoring Hul.

"Please," Kyle said. He held out his half-empty bowl, aware that doing so complimented her cooking more than any spoken word of praise.

She bestowed a motherly smile on him as she topped off his bowl with hot gravy and another lump of meat.

"Women," Hul said with a shake of his head after his mother went back inside.

Most of the women and children there took their stew and bread home with them.

Gilbert's foot seemed to bother him, so rather than limp back to his house, he sat on the cobblestones near the bench to eat.

From what Kyle could see, the boy appeared to be around twelve years of age and in the midst of a growth spurt, for the frayed hem of his brown tunic ended well above his knobby knees. His coloring was fair like his mother, with the same gray eyes and sharp features. He possessed the voracious appetite of a healthy adolescent in that he consumed all of his stew and every crumb of bread, and then he went on to lick the bowl as well.

"Gil, lad," Hul said. "What happened to that foot of yours?"

Gilbert looked up at Hul with a guarded expression on his youthful face, as though suspicious of the man's sudden concern for his well-being. "Why do ye want to know?" he said.

"No reason in particular," Hul said. He turned back to his stew, as though he could care less whether the boy told him or not.

Gilbert's reluctance to answer that simple question gave Kyle the impression there was more to the incident than met the eye. He busied himself with gnawing on a meaty bone, while watching the boy from the corner of his vision.

"I trod on a sharp stump," Gilbert said after a moment.

"That must have hurt," Hul said around a mouthful of bread.

"It did," Gilbert said. "I didn't see it there until I ran over it."

"See what?" Hul said.

"The stump," Gilbert said. "Somebody cut off a sapling at an angle low to the ground. That's what tore open the side of my foot."

"How did ye get home?" Hul said.

"We walked," Gilbert said. "My foot hardly bothered me at all."

" 'We'?"

"Rollo and me."

"So Rollo was there, too," Hul said. "Where were the pair of ye?"

"In Cragston Forest," Gilbert said, his eyes averted.

"It's dangerous to go that far down the coast by yerselves," Hul said with a stern demeanor. "What were the two of ye doing there, anyway?"

Gilbert glanced at Hul, his manner defensive. "Rollo dared me to go into the forest with him," he said.

"Are ye daft, lad?" Hul said. "Don't ye know it's haunted?"

"I know it," Gilbert said. "That's why I waited for him at the ravine. Rollo went into the woods by himself."

"Did ye see a wraith, then?" Hul said, chuckling. "Is that why ye were running?"

"I ran because the Southrons were chasing after us."

"The Southrons?" Hul cried, sitting up straight.

"Aye," Gilbert said. "Four of them, soldiers all. We hid in a crevice to get away from them. They rode up and down looking for us. When they couldn't find us, they gave up and left."

"Why were the Southrons after ye?"

"Rollo told me they caught him spying on them as they beset a big fellow in the forest."

"Did they kill him?"

"I don't know," Gilbert said. "Rollo didn't say. After the Southrons quit searching for us, we hurried back to town."

"I ought to tell yer mam what ye did," Hul said, "but I don't want to worry her. Go home and soak yer foot in hot salty water, lest it fester and fall off. I'll come over later to take a look at it."

"Is that true?" Gilbert said, thoroughly alarmed. "Will my foot really fall off?"

"It will, if the rot sets in," Hul said. "Now hop to it."

Gilbert scrambled to his feet and limped home as fast as he could.

"What do ye think of the lad's tale?" Hul said, turning to Kyle.

"I think we, or rather you," Kyle said, "need to speak with Rollo to find out what he saw."

"I think ye are right," Hul said. He caught the eye of one of the ruffians and jerked his head meaningfully toward one house in particular on the far side of the street.

The man got up and sauntered away.

"I don't know what possessed Rollo," Hul said, "to tangle with those Southrons."

"I don't think he did it on purpose," Kyle said.

"Maybe not," Hul said. "His uncle will have a fit when he finds out about it."

The man came back after a moment and resumed his seat near his tough-looking companions.

A minute later, an adolescent boy walked out of the house across the street and advanced on Hul with the sinewy grace of a feline. He was shorter and thinner than Gilbert, with small delicate bones and smooth pale skin. An unruly mop of flaxen curls framed his pixie-like features, and the large brown eyes in his oval face were bright with mischief. "Ye sent for me, Master Hul?" he said in a light, almost girlish voice.

"Set a while, Rollo," Hul said. "I want to talk to ye."

In a single fluid motion, the boy folded his slender tunic-clad body into a cross-legged position on the cobblestones.

"Tell me about those Southrons in Cragston Forest," Hul said. "Ye won't get in trouble if ye tell me the truth of it."

Rollo's gaze shifted to Kyle, who occupied himself with eating his stew, and then back to Hul. "They threatened a man with drawn swords," he said in his girlish voice.

"Did he provoke them?" Hul said.

"Nay," Rollo said. "He was fishing at the time."

Kyle recalled that Macalister recently invited him to go fishing with him somewhere south of town. He dropped all pretense of indifference and intruded into the conversation. "Was the fellow a tall Scotsman, with cropped brown hair and a beard?"

"Aye," Rollo said with a nod.

"His name is Macalister," Kyle said to Hul. "He's the town blacksmith."

"I thought he looked familiar," Rollo said.

"What did they do to him?" Kyle said, taking over the interview. Hul appeared content to let him do so, and the boy hardly seemed to notice.

"It was more like what he did to them," Rollo said with a grin. "After he worked them over with a tree limb, they rode out of there like their horses' tails were on fire. That's when they spotted me."

"I take it they didn't hurt Macalister, then," Kyle said.

"I didn't stick around to find out," Rollo said. "I was too busy running from the Southrons. The other fellow who was there might know."

"Do you mean Gilbert?" Kyle said. "We already spoke to him."

"Not Gil," Rollo said. "There was somebody else in the forest that day. He saw what happened, too."

"Did you get a look at him?" Kyle said.

"Just a glimpse," Rollo said. "I don't think he was a Southron, though, because he helped me get away from them. They would have trampled me into the ground otherwise."

Kyle sat at the trestle table facing John and Colina, who was an attractive woman in her early forties and a bride of two months. The happy couple lived in a two-story house in Newton, located on the north bank of the river across the bridge from the town of Ayr.

Kyle held a chicken leg in his hand. The tender meat was tasty and practically fell from the bone, yet he could not bring himself to take another bite. He was still full from those two helpings of Abigail's stew earlier that morning. Although he mentioned it to John when he first arrived, no opportunity presented itself to tell Colina. That was just as well, for she looked so delighted with her new role as hostess. He hated to say or do anything that might dampen her high spirits.

Joneta sat in the chair beside him. A black cap covered most of her light auburn hair, except for the thick braid that hung down her back. A shiny gold ribbon—the one he bought in Glasgow and gave to her a couple of months earlier—secured the end, providing the only splash of color on her black widow's attire.

"Are ye feeling poorly?" she whispered, leaning close.

"A mite," Kyle said, glancing at her. "It will pass." A belch escaped from his lips before he could stifle it.

"Soon, I hope," she said, ducking her head as though to hide a smile.

"I checked the feed ye gave to me," John said to Kyle. "It was definitely laced with poison."

Kyle put the chicken leg back on the gravy-soaked trencher before him and wiped his fingers on a moist cloth. "Do you know what kind of poison was used?" he said.

"It came from a yew tree," John said. "Every part of the yew is deadly, from the bark to the leaves and the seeds. The person who did this made a decoction by steeping ground bark and crushed leaves in boiling water. The grain was soaked in the liquid, which caused the hard kernels to split open, thus letting in the poison. After the seeds dried, a measure of honey was added to cover the bitter taste. A single mouthful of that feed would be fatal."

"How fast does it work?" Kyle said.

"From two to four hours," John said, "depending on the size of the animal and the amount of poison ingested. Some of the seeds you gave me were safe to eat, which leads me to believe that not all of the grain in the sack was treated with poison. Enough toxic feed was mixed in with the good feed, though, to taint the lot."

"Now that I think on it," Kyle said, "no one else lodged a complaint about their stock dying under mysterious circumstances." He frowned at the implications. "That means the Rylands were singled out on purpose."

"But why go through so much trouble just to kill a few animals?" John said.

"That is a good question," Kyle said. "Unfortunately, I don't know the answer."

"Well, the Rylands are Southrons," John said. "That could be a factor, and they did usurp Cragston Castle from the former owner, who is a countryman of ours."

"The shire is rife with English nobles guilty of doing the same thing," Kyle said. "Why not punish them as well?" He shook his head. "Nay, I think this personal, in that it is directed only at the Rylands."

At that moment, Colina rose from her chair and went over to the sideboard. She picked up a tray with four cups of custard on it and returned to the table. She set a cup before each of her guests, then her husband, and took the last one for herself. "I hope this turned out all right," she said. "I made it myself."

Since there was always room for dessert, Kyle helped himself to the pudding made from milk and eggs and sweetened with honey. "It is delightful," he said, after sampling it. "As was the entire meal."

"Ye hardly touched a thing," Colina said without reproach. "I suspect ye ate before ye came here."

"As a matter of fact," Kyle began, about to launch into an explanation.

"I don't blame ye at all," Colina said, interrupting him with a laugh. "Especially if ye thought it was my cooking ye had to eat." She glanced over at her new husband. "I finally took John's advice and hired a cook. He would never admit it aloud, but I'm sure he is quite relieved that I did so."

"Dearest," John said, patting her hand. "I only suggested it to save ye from drudgery in the kitchen. I want ye to be a lady of leisure."

"Oh, John," Colina said, blushing. "Ye always say the right thing."

Kyle finished the last of his custard with gusto and set the empty cup on the table. "Good food, good company," he said. "What more can a man ask for?"

"Knowledge," John said, leaning back in his chair. "Speaking of that, I went poking around the priory archives the other day and located some old tomes down in the cellar."

"Did you find anything of interest in them?" Kyle said, loosening his belt a notch.

"I did, believe it or not," John said. "I came across entries penned by Brother Demas, a monk long dead, who wrote at length about druids. According to him, druids of ancient times served as priests, like the clergy today, to intercede with the gods and goddesses on behalf of the people. It seems they were not as bloodthirsty as Prior Drumlay made them out to be, either."

"How so?" Kyle said.

"They used cattle in their sacrificial rituals, with a preference for white bulls. They purified the carcass with fire, one of the three elements integral to their ceremonies. After they ate their fill of the roasted meat, they burned the leftovers to prevent it from being defiled by those uninitiated into their brotherhood. Water was the second element essential to communing with their gods, though Brother Demas was a mite vague as to how they used that in their rituals. Only on occasion did they put a human to death. Those were mostly criminals, though."

"Mostly?" Kyle said.

"During times of war," John said, "they evidently chose an unblemished male from among the prisoners captured in battle to offer as a sacrificial victim for their deities to ensure victory."

"I see," Kyle said.

"Nobody really objected to the druids carrying out the sentence of death on a condemned prisoner or on dispatching a hated enemy so that all may benefit from it."

"Did they cook the prisoners and eat them, too?" Colina said, horrified.

"Nobody ate the prisoners, dearest," John said. "Only those initiated into the druidic rites attended their ceremonies, and those present only ate the flesh of the animals that were sacrificed."

"I'm relieved to hear it," Colina said.

"Me, too," Joneta said.

"Druids were mystics, not cannibals," John said. "They foretold the future by observing signs and portents in the world around them. They could predict the outcome of the next planting season by reading the entrails of the sacrificial bull. They did that with criminals, too. Thus, the villagers knew ahead of time which crops would flourish and which would fail."

"Where does mistletoe fit into this?" Kyle said.

"I'm getting to that," John said. "Druids revered above all other trees the mighty oak, the third element vital to their rituals. In fact, the word 'druid' means 'men of the oak trees.' Thus, mistletoe that grew on the sacred oak was considered sacred as well. It was reputed to possess magical powers, either for healing or for killing, as long as it never touched the ground."

"How old are those writings?" Kyle said.

"Brother Demas penned them about four hundred years ago," John said. He held up both hands, as if to ward off a critical remark. "I know ye are going to say that none of it applies today."

"On the contrary, my dear John," Kyle said, smiling. "You have stumbled across a font of information that may well lead to Sir Humphrey's killer."

"How so?" John said, puzzled.

"Everything Demas wrote about druids seems to have a bearing on the case. The oak-leaf-and-acorn pattern on Sir Humphrey's belt is reminiscent of the sacred oak. The sacrificial death of a condemned man indicates that the murderer likely considered Sir Humphrey a criminal worthy of execution. The mistletoe thrust down his throat denotes a judgment of death, even though it did not actually kill him. He drowned in water, one of the three elements used in druidic rituals."

"Where does fire fit into this scenario?" John said.

"I'm still working on that," Kyle said.

Joneta turned to Kyle, her smooth brow furrowed in thought. "What if druids are not involved at all?" she said. "What if the killer knows enough about druids to shift the blame to them? Wouldn't that serve to throw you off his scent?"

"It would have done so an hour ago," Kyle said, his eyes on her. "But not now, thanks to Brother Demas." He looked over at John. "I think I know who murdered Sir Humphrey."

"Who?" John and Joneta said in unison.

"His own nephew," Kyle said grimly. "I believe I shall pay Sir Peter a visit later this afternoon."

CHAPTER 10

Kyle drove down the coastal road in John's wagon, which he borrowed to take Joneta home after lunch. She sat in the high seat beside him, cradling her sleeping baby in her arms. The gelding trotted alongside, its reins tied to the wooden slats.

He brought Vinewood and Hoprig along with him in anticipation of arresting Sir Peter Ryland. The two English soldiers rode a hundred feet behind the wagon so that he and Joneta could speak without being overheard.

"I am not really convinced that Sir Peter killed his uncle," Joneta said, giving Kyle a sidelong glance. "I met Sir Peter once when Marjorie and I were coming back from town in the carriage. He was riding in the opposite direction. Marjorie stopped the carriage to introduce me to him."

"What was your impression of him?" Kyle said.

"I thought him pompous and arrogant, like most Southron nobles. However, he didn't strike me as a man who would murder a member of his own family."

"Sir Peter is the only one who stood to benefit from Sir Humphrey's death," Kyle said. "The obligation to repay his mounting debt ended with his uncle's demise."

"Sir Peter is presently working on a marriage alliance between Marjorie and some influential Southron family," she said. "He will surely need extra money to cover the expense of the wedding, meals, and lodging for the groom and his family, and the cost of the reception afterward. Why dispose of his only source of revenue—his uncle—prior to such an important occasion? It doesn't make any sense."

"Perhaps Sir Peter did ask for another loan. Maybe Sir Humphrey turned him down. That led to a quarrel, which then led to blows. It could happen."

"That does not explain the mistletoe found in Sir Humphrey's throat."

"It is that very fact that points directly to Sir Peter," he said. "He is the only other person involved in this matter who knows the meaning behind the use of mistletoe."

"The only other person that ye know of," she said. "There could be others."

"Indeed," he said with appreciation for her astute deduction. "You may be right."

At that moment, a cooling breeze blew in from the firth to temper the warmth of the summer afternoon.

Kyle turned his gaze seaward and spotted a merchant vessel with furled sails some distance from shore. The moored ship looked like the same one at anchor there for the last couple of days. The configuration of the hull looked vaguely familiar, but being no expert in things of a nautical nature, he dismissed the notion that he had seen it before as absurd. He told Joneta about the signal light he saw flash across the water while riding back to the garrison on Monday night.

"They're flying the Scottish flag," she said, shading her eyes with her hand against the glare of the sun. "Are they smugglers, do ye think?"

"If they were," he said, "they wouldn't drop anchor that close to shore, nor would they linger there for days."

"They must be up to no good," she said. "Otherwise, why hang about this far down the coast?"

"Maybe they're waiting for something," he said. "Or someone," he added, frowning at the notion. "I wonder if Sir Peter hired that ship as a means of escape."

"If he did murder his uncle," she said, "why not flee immediately afterward? Why wait around for days and risk getting caught?"

"Why, indeed?" he said. He could not help but admire her reasoning yet again.

The baby stirred in her arms. She shifted him to her shoulder and patted his back until he settled down.

"I wonder how Simon fits into the picture," he said, thinking aloud.

"Simon?" she said with a laugh. "What makes ye think he's involved in any of this?"

"He lives near the coast," he said. "That's rather convenient for a smuggler, is it not?"

"I live near the coast, too," she said. "I'm no smuggler, nor do I traffic in stolen goods."

"Cragston Castle is not that far from his house," he said.

"Nor from mine," she said.

"He owns a pony and a cart, which allows him to drive to and from town whenever he chooses, no matter the hour of day or night."

"Simon is harmless," she said. "He's too scared of his own shadow to get mixed up in any dangerous undertakings."

"Possibly," he said, unconvinced. He was sure Simon was guilty of something, but unsure of precisely what. "He seems to enjoy taking you to town in his cart."

"Of course, he does," she said. "I pay him well enough to take me or Meg when he is going in that direction."

"Oh," Kyle said, feeling rather silly that he thought she might be interested in someone like Simon. He stopped the wagon where a rutted track intersected with the coastal road and waited for Vinewood and Hoprig to catch up with him.

"Stay here while I take Mistress Joneta home," he said to the

English soldiers. "I shall be back shortly."

He shook the reins, and the wagon lurched forward. He turned onto the track and followed it inland through a field of green clover to the hill beyond.

"I never got the chance to ask you about Cragston Forest," he said. "Have you ever gone there alone?"

"Many times," she said. "I cut through it on the way to Cragston Castle to visit Marjorie. It shortens the distance by a full mile."

"Have you ever done so at night?"

"Never had to," she said. "Marjorie is kind enough to take me home in the carriage."

"Do you believe the forest is haunted?" he said.

"Derek seems to think it is," she said.

"What about you?" he said, glancing at her lovely profile. "Do you think it's haunted?"

"I do," she said. "But not by wraiths."

"By what, then?" he said.

"By those who cannot find peace by day or by night," she said.

He cocked a skeptical eyebrow at her. "Do they wear white robes?" he said.

"They dress as ordinary men."

"How do you know about their not finding peace?"

"I overheard them as I passed by."

"Did they see you?"

"Of course not," she said. "Otherwise, they would not speak so freely."

"Where is this place?"

"They won't be there now, if that's why ye are asking," she said. "They were but visiting the old man at the time."

"What old man?"

"The old man in the forest," she said. "The one who lives in a tree."

He laughed out loud. "You really had me going there for a minute," he said, grinning.

"Every word I spoke to ye is true," she said. "Go see for yerself." She described the location to him and told him how to get there.

The wagon bumped along the dirt road through the woods and across the open meadow to Joneta's house. Wildflowers abounded in the open field. Blossoms of blue and red and yellow dotted the verdant landscape. Windflowers quivered in the soft breeze. A brown hare reared its head above the green grass for only an instant before darting away.

Kyle brought the wagon to a halt in front of the wooden house. He jumped to the ground and went around to the far side to lift Joneta and the baby from the high seat.

"It was kind of ye to take me home," she said, gazing up at him.

He looked down at her, enthralled. "I wouldn't have it any other way," he said. He wondered why he never before noticed the flecks of gold in her hazel eyes.

She stood on her toes and kissed him on the lips.

A warm flush of pleasure washed through his body. The expression on her face left no doubt in his mind that she loved him. If there was ever a moment ripe for a marriage proposal, this was it.

He opened his mouth to speak the words, but no sound came out of his stiff throat. His courage never failed him in battle, yet at that moment, his mouth went dry, and his stomach turned a somersault.

"Is anything wrong?" she said with concern.

He shook his head, trying not to look as foolish as he felt. "My men are waiting for me," he managed to choke out at last.

"I should go now."

Her lips twitched, giving him the impression she was enjoying this a little too much.

"I look forward to seeing ye again," she said.

"Me, too," he said. He clambered up into the high seat and jiggled the reins. He waved as the wagon lumbered away, glad to put that awkward moment behind him.

The trip to Cragston Castle an hour later proved to be a waste of time. Mistress Ryland claimed her son, Sir Peter, never showed up for dinner last night. Marjorie, the daughter of Sir Fulbert and Mistress Ryland, was out on an errand, so he could not question her about her uncle's demise or her brother's whereabouts.

The only thing that kept the visit from being a total loss was the opportunity to speak with Arnald the groom. Kyle confirmed that the feed the young man purchased for the stock was indeed toxic, and that the Rylands should consider purchasing their grain elsewhere from here on out.

When Kyle was ready to depart, he walked over to John's wagon parked in the courtyard and untied the gelding's reins from the slatted side.

"Vinewood," he said, mounting his horse. "Drive this rig back to town and drop it off at the apothecary shop." To Hoprig, he said, "Come with me."

The three of them left Cragston Castle together. On reaching the coastal road, Vinewood continued on toward town with the wagon. Kyle and Hoprig turned inland to ride through the rocks and shale to the trees beyond.

"Where are we bound?" Hoprig said, urging his chestnut mare up the slope of a shallow ravine behind the gelding.

"Cragston Forest," Kyle said. "We're on the hunt for an old man who lives in a tree."

"Right," Hoprig said, evidently untroubled with the odd response he received to his query.

They rode deep into the woods, following game trails through thick underbrush and tangled vines. Before long, the ground rose gently beneath the hooves of their horses, an indication they were now in Cragston Forest.

Kyle wended his way through the trees looking for a creek bed. After searching in vain for nearly an hour, he was about to turn back when he heard the gentle purling of water.

He paused to listen for a moment. "Do you hear that?" he said.

"It's coming from over there," Hoprig said, pointing to a dense thicket of alder.

Kyle guided his mount toward the sound, pushing through the undergrowth until he came to a stream that cut a crooked path through the rocks in a series of shallow waterfalls.

He paused to sniff the air. "I smell smoke," he said. "That means we're getting close."

He and Hoprig followed the stream for a hundred yards to a place where the trees grew closer together. Twining vines and dense foliage blocked most of the sunlight filtering through the branches overhead. An unnatural hush seemed to grip that part of the forest, broken only by the intermittent twitter of a mockingbird somewhere nearby.

Kyle looked for moss growing on tree bark to determine the northward side. Unfortunately, moss covered all surfaces of the trunks due to a lack of sunlight in that location.

"Do you know where we are?" Hoprig said.

"I'm not sure," Kyle said, reining in.

"Are we lost, then?" Hoprig said.

"I'm not sure of that, either," Kyle said.

"Maybe that fellow can help," Hoprig said, indicating the direction with his chin.

Kyle turned his head to see an old man sitting on the trunk of a fallen tree in a small clearing a short distance away. A campfire burned in a shallow pit in the ground before him.

The old man rose to his feet and leaned on a gnarled staff, evidently waiting for them to approach. His long brown robe blended with his surroundings. Only his white hair and beard stood out against the dark trunks of the trees behind him.

Kyle nudged the gelding toward the old man. "Good morrow," he said on entering the shadowed clearing.

"Good morrow to you, Master Deputy," the old man said, his voice mellow and soothing. He spoke in the perfect English of an educated man.

Kyle schooled his countenance to hide his astonishment that the man knew his identity. The next words he heard amazed him even further.

"I've been expecting you." the old man said.

"Me?" he said. He cast a puzzled glance at Hoprig. "I didn't even know I was coming here until an hour ago." He gave the old man a long hard look. "Who are you, good sir?"

"You may call me Rolf," the old man said. "The lady surely mentioned me to you."

"She did, but not by name," Kyle said. "I'm pleased to make your acquaintance, Master Rolf." He swung down from the saddle to face the old man on his own level.

That was when he got a closer look at the gnarled staff in Rolf's hand. The knob at the top depicted a man on one side and a woman on the other. Instead of hair, carved leaves sprouted from their heads and framed their naked bodies.

Hoprig stayed in the saddle, apparently content to watch from the back of his horse.

"Do you live nearby?" Kyle said. "In a tree, perhaps?" he added in jest.

"You could say that," Rolf said with a smile. He waved a

hand at a thicket of saplings on the opposite side of the small clearing.

At first glance, Kyle saw what appeared to be a stand of young beech and maple trees. Upon closer examination, he spotted a small croft nestled in the middle of the thicket, half hidden in a tangle of brush. Green and brown lichens covered the stone walls, and a carpet of grass on the sod roof camouflaged the humble dwelling from prying eyes. Anyone passing through the clearing would miss it completely, unless they knew exactly where to look for it.

"There are few who know where I dwell," Rolf said. "I keep it so to avoid the curious and the profane who mock."

"Mock what?" Kyle said.

"Things that are holy," Rolf said.

"Are you a priest?"

"In a manner of speaking."

"Have you taken holy orders, then?"

"I do not need holy orders to compel me to spend my day in prayer and contemplation. I do that of my own accord."

"So you are a holy man, then," Kyle said. "A hermit."

"Something like that," Rolf said.

"I don't suppose you get many visitors out here."

"Not too many."

"What about Sir Humphrey Ryland?" Kyle said. "Did he ever stop by to see you?"

"He did, actually," Rolf said. "A troubled soul, that one," he added with a shake of his head.

"Not anymore," Kyle said. "He's dead, I'm afraid. We pulled his body from the River Ayr two days ago."

Rolf received the news without a blink, as though he already knew. "I suspect he was the victim of foul play," he said, regarding Kyle with hooded eyes as black as ebony.

"What makes you say that?" Kyle said, curious as to how the

old man arrived at that particular conclusion.

"He would never go near the river on his own," Rolf said.

"Was it because he couldn't swim?" Kyle said, recalling what Arnald the groom told him earlier.

"It was far more than that," Rolf said. "There was an incident on his journey home from the Holy Land. The ship he hired to cross the English Channel began to take on water. By some miracle, they finally made it to home port. That was when he swore he would never leave dry land again."

"How well did you know Sir Humphrey?"

"Well enough to know he was a good man," Rolf said. "He came practically every day, rain or shine. He always brought fresh game with him. We would sit and talk while the meat roasted over the fire." He stared into the middle distance for a brief moment, as though gazing out upon some fond memory. "I shall miss our lively discussions," he added softly.

"What was it that troubled him?" Kyle said.

"What is it that troubles any of us?" Rolf said with a sigh. "The things we did, or perhaps the things we should have done."

"What exactly did Sir Humphrey do that vexed him so?"

"Surely you cannot expect me to reveal that which was told to me in confidence?"

"I expect you to be forthcoming about everything that might have a bearing on Sir Humphrey's death."

"I know nothing that would be of use to you," Rolf said. "Sir Humphrey sought redemption for sins committed years ago in another land. He came to me looking for peace of mind and heart, but I could not provide it to him. His was a path only he could travel."

"Why should he come to you for absolution?" Kyle said. "You are neither his priest nor his confessor."

"He was a friend who bore a great burden," Rolf said. "When he first came to me with his troubles, I could see he was not long for this world. I told him so, and he took the news quite well. He welcomed it, in fact."

"Was he ill?" Kyle said.

"Only in spirit," Rolf said. "He will come back, though, as all men do in the circle of life."

Kyle grunted by way of response. He refused to take the bait to engage in an argument over the mysteries of the afterlife. His knowledge of theology was limited by choice. Thus, he thought it best to steer clear of such matters.

A sudden breeze rustled the leaves overhead, letting the late afternoon sun shine through the gaps between the branches.

Kyle noted the slant of the shadows and the direction of the sun. "It's getting late," he said. "I must go."

As he swung up into the saddle, he could not shake the feeling that Rolf had purposely withheld information from him. It might be unimportant, like the sins Sir Humphrey committed years ago in a foreign land. But then, it could be something he needed to know. Whatever it was, he would attempt to ferret it out some other day.

"Now that Sir Humphrey is gone," he said, looking down at the old man, "can you manage out here on your own?"

"Quite well, thank you," Rolf said. "I rely on Mother Earth for my care and keeping. She will never fail me."

"I bid you goodbye, then," Kyle said, taking his leave. He turned the gelding's head to the west and set out through the forest for the coastal road, with Hoprig following behind him.

Rolf watched the deputy and the English soldier ride away until the trees hid them from view. "They're gone," he said as he lowered himself onto the fallen tree trunk near the campfire. "You can come out now."

A man in the white linen robe of an acolyte in the service of a priest emerged from behind the croft and pushed through the undergrowth to step into the clearing.

"Did you hear any of that?" Rolf said.

"I heard every word, Master," the acolyte said.

"I fear that man of law will not rest until all things come to light," Rolf said.

"But that will ruin everything," the acolyte said.

"Nothing ever stays the same," Rolf said, his expression wistful. "We must keep up with changing times or be left behind."

"The precepts of the Order never change," the acolyte said. "Ye taught me that."

"So I did," Rolf said. "You must never forget the unwritten tradition, for only then can you pass it on just as it was given to you."

"Shall I fetch yer mantle, Master, that ye may instruct me further?"

"You may," Rolf said, poking at the charred limbs with the butt end of his staff. He stared into the blaze, undaunted by the specter of death that leered at him from within the orange and yellow flames. "Let us finish this while there is still time."

The hollow clop of hooves drummed in Kyle's ears as he and Hoprig rode over the garrison drawbridge later that afternoon. Inside the curtain walls ahead of them, English soldiers with halberds grounded encircled the raised wooden platform situated in the center of the courtyard. They stood with their backs to the rectangular structure, facing a crowd of Scottish burghers that grew larger with each passing moment.

The gibbet on one end of the platform cast a menacing shadow across the sullen faces of the townsfolk gathered there.

Captain Morhouse, clad in black bull-hide armor, stood on the platform with his feet braced and his hands clasped behind his back.

The English marshal, a grim-faced officer with a barrel chest, stood beside Morhouse with a plaited leather horse whip in his hand.

Blackwell and five other soldiers held a shackled Scotsman at the bottom of the stairs leading up to the platform.

"Carry him if you must, but get him up here," Morhouse barked at Blackwell. "And be quick about it."

Kyle drove his heels into the gelding's belly, for he recognized the prisoner. It was his friend, Macalister the blacksmith, who towered head and shoulders above the soldiers restraining him.

Macalister's left eye was swollen shut, and a purple bruise stained his cheekbone on the same side of his bearded face. Blood from a cut over his right eye flowed down beside his nose and dripped from his chin. His brown tunic was torn in several places, and his bare arms and legs were scratched and abraded, as though from being dragged along the ground.

The onlookers moved aside to let the mounted deputy through. Not one of them uttered a word. Their animosity, though, was palpable as they watched the English soldiers haul one of their countrymen up each of the four wooden steps.

The soldiers shoved Macalister onto the platform just as Kyle rode up to the wooden guard rail around it. "What is the meaning of this?" he demanded.

Morhouse spared him a fleeting glance. "This is none of your concern, Master Deputy," he said. "You better move along."

Kyle disregarded the warning. "What did this man do to be treated so?" he said.

"He resisted arrest," Morhouse said.

"Arrest?" Kyle said. "On what charge?"

Morhouse fastened a scornful gaze on Kyle. "He assaulted English soldiers without provocation," he said, "at which time he inflicted serious bodily injuries upon them."

Kyle looked over at Macalister, who shook his shaggy head in denial of the accusation.

"The prisoner will receive twenty lashes for refusing to come along quietly," Morhouse said. "He will then swing from the gallows at dawn as a warning to other rebels who dare beset the King's troops."

At a nod from the Captain of Horse, the six soldiers wrestled Macalister over to the gibbet post and shoved his face against it. While one soldier tied his hands around the upright support, another ripped his tunic at the neck to expose the bare skin of his back.

The soldiers stepped away to stand at attention as the English marshal walked forward with the horse whip in his hand.

Kyle shook his booted feet clear of the stirrups and stood up in the saddle. He leaped onto the platform and bounded over the side rail to intrude himself between the English marshal and Macalister. "Has this man been tried in court?" he said in a loud voice for the burghers to hear. "Has he even had a hearing?"

His words sent a murmur of agitation rippling through the onlookers. They began to inch closer to the platform. The hum of their voices rose to the hostile growl of an angry crowd about to erupt into an unruly mob.

The soldiers surrounding the platform leveled their halberds, aiming the sharp tips outward at the burghers closing in on them.

"Stand down, Master Deputy," Morhouse said, "or you shall rue your rash deed."

Kyle placed a hand purposefully on the hilt of his sword. "What has Sir Percy to say about this?" he said. "Does he even know about it?"

"You overstep your authority, deputy," Morhouse ground out between his teeth, his face flushed. "Stand down, I say."

"Nay," Kyle said, shaking his head. "Not until this man is

tried in a proper court of law to determine his innocence or guilt."

"Will you step aside or not?" Morhouse said in a mild voice at odds with the formidable scowl on his face.

"I will not," Kyle said, folding his arms across his chest.

Morhouse pointed his finger directly at Kyle. "Arrest that man," he said. "He is interfering in the King's business."

CHAPTER 11

Kyle caught the smirk of satisfaction on Morhouse's lips just before Blackwell and the five other soldiers pounced on him from either side. He struggled to free himself from their grasp, but the weight of three men in full armor clinging to each arm was difficult to shrug off. "Sir Percy will hear about this," he said.

As the English soldiers hustled Kyle from the platform, he spotted Hoprig astride his mount on the fringe of the crowd. "Fetch Sir Percy at once," he cried out to him.

The burghers at the foot of the stairs stood their ground, refusing to give way to the soldiers trying to manhandle Kyle through their midst.

The halberdiers stepped forward, their halberds aimed with deadly intent. Only then did the burghers part ranks, slowly and with obvious reluctance, to clear a path for the arresting soldiers to pass through.

Behind him, Kyle heard Morhouse give the order for the marshal to lay on with the whip.

An ominous silence fell over those looking on. In the hush that followed, the crack of leather on bare flesh sounded like the breaking of a quarterstaff.

Kyle cringed inwardly at each stroke delivered to Macalister's back. His inability to prevent the flogging left him angry and frustrated. That, though, was not as serious as being thrown into the dungeon, for such confinement would prevent him from taking action to stop the hanging in twelve hours.

Blackwell and the English soldiers half-dragged, half-carried Kyle across the courtyard toward the dungeon. They moved at a snail's pace, for he kept setting his heels in the ground to impede their forward progress. On the way, they drew abreast of the main hall, which housed the garrison's administrative offices on the second floor.

Sir Percy's office window, which overlooked the courtyard, was wide open to let in the late afternoon breeze.

"Sir Percy!" Kyle bellowed in an effort to attract the attention of the Castellan of Ayr Garrison. "Sir Percy!"

Sir Percy appeared in the unshuttered window and gazed down into the courtyard. Walter the clerk walked up to join him, looking with keen interest upon those gathered below. Hoprig stood behind the two men, his face flushed from running.

"You there," Sir Percy said, addressing Blackwell. "What is going on?"

"Nothing important, m'lord," Blackwell said. He dug his fingers into the muscles of Kyle's arm, as though to warn him to hold his tongue.

Kyle gritted his teeth against the pain. "On the contrary, m'lord," he said. "There is a grave miscarriage of justice taking place as we speak."

"Release the deputy," Sir Percy said. "I will hear what he has to say."

"But m'lord," Blackwell said. "This man is under arrest."

"Unhand him," Sir Percy said, annoyed. "That is an order."

The soldiers released Kyle, but the six of them stayed within easy reach of him.

"Speak up, man," Sir Percy said to Kyle.

"Thank you, m'lord," Kyle said. "A prisoner is being flogged at this very moment for a crime he did not commit. I appeal to you for justice on his behalf."

"The prisoner is guilty, m'lord," Blackwell said. "I am one of those he assaulted for no reason." He removed his nasal helm to show the purple bruising under both eyes. His nose was swollen and discolored where the bridge was broken.

"That man is a liar, m'lord," Kyle said. "A companion of his did that to him because he tried to trample a girl with his horse."

Blackwell's face turned scarlet. "Such a thing never occurred, m'lord," he said, blustering. "It is he who is lying."

"Enough!" Sir Percy said. His gaze settled on Kyle. "What is it you want from me?"

"I respectfully request that you hear what the prisoner has to say in his own defense," Kyle said. "It is his right under English law."

"The prisoner is not English, m'lord," Blackwell said to Sir Percy.

"All the more reason to hold a hearing before he is executed," Kyle said. "The heavy-handed treatment of a Scotsman these days will surely incite his countrymen to violence."

"Three others besides me suffered injury at the hands of the prisoner, m'lord," Blackwell said. "They and I will swear that the man in custody is the one responsible."

"Sir Percy," Kyle said. "There is a witness who says otherwise."

Blackwell turned on Kyle. "Where is he?" he demanded.

Kyle ignored him. "Besides that eyewitness," he said to Sir Percy, "there is another person who saw what happened that day."

"Then bring them forward," Sir Percy said.

"I shall, m'lord," Kyle said. "I ask for a week to gather evidence and to prepare a defense." He thought it prudent not to mention that the second witness was unknown at present and that he needed time to find him.

Sir Percy looked displeased at the suggestion of any delay at all, until he noticed Walter the clerk watching him closely. "This day is practically spent," he said after a moment of thought. "Therefore, you may have two full days to prepare, starting on the morrow. When the church bells ring at terce on Saturday morning, I shall review the facts that you present to me."

"Thank you for that, m'lord," Kyle said. "I beg your indulgence a minute longer, as there are still two pressing issues to address."

"You got the hearing you requested," Sir Percy said, his tone peevish. "What more do you want?"

"Captain Morhouse seems determined to hang the prisoner at dawn tomorrow," Kyle said. "Perhaps if you spoke to him . . ." He left the sentence unfinished, unwilling to push too hard, for the young castellan could be downright obstinate at times.

"I see," Sir Percy said. He caught Blackwell's eye. "Ask Captain Morhouse to attend to me in my office without delay." His gaze returned to Kyle. "And the other pressing issue?"

"There is the matter of my arrest," Kyle said. "I cannot undertake the prisoner's defense from behind bars. Since his life hangs in the balance, I appeal to you for clemency."

"Why were you arrested?" Sir Percy said.

"I attempted to prevent the unjust flogging of an innocent man," Kyle said.

"A flogging that Captain Morhouse ordered?"

"Aye, m'lord," Kyle said.

"I shall defer judgment on that issue until after the hearing on Saturday," Sir Percy said. "If you prove that the prisoner is innocent, you and he will go free."

"Thank you, m'lord." Kyle said.

"However," Sir Percy continued, "if the prisoner is found guilty, he will go to the gallows and you will go to the dungeon."

"As you say," Kyle said with a slight bow. That was not quite what he hoped for, but he could live with it for the time being. He turned on his heel and pushed through the English soldiers flanking him, headed back to the platform to see to Macalister's needs.

"Master Shaw," Sir Percy said, calling after him in a raised voice.

Kyle paused to look over his shoulder. "What is it, m'lord?" he said.

"Try to stay out of trouble."

"I'll do my best, m'lord."

The bells of St. John's rang in the hour of vespers shortly before sundown. Hoprig rode through the priory gates and on to the church, hardly able to contain his excitement at the prospect of seeing Isabel once again. The grounds were deserted, for every cleric in the enclave attended the worship service at that time of day.

He swung down from the saddle in front of St. John's Church and tied the reins to the rail alongside a handful of other horses standing there. A one-horse open carriage was parked nearby, its driver nowhere in sight.

Hoprig touched the spot on his chin where he cut himself shaving and glanced at his finger to make sure the bleeding had stopped. He hung his sword belt on the saddle bow and straightened his brown velvet cotte before mounting the church steps.

He opened one of the huge double doors and stepped into the cool gloom of the dimly lit vestibule. The cloying scent of irises mingled with the smell of beeswax candles. The only sound he heard was Prior Drumlay's voice droning on in Latin.

He trod with care on the flagstones so as not to disturb the small crowd of townsfolk standing in the nave, facing the altar.

His gaze roved over each person present in search of one in particular.

A woman in a royal blue silk gown stood near the front of those gathered. An ivory comb anchored a beaded black veil to the dark hair piled on her head. She shifted from one foot to the other, as though the shoes she wore hurt her feet.

The movement, though slight, drew Hoprig's eye. He was glad it did, for that was when he saw Isabel dressed in a white linen tunic, standing beside the restless woman.

At that instant, his world shrank to encompass only Isabel. He stared at the back of her head, willing her to look over her shoulder. His heart missed a beat when she finally did.

She turned to whisper something to the woman before stepping out from the small assembly to walk toward the rear.

He intercepted her in the vestibule and held out a hand to her. To his delight, she took it without hesitation. Her skin felt warm beneath his fingers, her bones small and delicate.

She led him out through the double doors and down the front steps. Together, they ran around to the side of the church building, laughing like carefree children for the sheer joy of it. They ducked into a shadowed niche, their hands still clasped and their eyes on each other.

"You came," she said, smiling up at him.

He grinned down at her. "Of course, I did," he said, giddy with happiness for the first time in his life. He clung to that feeling with all his might, refusing to let reality intrude for even an instant. He stood only inches from her, his gaze on her youthful face so close to his own. Her nearness sent a flood of heat coursing through his body, causing his breath to quicken.

A warning sounded in his conscious mind that any crass advance on his part would swiftly change the trust in her eyes to hatred. That was the last thing he wanted, so he stepped back half a pace to break the spell. "It is such a fine evening," he said. "Let us walk a bit before the church service ends."

He took her hand and tucked it under his arm, hoarding the warmth of her fingers through the thin fabric of his sleeve.

They set out at a slow pace, headed nowhere in particular, completely oblivious to their surroundings.

She listened as he told her about the encounter with the old man in the woods earlier in the day.

"His name is Rolf," he said. "From what I gather, he's a holy man."

"Is Master Rolf a seer, do ye think?" she said.

"He must be," he said. "He knew we were coming before we did."

"Ye say he spoke of Sir Humphrey," she said. "Is he the Southron who drowned the other day?"

"Aye," he said.

"If Master Rolf is a seer," she said, "why did he not warn Sir Humphrey of his fate?"

"Perhaps he did," he said. "Sir Humphrey may have paid no heed."

"I find that hard to believe," she said. "He seemed like a sensible person."

"Did you know him?" he said.

"Not me," she said with a shake of her head. "Lady Catherine did, though. She met with him after vespers about two weeks ago."

"Do you know what they spoke about?"

"I heard Sir Humphrey mention Sir Victor's name," she said. "Sir Victor is Lady Catherine's son," she added by way of explanation.

"I didn't know Captain Morhouse had a son," he said, mildly surprised.

"He doesn't," she said. "Sir Victor is my lady's son by her first husband. She was widowed shortly after the birth of her only child."

"What did Sir Humphrey say about Sir Victor?"

"They spoke too low for me to hear anything further," she said. "I do know that my lady's son went missing years ago in the Holy Land, and that she has been praying for his safe return ever since."

They came to a row of bushes planted along the east wall of the priory grounds. Pure white gardenias bloomed in profusion on every bough.

She paused to inhale the fragrant scent.

He plucked a blossom from the nearest branch and presented it to her with a flourish.

She accepted the flower with a smile and held it against her breast like a cherished possession.

They resumed their stroll about the grounds.

"The conversation with Sir Humphrey upset my lady something awful," she said. "She spoke not a word all the way home. Edgar noticed it, too."

"Has Lady Catherine known Sir Humphrey long?"

"I had no idea she knew him at all until I saw them together that one time."

"Did she approach him?"

"It was more the other way around," she said. "He appeared anxious to speak with her. Since they were on the priory steps at the time, there was nothing scandalous about their meeting."

"Did they talk for a long while?"

"Not really," she said. "By the time I walked over to tell Edgar to bring the carriage around for Lady Catherine, Sir Humphrey had already left."

They were meandering in the direction of the church when the huge double doors opened wide. They stopped to watch the vespers attendees pour outside into the waning light of day.

"I must see to my lady now," she said, slipping her hand from under his arm. As she turned to him, the breeze blew a strand of hair across her face. "When will I see ye again?"

"Soon," he said, brushing the errant tress back with his fingers. "I promise."

With the gardenia cradled so as not to crush its tender petals, she kissed him on the cheek. She turned and ran over to catch up with Edgar, who was driving the carriage around to the front of St. John's Church.

He watched her go, torn between hope and despair, unwilling to look beyond tomorrow where she was concerned. His rational mind warned him that such an entanglement could only lead to grief. In his heart, though, he counted the hours until their next meeting.

The garrison dungeon was a one-room outbuilding set against the curtain wall next to the stable. The gaps between the timber-planked sides and the roof rafters let in air and light. A solid oak door with a keyed latch barred the way to freedom.

The prison-like structure was large enough to hold twenty prisoners. The only amenities were two chamber pots and sufficient straw to cover every square inch of the earthen floor. Unfortunately, the pots needed emptying and fleas infested the straw. Rats lived there, too, although they only crept out from the dark corners after nightfall.

It took nearly an hour for Kyle to secure written permission from Sir Percy to bring John Logan into the dungeon to attend to Macalister's injuries. He showed the official-looking missive to the guard, who then unlocked the door to let the two of them inside.

Macalister was easy to spot, for there were only four prisoners in the dungeon that day. Kyle and John walked over to where he lay on his belly in the straw. John knelt down to examine the red stripes crisscrossing his back.

"It burns like fire," Macalister said.

John dug in his leather medicament bag and withdrew a tiny clay pot stoppered with a cork. "The woad in this will numb the pain," he said. He applied a thin layer of blue salve to the affected area visible through the torn tunic. He then cleaned the dirt and dried blood from the cuts and abrasions on Macalister's face and arms and bandaged them with a strip of linen.

"The Southron marshal must be going soft," Macalister said. "There was a time when he could flay the skin off a man's back."

"Consider yerself lucky, then," John said, putting away the salve.

"I don't feel all that lucky just now," Macalister said, sitting up with a grunt of pain. "Not with having to face the noose in the morning."

Kyle hunkered down on his heels to tell John and Macalister about his conversation with Sir Percy. "The hearing is set for Saturday morning," he said.

"That doesn't give us much time," Macalister said.

"There's more to tell," Kyle said. "Morhouse won't let me question the four soldiers who brought the charge against you. He says I must wait until the hearing to do that."

"Those Southrons started it," Macalister said. He related the details of the incident to them. "I should bring charges against them for harassment and unlawful assault."

"Before you make accusations against anybody," Kyle said, "let us clear your name first. A boy from town saw everything that happened to you. I plan to speak to him in the morning about standing up for you at the hearing."

"Will Sir Percy accept the testimony of a child?" Macalister said.

"He may not have to," Kyle said. "There was another witness in the forest that day besides the boy," Kyle said. "I suspect it was old Rolf." He gave them a brief description of the holy man.

"I've seen him in Cragston Forest on occasion," Macalister said. "He'll make a credible witness, but only if he consents to attend the hearing. He is a hermit, ye know."

John climbed to his feet. "What possessed ye to go to Cragston Forest?" he said, appalled. "Don't ye know it's haunted? People have gone in there and never came out again."

"Well, that explains why the fishing is so good out that way," Macalister said. "Nobody goes there."

"Do you need anything?" Kyle said.

"I could use something to eat," Macalister said. "A blanket to sleep in, too, though I probably won't get much rest tonight."

"I'll get those for you now," Kyle said, rising. "Just don't make yourself too comfortable, my friend," he added as he dusted the chaff from his leggings. "You won't be in here that long."

"Ye are right," Macalister said. "In three days' time, I shall either gain my freedom or face the hangman."

Early the next morning, Kyle rode from the garrison, bound for the older part of town. Droplets of dew gleamed like cut diamonds on the trees and shrubs along Harbour Street. A residue of moisture covered the cobbled paving ahead of him. The River Ayr on his left flowed like liquid silver in the brilliance of the rising sun.

He traversed a maze of shadowed alleyways and winding lanes before he finally arrived at his destination. The metallic ring of the gelding's shod hooves on stone brought a pack of barking dogs out from behind the houses on the dead-end street.

Hul flung open his front door and hollered at the dogs. "Ah, Master Deputy," he said after the surly creatures scuttled away. "What brings ye here at this hour?"

"Ill tidings, I'm afraid," Kyle said, dismounting. "Morhouse arrested the blacksmith yesterday for assaulting those English soldiers in Cragston Forest. It is important that Rollo attend the hearing on Saturday to set the matter straight."

"Rollo isn't here," Hul said.

"When will he return?"

"He's not coming back."

"What?" Kyle said, dismayed. "Why not?"

"Word is already out about the arrest," Hul said. "Rollo's uncle figured those Southrons would come looking for the boy since he saw what they did. Rollo and his uncle packed up and took to the road shortly before midnight."

Kyle blamed neither Rollo nor his uncle for taking flight. Nothing could save them if Blackwell and his men got their hands on them. Had he been in the uncle's position, he would have done the same thing. Unfortunately, the boy's absence made Macalister's innocence all the more difficult to prove. "I don't suppose you know where they went?" he said.

Hul shook his head. "Even if I did," he said, "I wouldn't tell ye. If those Southrons ever caught up with Rollo or his uncle, they would kill them both to save their own worthless hides."

"What about Gilbert?" Kyle said.

"He's gone, too," Hul said. "As soon as his mother heard the news, she left with him and the babe to stay with kinfolk in the east."

"I'm glad to hear that," Kyle said. "Although Gilbert saw nothing that could incriminate Blackwell or his men, they would get rid of him, too, just to make sure he doesn't tell any tales about them."

He climbed into the saddle and gazed down at Hul. "Have a care around Blackwell and those men of his," he said. "Until the day of the hearing, Rollo presents a threat to them. They may seek you out to bully you into telling them where the boy went."

"I'd like to see them try," Hul said with an unpleasant smile.

Kyle took his leave and rode slowly back to Harbour Street, his mind on locating the second eyewitness. He hardly noticed the bustle of activity around him, with men loading dog carts to take their goods to market, and women sweeping their steps or fussing at their children to come inside to eat or to go outside to play.

With Rollo out of the picture, he could only hope that the other witness was indeed Rolf, for Macalister's sake. If not, then he faced an uphill battle to prove what actually occurred that day.

The gelding was plodding past the Bull and Bear Tavern when Kyle heard someone in the courtyard call out to him. He reined in at the signpost to wait for the lanky man whom he recognized as the tavern groom to hurry over to him.

The gray hair on the groom's head was still rumpled from his pillow, and his tan homespun shirt hung unbelted over his brown leggings, as though he dressed in haste. "Master Deputy," he said, his long face pale with strain. "Ye must come at once."

Kyle turned aside and rode through the gated entryway into the courtyard beyond.

No patrons moved about the small open area at that early hour, only a young man with the same high cheekbones and hatchet nose as the groom.

Kyle dismounted and handed the reins to the young man. "What seems to be the problem?" he said to the groom.

The groom led the way into the warm darkness of the stable. "Me and my son, we just found him," he said.

Kyle followed the anxious groom down the aisle between vacant box stalls that smelled of old hay and fresh manure. "Found who?" he said.

"Him," the groom said, pointing to the body of a man dangling from one of the sturdy rafters supporting the roof over the last stall.

CHAPTER 12

Inside the empty stall, dust motes drifted in the air, trapped in a shaft of sunlight coming through a crack in the wall boards.

Kyle opened the half-door to enter the stall. The sudden draft sent the dust motes into frantic motion. Even though the dead man faced the other way, he knew who it was from the shape of his body and the silver-trimmed black velvet cotte he wore.

"It's Sir Peter Ryland," he said.

The groom made the sign of the cross on himself. "Why would a Southron nobleman take his own life?" he said.

The noose around Sir Peter's neck drew Kyle's eye. Instead of common hemp, the rope appeared to be made from a long strip of white linen twisted into a sturdy rope-like cord. The entire length of it showed signs of fraying, as though from being dragged across the rough wood of the rafter. "I don't think he did this on his own," he said.

The groom glanced over at Kyle, his eyes wide with fear. "Ye mean he was murdered?" he said.

"That's what I aim to find out," Kyle said. He peered closely at the wooden beam from which Sir Peter hung. "That rafter looks different from the others."

"It's made of oak," the groom said. "The old one was pine, like all the rest. It rotted through because of a leak in the roof, so the owner replaced it with whatever wood he had at hand."

"Interesting," Kyle said. His gaze swept the unoccupied stalls on either side of the aisle. "Where is Sir Peter's horse?"

"He came for it last night," the groom said.

"What time was that?" Kyle said.

"Nigh on midnight, as best as I can recall," the groom said, frowning in thought.

"Did you see him ride away?" Kyle said.

"Not really," the groom said. "I handed the reins to him and held the bridle while he mounted. I went back to my room after that."

"Did he return later in the night?" Kyle said.

"He did, now that you mention it," the groom said. "He waved me away when I tried to attend to him. He must have come back for something he left behind, because he rode out again a few minutes later."

"Did you see him leave the second time?" Kyle said.

"I heard him," the groom said. He walked up the aisle to show Kyle the timber planking on the ground just inside the open entryway. "No horse can tread across that without me hearing it."

"How do you know it was Sir Peter?" Kyle said.

"He was the only person here at the time," the groom said. "It had to be him."

"Was your son with you last night?" Kyle said.

"He only works here in the mornings to muck out the stalls," the groom said. "I tend the horses by myself, day and night."

"Where do you sleep?" Kyle said.

The groom showed him a small room at the head of the aisle near the entrance of the stable.

"Do you know where John Logan's shop is located?" Kyle said.

"I've been there a time or two," the groom said.

"Fetch him here, will you?" Kyle said. "You may use my horse." He started back down the aisle, but halted after a couple of steps. "Be sure to tell John to bring the wagon."

The groom hurried away to do as he was bidden.

Kyle continued on to the stall at the end of the row. He looked for footprints leading up to the half-door, but he found only his own and those of the groom impressed into the churned earth. He inspected the stall and sifted through the straw in it, but he found nothing of interest.

Since there was no more for him to do until John arrived, he shut the double doors to the stable. "Don't let anybody go inside," he said to the groom's son. "Come get me when John arrives. I'll be in the tavern." He crossed the courtyard and went inside to get something to eat.

Half an hour later, Kyle stepped through the tavern door into the sunlight. He watched John drive the wagon through the tavern gates with the groom on the wooden seat beside him. The gelding trotted behind them on a lead rope.

News of Sir Peter's death must have spread through town like a wildfire, for a dozen or so curious burghers followed the wagon into the courtyard and gathered in groups of twos and threes to look on in silence.

Kyle called out a greeting as John climbed down from the high seat. The two of them then headed for the stable.

"I can hardly believe it," John said with a shake of his head. "That's the second Ryland in three days." He glanced over at Kyle. "Have ye cut him down?"

"Not yet," Kyle said. "I was waiting for you." To the groom, he said: "Back the wagon up to the last stall so we can load the body onto the bed."

While the groom set about coaxing the mule into compliance, Kyle and John opened the stable doors. They walked down the aisle with the groom's son to the last stall at the far end.

John entered through the half-door to test rigidity of the dead man's limbs. "My guess is that he's been here for about five or six hours," he said.

Kyle and the groom's son each got a grip on the twisted linen cord. When John cut it just above the knot that secured it to the post, they lowered the hefty body until it rested on its back on the floor of the stall.

The face of a hanged man is particularly unpleasant to gaze upon. The young man took one look at the protruding tongue and the bulging eyes and stumbled from the stall to vomit against the back wall. Kyle slipped the noose from around Sir Peter's neck and checked over the man's clothing. The fabric showed no tears or slashes to indicate a violent attack. The presence of a large gold signet ring on his middle finger and a bulging coin purse hidden inside his shirt ruled out robbery. The only things worthy of note were the bruising on the face and knuckles, the smear of blood on the ring, and the smudge on the front of the black velvet cotte.

In deference to the young man's squeamish stomach, John covered Sir Peter's face before the four of them lifted the dead weight and heaved it onto the wooden bed. Kyle coiled the linen rope into a neat bundle and tossed it into the wagon beside the body.

The onlookers, who had infiltrated the stable by that time, pressed forward to gawk at the body and to speculate about the incident in excited voices.

John climbed into the high seat and drove the wagon up the aisle toward the stable entryway.

Kyle followed on foot to the courtyard, where he mounted the gelding. He thanked the groom and his son for their assistance, after which he rode out into the street.

He escorted John through town and on to St. John's Priory. He entered the iron gates and rode around to the mortuary chapel behind the church.

Once again, Prior Drumlay came out to meet them in a jingle

of keys. "Who is it?" he said as he turned the latch in the chapel door.

"Sir Peter Ryland," Kyle said.

"Ill fortune has certainly plagued that family of late," the prior said. "How did this one die?"

"The groom found him hanging in the stable at the Bull and Bear," Kyle said.

Prior Drumlay paused in the act of pushing open the chapel door. "A suicide cannot be buried in consecrated ground," he said.

"I seriously doubt it was suicide," Kyle said. "I'm just waiting for John to confirm it."

A short while later, Sir Peter Ryland lay naked on a makeshift table in the mortuary chapel, his private parts covered with a strip of linen. The remains of Sir Humphrey Ryland reposed on a cold marble slab nearby.

Prior Drumlay went to arrange for a Requiem Mass to be held for the newly departed nobleman, leaving Kyle and John in the chapel to attend to the grisly business at hand.

John bent over Sir Peter's body to examine every square inch of it, front and back. He even looked down the dead man's throat. When he finished, he wiped his hands on his brown tunic. "There is extensive discoloration here," he said, indicating the area below the chin.

"Of course," Kyle said. "That would be from the cord."

"The affected area is too broad to come from a cord as narrow as the one used. It appears he was choked first, and then strung up afterward while he was unconscious, but still very much alive." He rolled the body onto its side and swept the strands of hair out of the way. "Do you see these eight purple spots on the back of his neck? See how they line up, four on each side."

"I've been a man of law long enough to recognize marks like those," Kyle said. "They came from a pair of hands around his throat."

"Exactly," John said. "Look closely at this." He pointed to the only bruise that was out of line with the others. "The little finger on this left hand is shorter than the one on the right."

"Are there any other signs of violence on him?" Kyle said.

"Shortly before his death," John said, "he engaged in a fight with his fists. There is bruising around his mouth and chin where his face was hit, and the knuckles of both hands show discoloration consistent with landing a few punches of his own on his opponent."

"Good for him," Kyle said. "I hope he did some damage."

"He probably did with that ring he wore," John said. "I put it there with his garments." He went over to the altar to pick up the gold signet ring and hand it to Kyle. "As ye can see, there's dried blood on it."

"Interesting," Kyle said. He tucked the ring into his pouch along with the dead man's coin purse.

"One last thing," John said. "I didn't find any mistletoe down his throat, like I did with Sir Humphrey. I suppose that means there is a second murderer at large."

"Maybe that is the impression the killer would like to give," Kyle said. "In my opinion, however, two deaths in the Ryland family is no coincidence."

"The first man was drowned, the second hanged," John said. "Mistletoe was found on one, a linen cord used on the other. I don't see a pattern here."

"I still say the same man killed both of them," Kyle said. "Whatever he has against the Rylands is serious enough for him to commit murder."

"What if it's the other way round?" John said. "What if the Rylands have something he wants, and this is his way of coercing them into giving it to him?"

"Perhaps," Kyle said, frowning at the possibility. "The family that the Rylands displaced at Cragston Castle moved into another of their own holdings in the north. If they did come back here to seek revenge, news would have reached me by now." Twin lines appeared between his tawny eyebrows. "What if this really does involve the cult that Brother Demas wrote about?"

"Druids?" John said. "I thought ye already leaned in that direction."

"That was just a guess earlier," Kyle said. "Too many factors now point toward their involvement. As I recall, the three elements essential to their rituals are water, oak, and fire."

"So says Brother Demas in his writings," John said.

"The murderer drowned Sir Humphrey in water," Kyle said. "He hung Sir Peter from an oaken rafter. That's two elements right there."

"So you think the next victim will die by fire?" John said.

"I do," Kyle said.

"Perhaps ye should warn Sir Fulbert, seeing as he is the only Ryland left."

"What about Sir Fulbert's daughter?" Kyle said. "She's a Ryland, too, which puts her in harm's way as well."

"But druids only sacrificed males, whether animals or humans," John said.

"What about the criminals they executed?" Kyle said. "Were they always males, too?"

"I assume so," John said. "It is unusual for a woman to be condemned to death. They don't have the physical strength to assault or batter, like a man does. I suppose that is why most convicted felons are men."

"Getting back to Sir Fulbert," Kyle said, "I plan to pay him a visit later today to inform him of Sir Peter's death. Even if I warn him that his life may be at risk, I cannot tell him what he needs to know, which is who the killer is or why he has it out for the Rylands." He fingered the twisted linen cord. "While I am there, I will ask him about this. I just hope I get an answer this time."

"He never cooperated in the past," John said. "Why should he do so this time?"

"Because now he has something precious to lose," Kyle said. "His own life."

"What if Sir Fulbert is the murderer?" John said.

"I know he hated his brother enough to kill him," Kyle said. "I have my doubts, though, as to whether he would murder his only son and heir."

"Let us assume for a moment that the killer was in fact a woman," John said. "Could Sir Fulbert's wife have done it?"

"Mistress Ryland is far too emotional to kill in cold blood," Kyle said. "The murderer, on the other hand, plotted and planned to eliminate his victims one at a time as the opportunity arose."

"What about the daughter, or even the daughter-in-law, Sir Peter's wife?"

"I haven't met the daughter yet, so I reserve judgment on her. However, I did meet Sir Peter's wife. She is cold and calculating enough to carry it out. She lacks motive, though, especially since she relies on the Rylands for her support. She may be capable of murder, but she's no fool."

"I seriously doubt a woman did it anyway," John said. "How could any female throttle a big man like Sir Peter, and then hoist his body into the air at the end of a rope?"

"I agree it would take a man's strength to choke another man, especially if the victim offered resistance. However, there is a way that any woman could easily haul Sir Peter aloft."

He presented the twisted linen cord for John's inspection.

"Do you see where the edge of the fabric is tattered all along the length of it?" he said. "My guess is that the killer tied the noose around Sir Peter's neck, slipped the cord over the rafter, and then secured the end to the saddle bow. All he had to do was urge Sir Peter's horse to take a few steps forward to lift the body off the ground, thus fraying the linen fibers in the process. After tying the loose end to the post, he rode the horse from the stable. The groom assumed it was Sir Peter, just as the killer anticipated the man would."

"It appears this murderer is a professional," John said. "He kills his victims cleanly and quickly, leaving behind neither a trace of his presence nor a witness to incriminate him."

"On the contrary, my friend," Kyle said. "The imprint of those fingertips on Sir Peter's neck reveals a singular defect on the killer's left hand." He picked up the black velvet cotte. "And there is this," he added, indicating the smudge on the front. "Do you recognize it?"

John examined the spot. "Should I?" he said. "It looks like any other fine powder."

"It is cold fire," Kyle said. "Sir Peter spilled it the other day when he came into the chapel to identify his uncle's body." He touched the smudge and showed John the residue on his finger. "Some of this may have rubbed off on the killer's clothing."

"Even with a bit of that on him," John said, "he may not be so easy to find. Cold fire glows only in the dark."

"Easy or not," Kyle said, "it is better than nothing."

It was nearly noon by the time Kyle, Hoprig, and Vinewood rode into the bailey at Cragston Castle. They followed Arnald the groom up the hewn stairs to the second floor, where they entered the main hall with the vaulted ceiling and tapestry hangings on the stone walls.

Sir Fulbert hunched over a pewter mug at the trestle table in the center of the floor. His green shirt was wrinkled and stained, his face unshaven, his hair disheveled. His countenance was haggard, like that of a man dragged through hell by the scruff of his neck.

Mistress Ryland and Eleanora sat across the table from Sir Fulbert eating the remnants of their midday meal. They wore linen gowns the color of oatmeal. Frilly white caps covered their hair, as was customary for married women.

"Kyle Shaw, Deputy to the Sheriff of Ayrshire," Arnald said in a loud voice. He then withdrew from the main hall and closed the doors behind him.

Kyle approached the table with a wrapped bundle under his arm and greeted each of the Rylands by name.

Mistress Ryland acknowledged him with a nod of her head, though she kept her face slightly averted.

Eleanora eyed him like a hungry lioness surveying its next meal.

Sir Fulbert glanced over at him. "What do you want now?" he said, his tone harsh.

Before Kyle could respond, a young woman barely twenty years of age burst into the main hall.

"I will never marry Charles Ettwick!" she cried. She flounced across the wooden floor in a violet silk gown and stopped in front of Sir Fulbert, her hands on her slim hips. "I don't care how rich he is. I will not marry him!" She stamped her foot to emphasize her words. Blond curls framed her angelic face, which at that moment was flushed with anger.

Sir Fulbert stood up so abruptly, the bench toppled over behind him. "You will do as I say!" he roared, his face scarlet. Blue veins throbbed in his temples.

"You can't force me to marry him," the young woman said, her voice brittle with disdain.

Sir Fulbert raised his arm in such a way as to strike the young woman with a backhanded blow.

She lifted her chin in defiance. "Go ahead," she said. "Beat me black and blue. It won't work this time. I refuse to marry him."

Sir Fulbert lowered his arm. "Lock her in her room," he bellowed at Mistress Ryland, who flinched at the loudness of his voice. "She will stay there until I see fit to let her out."

"I hate you," the young woman said in a low tone seething with contempt. She whirled in a rustle of silk and fled from the main hall.

Mistress Ryland got up from the bench, her face stricken with mortification. "Please excuse my daughter," she said to Kyle. "I don't know what got into her."

That was when Kyle noticed the bruise on her cheekbone. She cast a scornful glance at her husband before she walked with quiet dignity from the main hall.

Sir Fulbert reached for his mug and drank deeply from it. His gaze settled on Kyle and the two English soldiers standing by the table. "Get out," he said in a calm voice. His expression showed no remorse over his outburst.

"I bring you news of Sir Peter," Kyle said.

"What about him?" Sir Fulbert said.

"I regret to inform you that your son is dead," Kyle said.

Eleanora arched a skeptical eyebrow, as though she doubted his words.

Sir Fulbert focused his bloodshot eyes on Kyle with an effort. "Dead, you say?" he said. "How did it happen?"

"Hanged," Kyle said. He related how the groom found the body in the stable at the Bull and Bear Tavern.

"There must be some mistake," Sir Fulbert said, clearly at a loss. "Peter just finalized the contract for his sister's impending nuptials. Our troubles are nearly over."

"I'm sorry to be the one to tell you," Kyle said. "Sir Peter is in fact dead. I saw his body myself. He now lies in the mortuary chapel at St. John's."

"He would never hang himself like a . . ." Sir Fulbert said. He paused to grope for the right words. "A common criminal."

"He didn't," Kyle said. "He was murdered." He put the wrapped bundle on the table and laid back the edges to reveal the twisted linen cord. "This is what was used to hang him."

The color drained from Sir Fulbert's face at the sight of the white cord. The only sound that broke the silence was the harsh rasp of his breathing.

Kyle righted the overturned bench in time for Sir Fulbert to sit heavily upon it, as though his knees suddenly gave out under him. He refilled the man's mug from the pitcher on the table and placed it before him.

Sir Fulbert brought the mug to his lips with a shaking hand and drank deeply of the amber brew within.

"Tell me why the killer used a long strip of linen instead of hemp rope," Kyle said.

"It doesn't matter now," Sir Fulbert said, his tone flat. He set his mug on the table and clung to it with both hands.

"The rafter from which Sir Peter was hanged is made of oak, rather than pine," Kyle said. "Is that significant, do you think?"

Sir Fulbert's brows drew together, and the muscles tightened along his jaw. He put his head in his hands and let out his breath in a weary sigh. "Leave me be," he said, his voice muffled.

"Sir Fulbert," Kyle said. "You must know by now that your life is in danger. I can arrange for a troop of soldiers to stand guard over you, if you wish."

Sir Fulbert lifted his head. "It won't stop the hashshashin," he said, his expression reflecting the despair in his voice. "Nothing will."

"Do you know who the killer is, then?" Kyle said.

"Not by name," Sir Fulbert said. "I just know he won't quit

until the score is settled."

"How do you know that?" Kyle said.

"That is what the hashshashin do," Sir Fulbert said. He got up from the bench and walked on unsteady legs toward the doorway.

Seeing that he would get nothing further from Sir Fulbert, Kyle turned to Eleanora, who sat on the other side of the table. "I am sorry for your loss," he said.

She perked up under the handsome deputy's gaze. "Thank you," she said.

"Do you feel up to answering a few questions just now?" Kyle said. "I could come back another time, if you prefer."

"Now is as good a time as any, Master Deputy," she said.

"Can you tell me what hashshashin is?" he said.

"This is the first time I ever heard of it," she said.

"Never mind, then," Kyle said. "Tell me about Sir Charles Ettwick. Have you ever met him?"

"Of course," she said. Her hands fluttered up to adjust the frilly white cap on her head. "He is Peter's friend."

"What do you think of him?" Kyle said.

A spot of pink appeared on her cheeks. "He is quite charming," she said. "Marjorie should be grateful she's engaged to someone like him."

"Why is that?" Kyle said.

"He has wealth and position," she said. "He is also very good looking."

"I don't think she's too happy about the prospect of marrying him," Kyle said.

"She will do her duty when the time comes," she said. Her voice took on a hard edge. "I had to do it, and so must she."

"When did you last see Sir Peter alive?" Kyle said.

"The day before yesterday," she said. "Right before he left for town to identify his uncle's body."

"Did he seem depressed to you?" Kyle said.

"Quite the contrary," she said. "Charles agreed to the marriage contract, and Peter was elated about it." She licked her lips, her gaze intent on his face. "Tell me," she added, her fingers gripping the edge of the table. "Was he robbed, too?"

"He was not," Kyle said. "I found these on his body." He removed the gold ring and the coin purse from the pouch at his side and set them before her.

Her whole body appeared to relax. She tucked the ring into her bodice between her breasts. She then loosened the binding ties on the small purse and dumped the contents onto the table. Her eyes lit up at the sight of the gold coins on the wooden surface before her.

It came as no surprise to Kyle that she professed more interest in her husband's money than in his fate. In his opinion, that was consistent with the kind of woman she was.

"Sir Peter's horse went missing," he said. "I shall keep an eye out for it. The animal is too distinctive-looking to sell, and being a gelding, it has no value as a breeder. It should turn up soon."

"I am sure it will," she said, tearing her gaze away from the gold coins to glance up at him. "I shall attend to burial arrangements on the morrow."

"One more thing before I go," Kyle said to her. "It's about Sir Humphrey. Did he ever mention meeting anyone on his outings?"

"Not to me," she said, "but I suspected as much."

"Suspected what?" Kyle said.

"That he met with a lover," she said. "No man hunts in foul weather. Yet, he went out with that hawk every day without fail."

"Do you have any idea who his lover was?" Kyle said.

"Not a clue," she said. "Sir Humphrey kept his own counsel."

Her lips stretched into a smile that did not touch her eyes. "But then, he wasn't like the rest of us, if you know what I mean."

"What do you mean?" Kyle said. He knew very well the implication of her statement, but he was determined to make her say it.

"That his liaison may not have been with a woman," she said.

"I see," Kyle said.

"I shouldn't have mentioned that," she said, not at all contrite. "One must never speak ill of the dead, you know." She gathered the coins and dropped them back into the purse.

"What will you do now that you are widowed?" Kyle said.

Her hand tightened possessively around the coin purse. "First, I shall bury my husband," she said. "Then, I shall book passage on the next ship bound for England."

CHAPTER 13

Kyle rode from Cragston Castle with Hoprig and Vinewood beside him. He reined in when they reached the coastal road to gaze out over the Firth of Clyde. Beyond the edge of the cliff, the incoming tide crashed against the rocks far below, only to rush back out to sea once again. The sound of the restless waves lulled him into a drowsy state, as did the warmth of the noon sun on his bare head.

He shook himself mentally, for this was not the time to nap in the shade of the nearest tree. There was a murderer roaming the shire, and as surely as the sun rose in the east and set in the west, the man would strike again. How soon that might happen, however, was anybody's guess.

"Have either of you ever heard of hashshashin?" he said to the English soldiers with him.

Vinewood shook his head. "Never," he said.

"It has a foreign ring to it," Hoprig said. "Much like the words my father picked up in the Holy Land during the last crusade."

"That must have been a difficult time for your father," Kyle said.

"Difficult," Hoprig said with a mirthless laugh. "According to Father, it was horrendous."

"Did he ever mention what happened over there?" Kyle said.

"He did," Hoprig said. "If even half of what he told me is true, Sir Peter got what he deserved. And, if there is any justice in this world, Sir Fulbert will, too."

"Exactly what did happen?" Kyle said.

With his fair brows locked in a frown, Hoprig opened his mouth and began to relate the things his father told him.

Naked steel flashed in the sunlight as Christian and Saracen hacked and slashed at each other under the Syrian sky. The battle raged on within sight of the walled city of Acre, the prize of that particular conflict. Even the cool breeze blowing in from the Mediterranean Sea failed to dispel the smell of blood, sweat, and fear that hung in the air over the combatants. The heaving mass of men and horses ebbed and surged. Pockets of English knights regrouped to attack or retreat, whichever seemed more expedient at that moment.

Lord Hoprig barely heard the clang of metal, the angry shouts, and the anguished cries of the wounded and the dying on the field of battle. The three Saracen warriors who bore down on him commanded his full attention. He raised his sword to block the stroke of the curved blade in the first man's hand. Before he could strike back, the man wheeled his horse and darted away. He twisted in the saddle to exchange glancing blows with the two other men before they, too, rode swiftly out of reach.

Beads of moisture slicked the brow of his bearded face, not from fright, but because of the infernal heat of the summer sun beating down upon him. His throat was hoarse from shouting, his mouth dry as parchment. The nosepiece of his Norman helmet partially obstructed his vision. His cumbersome bull-hide armor hampered his movements, unlike the loose flowing garb of the turbaned warriors. The Friesian he rode—a huge warhorse as black as midnight—was no match for the Saracens' fleet-footed mares, which literally ran circles around him.

He caught a glimpse of Sir Humphrey swinging his sword with deadly intent. He heard Sir Fulbert bellowing blasphemies

*somewhere to his left. On his right, Sir Peter seemed to be hold-
ing his own, his blade bloody, his white tabard streaked with
crimson.*

*The main body of English soldiers veered to the east as a
hundred Saracen troops on fresh mounts galloped into the fray
to join their countrymen in waging war against the infidel.*

*Sir Fulbert suddenly appeared in front of Lord Hoprig on a
muscular bay stallion. "We've been cut off," he shouted. "Come
this way." He beckoned to him with the sword in his hand.*

*Lord Hoprig turned his mount to follow Sir Fulbert, as did
Sir Humphrey and Sir Peter. The four of them rode in a wide
arc to circumvent the Saracen army. Before they could rejoin
their English comrades, a handful of Saracen warriors broke
away from their troop to chase after them. On overtaking them,
the Saracens tried to separate the knights from each other in
order to bring them down one at a time.*

*Lord Hoprig and his companions rode stirrup to stirrup
until, on Sir Fulbert's command, they pivoted their warhorses
and charged at their astonished pursuers. Steel rang against
steel as sword met scimitar. Neither Christian nor Saracen gave
ground, for this was a holy war, a fight to the death.*

*Light flared along polished metal as a curved blade came
down at Lord Hoprig's head. He threw up his arm to thwart
the stroke with his sword. The man then came up under his
guard to make a slicing sweep at his chest. The bull-hide armor
he cursed only moments before saved his life, for the tip of the
curved blade merely hewed out a chunk of stiffened leather,
rather than cleaving the flesh beneath. He lashed out with his
sword in a mighty backhanded stroke leveled at the man's neck,
separating the head from the body in a gush of blood.*

*Within minutes, five Saracen warriors lay dead in the grass.
Blood oozed down Sir Humphrey's arm from a breach in the
chain mail links protecting his shoulder. The others suffered only*

minor nicks and scratches.

They looked around to get their bearings, for they were now isolated and alone, having strayed farther afield than they intended. Even the blast of the battle horns sounded remote. The pasture land around them was flat as far as the eye could see, except for distant hills that marched along the eastern horizon.

"Look there," Sir Fulbert said, pointing to a small cluster of stone houses half a league ahead of them. "Let us teach those heathen dogs a lesson." He raked his spurs across the belly of his horse and took off at a lope. The others set out after him.

Filled with bloodlust and spoiling for another fight, the four of them drew their weapons and galloped into the village square around which the flat-roofed houses were clustered. Before the people there could take flight, they cut a bloody swathe through their ranks. Women and children screamed. A crippled old man shouted in alarm. All within reach fell by the edge of the sword. Only two women, both beautiful in face and form, were spared.

Lord Hoprig was the first to regain control of his reason. He reined in beside Sir Fulbert's bay to stare in horror at the crumpled bodies of women and children scattered around the square. Blood poured from mortal wounds, staining the earth beneath them. The crippled old man sprawled face-down in the dirt, lying in a puddle of his own blood.

"What have we done?" he cried in dismay. "There isn't an able-bodied man among them."

"They are heathens," Sir Fulbert said. "It is God's will that they should die."

Sir Humphrey drew up alongside his brother. "I cannot believe," he said, intruding into the conversation, "that God approves of slaughtering the innocent."

"My sentiments exactly," Lord Hoprig said. He exchanged a long thoughtful glance with Sir Humphrey. "I think the time has come to depart."

"I do, too," Sir Humphrey said.

The pair of them turned their horses to head back the way they came.

"Where are you going?" Sir Fulbert said, calling after them.

"Home," Lord Hoprig and Sir Humphrey said in unison.

"Father later learned," Hoprig said, "that Sir Fulbert and Sir Peter raped the two women and slew them afterward. Father never forgave himself for leaving that day. Had he stayed, he might have saved those women from such a fate."

Vinewood looked on in quiet sympathy.

"I'm sorry," Kyle said. "I had no idea it was like that."

"After Father left," Hoprig said, "the Christian army, those Knights of Christ with Sir Fulbert and Sir Peter in the lead, went on to pillage the countryside and burn every mosque they came across, preferably with the Saracens still inside, all in the name of God."

"No wonder your father wanted to go home," Kyle said. "I would, too." He gazed out over the roiling sea for a long moment, pondering Hoprig's account of his father's sojourn in the Holy Land, half-convinced that the hashshashin, whoever he was, might actually be justified in his quest for vengeance, if that was truly what this was about.

He glanced over his shoulder at the trees a short distance behind them. "I'll bet old Rolf will know something about that linen cord," he said. He turned the gelding's head inland and started toward Cragston Forest.

After a brief search, they located a deer track, which they followed through the trees. Sunlight flashed sporadically through a canopy of leafy branches onto the path ahead. The only sounds in the forest around them were the twitter of sparrows and the crunch of dried leaves beneath the hooves of the horses.

"I think I shall call upon Lady Catherine while we're out in this direction," Kyle said at length.

Hoprig seemed to perk up at the notion. "Have you news about the missing pearl?" he said.

"I wish I did," Kyle said. "The purpose of this visit is to get a description of it from her."

Hoprig nudged his chestnut mare forward to come up alongside the gelding. "There is something you should know before you talk to Lady Catherine," he said. "Sir Humphrey met with her a couple of weeks before he died." He related what Isabel told him about it. "Lady Catherine took the news of her son's death rather badly."

"I imagine she did," Kyle said. "It is difficult to lose a child of any age." That was something he knew about from personal experience.

The three of them rode in silence for a while, each occupied with his own thoughts. Before long, they came to a stream cascading over the rocks.

Kyle knew he was getting close to where the old man lived when he caught a whiff of smoke drifting in the air. His pace slowed when he glimpsed two men in white garments moving about the small clearing. "Hold up," he said softly, bringing his mount to a halt.

Hoprig reined in beside him. "What is it?" he said in a low voice.

Kyle peered at the white-robed figures through the trees. "I'm not sure," he said.

They dismounted and tethered their horses to a low branch. They trod with a light step along the deer path until they drew close enough to see and hear without being seen or heard.

Rolf stood near the campfire with a dagger in his hand. His head was bare, and over his brown robe, he wore a white mantle that took on a gaudy brilliance in the sunlight.

The other man, who Kyle recognized as Simon from town, knelt beside a small copper basin filled with water. He, too, was bare of head and dressed in a bright white garment, except he clutched to his chest a hare with its paws bound with a white cord. He lifted the creature and closed his eyes, his head tilted back.

"It looks like some kind of ceremony," Kyle whispered.

"Oh, Mother Earth," Simon said. "I call upon you to accept this offering, humble though it may be. Our fires we build upon your breast. The flames reach into the air, and the smoke supports the sky. The mighty oak sends its roots down into the soil, and rain falling from the heavens makes it grow."

He lowered his arms and laid the hare on the ground. He held the struggling animal with one hand and slashed its throat with the dagger Rolf handed to him. When its legs quit jerking spasmodically, he slit open its belly and leaned close to study the intestines that spilled out onto the bare earth. "This cannot be so," he said at last, looking up at the old man with a frown.

"What do you see?" Rolf said.

"Death," Simon said, frowning.

"I see it, too," Rolf said.

"But whose death does it portend?" Simon said, rising to his feet.

Kyle took that as his cue to make his presence known. He pushed his way through the undergrowth and stepped into the clearing. "Whose death, indeed?" he said.

Neither Rolf nor Simon seemed disconcerted by the deputy's sudden appearance from behind the bushes.

"Ah, Master Shaw," Rolf said. "You are just in time for lunch."

"But, Master," Simon said in protest, although he appeared reluctant to voice the reason for his objection in front of Kyle.

"Not to worry, Simon," Rolf said. "Hospitality ranks high among the virtues a man may possess."

"Although your offer is generous," Kyle said, "I must decline. Just now, I would like to hear more about the impending death of which Simon spoke."

Rolf made himself comfortable on the trunk of the fallen tree by the fire, while Simon set about skinning and cleaning the hare.

"Haruspicy—the art of reading entrails—is not an exact science," Rolf said. "The configuration of that particular hare's viscera indicates a loss of life, other than for the hare itself, of course. That is all there is to it."

"How do you know what it means?" Kyle said.

"It is too complicated to explain," Rolf said. "You must take my word for it."

"Prior Drumlay would call that using uncanny powers," Kyle said.

"It is hardly that," Rolf said. "It is no different from ascertaining that spring is near when the grass turns green in the meadow, or that a hard winter is in store when the animals grow a thick coat of fur. It is not a matter of looking, as much as actually seeing that which lies before us."

Hoprig and Vinewood led the horses into the clearing just as Simon skewered the hare's carcass with an iron spit. After suspending it over the open flames, he rinsed his hands in the copper basin and poured the blood-tainted water out on the ground.

Kyle told the old man about Macalister's run-in with Blackwell and his men. "Were you there in the woods that day?" he said.

"Not I," Rolf said. He looked over at Simon, who shook his head. "I am afraid neither of us can be of any assistance to you."

Undeterred, Kyle walked over to the gelding and removed the bundle of twisted linen cord from his saddle roll. "Tell me about this," he said, presenting it for the old man's inspection.

"I've never seen it before," Rolf said.

"I beg to differ," Kyle said. He bent down to pick up the discarded cord, which earlier bound the hare's paws. "These look very much alike to me," he added, holding the scrap of white linen beside the bundle in his hand. "What do you think?"

Rolf chuckled. "I knew you would be trouble when I first laid eyes on you, Master Shaw," he said.

"Tell me what I need to know," Kyle said. "Then, I will trouble you no more."

Rolf stood up to shrug the white mantle from his shoulders.

Simon took the garment from the old man and went over to the croft to put it inside, along with his own linen robe.

Rolf sat back on the tree trunk by the fire and picked up the gnarled staff beside him to prod at the glowing coals. "I will not insult your intelligence," he said, "by claiming ignorance about the things you ask. Since it is likely you will gather misinformation from the profane and the uninformed, I shall respond to your queries, within reason, of course, so that you may divine fact from fiction."

Elated with the possibility of finally getting some answers, Kyle dragged a chunk of oak closer to the campfire and sat facing the old man across the blaze.

About that time, Simon stepped from the croft in a brown tunic belted at the waist with a hemp rope. He stepped over the tree trunk to stand behind Rolf, as though to guard the old man's back. Meanwhile, Hoprig and Vinewood ambled up beside Kyle, as if to show their support for the man of law.

They regarded each other across the campfire, three on one side and two on the other, while the meat on the spit sizzled and crackled over the flames.

"Are you a druid priest?" Kyle said, his pale blue eyes holding the old man's steady gaze.

"You get right to the heart of the matter, don't you?" Rolf said with a smile.

"Well, are you?"

"I am."

"I suspected as much."

"What gave me away?"

"You did," Kyle said. "The last time we spoke, you mentioned the circle of life and Mother Earth. You also knew things no one told you. This time, you were wearing white robes and reading entrails. How could I come to any other conclusion?"

"I see," Rolf said. "Will you now set the hounds on us and banish our heinous cult from the shire?"

"I am looking for a murderer who is either a druid or who knows enough about them to use that knowledge to his advantage. Are there any other members, besides you and Simon?"

A shadow of fear crossed Simon's face for an instant. He placed a hand on the old man's shoulder, as though to steady his nerves and bolster his courage.

Rolf gave Simon's fingers a reassuring pat. "Only three in this shire," he said. "Two of them are dead."

"What are their names?"

"Sir Humphrey, Sir Peter, and Sir Fulbert."

At Rolf's admission, certain pieces of the puzzle began to fall into place in Kyle's mind. No wonder Sir Peter and Sir Fulbert balked at disclosing their secret to him. Should it become known, the Church would excommunicate them for belonging to a forbidden sect of pagan idol worshippers, especially after returning from the last crusade as heroes. Sir Fulbert was the only male Ryland left, which meant he was either the next target or the killer.

"There are also those who come to me for relief of spirit," Rolf said. "They are not initiates nor do they aspire to be. They seek redemption through confession of past sins. They bring offerings in return for peace of mind."

"Why should they trust you with information that can be used against them?" Kyle said.

"I require that they write their transgressions on parchment," Rolf said. "Those who cannot write must draw symbols, of which they alone know the meaning. After I offer prayer on their behalf, they pass the parchment through the fire. Thus, their mental burdens go up in smoke, leaving them with a clear conscience and a renewed perspective on life."

"What is the significance of the mistletoe?" Kyle said.

"It is a hallowed plant, a gift from the gods that grows without roots on the sacred oak. When properly harvested, it can heal certain ills and protect against poison. It can enhance fertility or be used as an aphrodisiac. It is even reputed to open locks, although I never had occasion to witness that. In bygone ages, it served as a token for safe conduct to the underworld."

"What does proper harvesting involve?" Kyle said.

Rolf's countenance brightened as he warmed to his subject. "It should only be done on Midsummer's Eve," he said. "Mistletoe taken from the sacred oak on that night is especially powerful. A priest in a clean white robe must cut it with a sickle made of gold. Those beneath the tree must take care to catch it in a white cloth, lest it touch the ground and lose its potency. The priest must then sacrifice a pair of white yearling bulls so that the mistletoe and those who receive a portion of it might prosper throughout the coming year."

"Interesting," Kyle said. He glanced down at the bundle in his hand. "Sir Peter was hanged with this, instead of rope. What does that mean?"

"White symbolizes purity," Rolf said. "A sacrificial victim must be secured with a clean linen cord. Only then is it considered as pure and holy as the priest who officiates in white ceremonial robes. Any other kind of binding taints the blood offering. Thus, it is rejected as profane. The use of such a cord to kill an innocent man makes a mockery of all that is sacred."

"What about the druidic practice of human sacrifice?" Kyle said. "Did that not sometimes involve the shedding of innocent blood?"

"Never," Rolf said. "An executioner is not considered a murderer for hanging a condemned man in the public square, is he? Hundreds of years ago, when people held the druidic priesthood in high esteem, druids served as public executioners, although they did so in private, with the added bonus of ensuring a good harvest because of appeasing the gods in the process."

"It sounds like a cruel and barbaric practice," Kyle said.

"You make druids of old sound like bloodthirsty savages," Rolf said. "The passage of a condemned man from life to death must involve violence of some kind in order to carry out his sentence. Druids in ancient times executed a felon with the skill of a chirurgeon, unlike the English who choke, disembowel, and chop up anyone perceived as a traitor to king and country."

The old man drew his dagger and sliced a piece of roasted meat from the spitted carcass. He put the morsel in his mouth and licked the juice from his fingers before continuing. "The purpose was never to make the victim suffer," he said. "It was to observe the body upon its sudden demise. The way it fell, the convulsion of the limbs, and how fast or slow the blood flowed from the wound were all meaningful. A quick thrust to the chest with a sharp dagger was the most common method used to dispatch the victim. Of course, during times of famine or warfare, a more elaborate procedure was needed to pacify certain deities. Under those dire circumstances, the priest conducted a singular ritual reserved for special occasions."

"One that no doubt involved pouring out a great deal of human blood," Kyle said dryly.

"They spilled not a drop, actually," Rolf said. "A criminal or a prisoner of war was sacrificed, of course. His body, though, remained intact to the end of the ceremony. They even had a unique name for that particular ritual."

"What was it called?"

"Threefold death."

CHAPTER 14

On the way to Kilgate Manor, Kyle mulled over the information that Rolf imparted to him, especially the details concerning the druidic ritual known as threefold death. That was an apt description, for the methods employed during the ceremony were drowning, hanging, and burning, in that order.

The hapless victim suffered the first death by being thrust headfirst into a barrel of water, where he remained until he quit struggling. It hardly seemed necessary for the priest to proceed to the second step, yet proceed he did in his determination to placate the gods. The body was hung by the neck from the branch of an oak tree until the priest saw fit to advance to the third phase, a step that surely bordered on overkill by that time. To complete the rite, the body was placed in an elaborate cage made of wicker and suspended over a huge pile of wood arranged in such a way that, when ignited, would consume the remains of the victim, the wicker cage and everything within twenty feet of the blaze.

The similarity of that ritual to the means used to murder the Rylands did not escape Kyle's notice. It was evident the killer possessed an intimate knowledge of druidic rites in order to imitate them. Although Sir Humphrey did not die in a water barrel, he drowned nonetheless. The same went for Sir Peter, who departed this life at the end of a rope slung over an oak rafter, not an oak branch. Since Sir Fulbert was the only male Ryland left, he seemed doomed to immolation. Whether his death would involve a wicker cage dangling over an open fire remained to be seen.

Besides Sir Fulbert and his daughter Marjorie, the list of suspects now included Rolf and Simon. The old man was not really a serious contender due to his advanced age. However, he did admit to being a druid, and that alone kept him in the running. Simon, who was either a druidic priest or an initiate hoping to become one, was also a candidate. He lacked motive, though, unless he had a hidden agenda nobody knew about. Of course, there was always the possibility that someone whose company either Rolf or Simon kept was the one with the hidden agenda, which meant there were more persons of interest to seek out before they could be brought to justice.

"We're here," Hoprig said, breaking into Kyle's reverie.

They rode through the front gate of Kilgate Manor. The sandstone walls of the fortress-like house took on a reddish-gold cast in the afternoon sun. The air was still, without a breeze to relieve the heat of the summer day.

They left the horses with Edgar and followed Isabel up the outer stairway to the second level. She bade Hoprig and Vinewood to wait in the main hall while she conducted Kyle on to Lady Catherine's solar. She rapped on the door and opened it for him to go inside alone.

The room was not as bright as the last time he walked into it, for the sun was high in the sky at that time of day. There was enough light, though, to clearly see the mistress of Kilgate Manor.

She sat at a tapestry loom near the window, her gaze on the vibrant hues in the design, her brow puckered in deep thought. The hand that held the threaded needle rested idly on the edge of the wooden frame. The black gown she wore set off the diamond-studded silver pendant at her neck, but the harsh color of the cloth made her olive complexion look sallow and wan.

The clump of booted feet on the wooden floor seemed to bring her back from somewhere far away.

"Why, Master Shaw," she said in a thick Spanish accent. "How nice to see you." She stuck the needle into the thickly woven material and turned in her seat to face him.

"Good morrow, m'lady," Kyle said with a courtly bow. "I trust I find you in good health."

"As well as can be expected," she said. With a wave of her hand, she indicated that he should sit in the chair across from her. "What brings you here on this fine day?"

Kyle sat on the hard-backed chair with a clank of metal. "Two reasons, m'lady," he said, repositioning his scabbard for comfort.

"What is the first?" she said with polite interest, her hands folded in her lap.

"On my last visit," he said, "I failed to get a description of the pearl that went missing. May I impose upon you to describe it for me now?"

"Of course," she said. She launched into a brief but detailed account of the configuration of the setting, the clasp, the size and shape of the pearl, and even its blushing pink color.

"It sounds like a costly piece of jewelry," he said. He went on to mention how Hul and his associates agreed to participate in the search, but only for a price.

"I am not surprised to hear that," she said. "It is no different in my country. I will be glad to reimburse you for any expenses you incur on my behalf." She adjusted the black skirts about her knees. "Now, tell me the second reason you came to see me."

"I understand you spoke with Sir Humphrey Ryland shortly before his death," he said.

Her hands froze in the act of smoothing the wrinkles from the fabric. "Who told you that?" she demanded, holding his pale blue eyes in a penetrating gaze.

"Rest easy that it was no one of your acquaintance," he said. "After all, you did meet with him in a public place. I would appreciate if you would tell me what he told you."

"I do not mean to be rude, Master Shaw," she said. "Nevertheless, my private conversation cannot be of any concern to you."

"Sir Humphrey died less than two weeks later, foully murdered by person or persons unknown. It is my duty to investigate every move he made up to the time of his death. The slightest detail, unimportant though it seems, may be just what is needed to resolve this matter."

"As you wish," she said. She knotted white-knuckled hands in her lap. "My husband begged off from going on the last crusade. He claimed he could better serve his king by keeping the rabble under control at the garrison near Paisley, where we lived at the time. He encouraged my son, Victor, to go to the Holy Land in his stead." Her mouth twisted in bitterness. "He had no right to do that. Victor was not his child."

"Please go on," he said gently.

"Victor was more than happy to oblige," she said. "He was only sixteen, with high hopes and grandiose notions of glory. He trained hard to hone his skills, and by the time he left, he thought he was ready to take on seasoned warriors in battle. I pleaded with him not to go, but he was young and headstrong and would not listen to reason. He promised to make me proud by coming back as a conquering hero."

She covered her face with her hands. Her shoulders shook for a moment as she wept silently. After regaining her composure, she removed from the cuff of her sleeve a linen cloth with lace around the edges, which she used to daub the moisture from her eyes.

"Shortly after Victor's arrival in the Holy Land," she continued, "Sir Fulbert sent him to the front of the battle lines, where he did not last an hour. Sir Humphrey told me that my son's horse, weapons, and armor went to a man who needed them. I do not begrudge that man the use of my son's belongings, especially if they were instrumental in saving his life. What I do lament, and will to my dying day, is that Victor is buried in a foreign country, without a stone to mark the location. That means I can never visit his grave, ever."

She looked up at Kyle, her countenance unreadable. "I made Sir Humphrey tell me those things because, as Victor's mother, I had a right to know. My husband knew of my son's fate, yet he let me go on thinking he was alive and well for three long years. You can imagine my shock and dismay upon learning the truth."

"How can you be sure your husband knew what happened to Victor?"

"He admitted it when I confronted him."

"Others returned from the crusade," Kyle said. "Did you never question why your son was not among them?"

"I thought perhaps he had settled in the Holy Land with other Christians who chose to remain there, or that he went to Spain to stay with relatives. The hope that I would eventually hear from him kept me going. Now, that will never be. He is gone forever."

"I'm sorry," Kyle said. "Please accept my condolence on your loss."

"Loss!" she said, her voice harsh. "It was murder. My husband persuaded Victor to go on crusade against my will, and Sir Fulbert knew my son lacked experience on the field of battle. A Saracen may have struck the mortal blow, but the two of

them are equally responsible for sending my boy to slaughter."
A menacing light glittered in her black eyes. "They must pay for
what they did."

Hoprig and Vinewood sat at the trestle table in the main hall of
Kilgate Manor. They occupied a bench, not as guests, but
merely to wait in comfort while Kyle paid a visit to Lady
Catherine.

Despite the cool interior of the stone building, sweat beaded
Hoprig's brow and the upper lip of his clean-shaven face. His
fingers plucked nervously at the ties of his black leather jerkin,
his eyes on the closed door on the far side of the hall in the
hope of seeing Isabel once again before it was time to leave.

As though in answer to his prayer, she opened the door and
beckoned to him. She looked fresh and pretty in a sky blue
linen tunic belted at the waist.

"Wait here," Hoprig said to Vinewood. "I will be but a moment." He hastened across the chamber and stepped through
the doorway into a long corridor. He followed her until she
stopped before a dark stairwell. When he caught up with her,
she led the way up granite steps that brought them to the third
floor of the manor house.

She paused on the landing before a stone archway. "That is
my lady's chamber," she said, indicating the first door in the
hallway beyond. "It is quite grand in there."

"I can imagine," he said, admiring the blond oak panels inlaid
with walnut. "Is that where we are bound?"

"Nay," she said. "Come." She took his hand and continued
up the hewn stairs, which appeared to vanish into the shadows
ahead.

He mounted the steps with one hand clasping hers and the
other against the cold stone wall to feel his way in the gloom.
The stairs beneath his feet leveled onto a short landing. Without

warning, the passageway changed direction. That was when he saw the thread of light seeping around the square hatch above him.

He ascended the remaining steps to the top, where he pushed on the trapdoor and laid it open. He climbed onto the weathered-plank floor and extended his hand to help her up into the guard tower.

A timber parapet as high as a man's chest closed in the four sides of the tiny elevated platform. A sturdy post in each corner supported the peaked roof over it. The three-foot gap between the roof and the top rail of the parapet allowed for an unobstructed view in every direction.

"This is my favorite place," she said, looking out over the landscape. "I can see the whole world from up here."

A breeze stirred his reddish-blond hair as he stood beside her, gazing in awe at the countryside all around him. The land seemed to go on forever, with undulating hills to the south and east and grassy plains to the north. He even fancied he could see the blue water of the firth along the horizon to the west. The dirt road leading up to the front gate looked like a thin white ribbon. A stream in a wooded dale outside the wall coiled like a serpent through the trees.

"What do ye think?" she said, her brown eyes on him.

"It's magnificent," he said.

"I hoped ye would like it," she said.

"I do," he said. He took her hand and brought it to his lips. "The best part, though, is sharing it with you."

He smiled at the delicate blush that heightened the color in her cheeks.

"I didn't see Owen when I rode in," he said. "How is he doing?"

"He's fine," she said. "He's swimming in the stream with Tippy. Do ye want to go down and join them?"

"Maybe next time," he said. "By the way, I have news." He then told her about Sir Peter's murder and the visit with the old man in the forest.

"What is a druid?" she said.

"Some kind of priest, I think," he said. He released her hand to rest both elbows on the parapet to look out at the panoramic scene. "I do know the Church doesn't approve of their practices."

A frown clouded her features. "I don't think my lady would, either," she said. "She's pretty strict when it comes to her Christian beliefs." She turned to gaze at him. "Was it a druid who killed Sir Peter, then?"

"I'm not convinced it was," he said. "I don't think Master Shaw is either. There are too many things that point to them."

"Isn't that good?"

"Not really," he said. "It just makes me wonder whether someone is trying to shrug his guilt onto them."

"Who would do that?"

"Either a coward or a very clever fellow," he said, his gaze on the distant hills.

She lifted her arms to prop her elbows beside his on the parapet. A breeze ruffled her loose sleeves, causing the soft fabric to billow and flap.

On turning his head to smile at her, he glimpsed the yellowish-purple bruises on the upper part of her right arm. He lightly touched the affected skin with his finger.

"Who did that to you?" he said.

"What will ye do if I tell ye?" she said.

"I'll kill him," he said, deadly earnest.

"What makes ye think it was a man?" she said.

"Because of your reluctance to say who it was," he said.

"Ye must promise not to kill him."

An unexpected rush of jealousy burned through him. "Does

he mean that much to you?"

"He means nothing to me," she said with vehemence. "I don't want ye to hang because of him. He's not worth it."

"So, who did it?"

From the stubborn set of her jaw and the determined look in her eye, he gathered she would never let on until he gave his word not to strike the man dead.

"All right," he said with a scowl. "I won't kill him, but that doesn't mean I won't hurt him."

"Ye already did," she said.

Only one name leaped into his mind. "Blackwell?" he said, incredulous.

She nodded her head.

"I'll kill him!" he ground out between his teeth.

"Ye promised."

"So I did," he said, making an effort to get a grip on his temper. "Why did he grab your arm?"

"He tried to pull me into my lady's sleeping chamber when he was in the house the other day. He claimed he just wanted to talk, but the look on his face scared me."

"That dirty bastard meant to force himself on you."

"I knew he was up to no good," she said. "That's why I broke free and hid myself until after he rode away with the master."

The heat of his fury cooled to an icy calm more dangerous than the thrust of a halberd. He would deal with Blackwell later, but there was something that could be done now. He removed the sheathed dagger from his belt and presented it to her.

"Keep this with you at all times," he said. "Don't be afraid to use it. Men are swine. You can't trust any of us."

She accepted the dagger and slid it under the linen belt around her slender waist. "I trust ye," she said.

Before he could speak, she pressed her lips to his.

His arms instinctively closed around her to pull her against the length of his body. She felt warm and soft under his calloused hands. His heart began to pound in his chest.

Then, an intrusive thought spoiled the moment for him, for he longed to do with her what Blackwell tried to do to her. He grasped her shoulders and set her firmly away from him. "Why did you do that?" he said.

"Blackwell tried to kiss me," she said with a shudder. "It sickened me. I hoped it wouldn't be like that with you." She averted her eyes to avoid his gaze. "It wasn't," she added in a small voice.

He ignored the urge to prove that to her again. "We ought to go back down," he said. He released her and started toward the trapdoor.

She laid a hand on his arm to stop him. "Are ye angry?" she said.

"With you, never," he said.

"I am going to the marketplace tomorrow," she said. "Will ye meet me there?"

He tenderly cupped her cheek with his hand. "I would love to," he said. "My watch is over an hour before sundown."

"I shall look for ye then," she said. She turned her head slightly to nuzzle his palm.

He let his hand fall to his side. "What am I doing?" he said in despair. "I'm a common soldier, indentured to my king possibly for the rest of my life. I own nothing but my horse and my gear. I'm no good for you. Go find a nice young man who will marry you and make you happy."

Her solemn countenance reflected a maturity that had nothing to do with age. "Ye should have sent me away when I would have gone," she said. Her face softened as she gazed up at him. "It's too late now."

He wrapped his arms around her and captured her lips in a

lingering kiss that left both of them breathless.

For one precious moment, all insurmountable differences between them ceased to exist. They were but a man and a woman, their hearts joined by that mysterious and wonderful thing that happens between lovers.

He broke off the kiss with great reluctance and stepped back from her. With an effort, he quelled the fires of passion and desire that blazed within him. He wanted her, needed her in fact, but not like this. To seduce her on the floor of the guard tower would only prove that he was no better than Blackwell.

"We should go now," he said.

He offered his hand to help her down into the square hole in the middle of the wooden platform.

"You must remember what I told you," he said. "Let no man ever get you alone." To himself, he added: Not even me.

CHAPTER 15

Kyle rose early on Friday morning. He splashed water on his face and put on an off-white linen shirt and brown leggings. After buckling on his sword belt, he opened the door of the sheriff's office and stepped outside. The air was already hot and humid, a sign that portended the advent of another sultry summer day. Low clouds overhead trapped heat rising from the ground, only adding to the misery.

Beads of sweat formed on his face as he walked across the courtyard toward the main hall to get something to eat. There was much to be done and little time to do it, for this was the last full day to prepare for Macalister's hearing.

After breaking his fast, he went over to the dungeon and bade the guard to let him enter.

The stench of human excrement assaulted his nostrils as he sought out Macalister among the other prisoners.

"How are you holding up?" he said.

"I'll live," Macalister said. "At least, for the time being." He flexed his shoulders with a wince. "My back is still sore."

"It will be for a while," Kyle said. "Are they feeding you?"

"Like a king," Macalister said, brushing the bread crumbs from the front of his tunic. "Have ye any news for me?"

"I do, in fact," Kyle said.

"Good or bad?"

"Both. Which do you want to hear first?"

"The bad news," Macalister said. "That way the good news

205

will sound even better."

"Old Rolf of Cragston Forest was not the one who saw you and Blackwell in the forest the other day."

"That is bad news," Macalister said with a frown. "So, what's the good news?"

"I plan to enlist Hul's help to locate our elusive witness. He can spread the word through town in less than an hour."

"What makes ye think the man we're looking for will risk his life to testify against Blackwell and his lads?"

"The size of the reward I'm offering, for one thing," Kyle said.

"Ye may only attract those willing to bear false witness in order to claim the prize."

"I thought of that," Kyle said. "However, I know which questions to ask to weed out the liars prior to the hearing."

"It could work," Macalister said. He sounded hopeful.

"It has to," Kyle said. "We need that witness to back you up. Otherwise, it boils down to your word against Blackwell's."

"Aye," Macalister said grimly. "And we both know what a Scotsman's word is worth in an English court."

Kyle reviewed the facts with Macalister one more time before he left the dungeon.

He saddled the gelding and went straight to Hul's house, where the two of them chatted for a short while. After parting with a handful of silver coins, he convinced Hul to conduct an immediate search for the missing witness. To him, it was money well spent, for his friend's life hung in the balance.

Apart from the testimony of that single eyewitness, Macalister's credibility, even under oath, would be considered questionable in the eyes of the court. He was a brawler who used his fists on occasion to make his point in the local tavern. Most of his associates were suspected rebels. Worst of all, he made no secret of his disdain for the English. The fact that he was the only blacksmith in town carried some weight. Even so, he could still be replaced.

Kyle rode down Harbour Street, bound for the garrison. On the way, he passed several wagons, their empty beds evidence of a profitable day at the marketplace.

A few minutes later, Simon came driving up the street in his wagon. Turval the potter sat in the high seat beside him. A striped horse blanket covered a pile of goods in the wooden bed behind them. There was nothing suspicious about that, for although they were headed away from the market grounds, they might have been making a delivery.

Simon kept his gaze focused on the cobblestones in the street ahead of him, while Turval gave Kyle a tight smile as the wagon rumbled by.

On his return to the garrison, Kyle went on to the stable to feed, water, and brush the gelding. After that, he walked over to the sheriff's office, where he began to fidget from the moment he stepped through the door. He had cause to be concerned about the hearing on Saturday morning. Macalister was gallows-bound unless, by some miracle, Hul produced the much sought-after witness. His own fate of being thrown into the dungeon for defying Morhouse paled in comparison with swinging from the end of a rope.

He set out for the marketplace on foot. He needed time to think, to mentally review the facts as he understood them and to compose questions designed to expose flaws in the testimony of Blackwell and the three other soldiers involved.

Sir Percy was another factor to consider. Should he sit in the judgment seat after drinking or gaming into the wee hours of the morning, as young men his age were prone to do, he would be in no condition to render an objective decision. A well-prepared defense would hardly matter under those circumstances.

Kyle turned into the marketplace, oblivious to the bustle of people around him. Merchants and vendors hawked their wares. Children laughed and played. Men and women haggled with peddlers over the price of goods. Dogs fought over discarded scraps of food.

He ambled down the rows of stalls, absently nodding a greeting to this vendor or that merchant, his mind on the impending hearing. He was no stranger to court proceedings. As a man of law, it was his duty to produce sufficient evidence to convict the guilty. This time, though, he must save the innocent. Without solid proof in the form of an eyewitness to the deed, all he had were his wits and his words to tip the scales of justice in Macalister's favor.

As his idle gaze roved over the crowd, he spotted a boy in a ragged homespun tunic, whose slender build and flaxen hair looked very familiar to him.

With a sudden start, he realized why.

Though the boy was halfway across the grounds, he was sure it was Rollo. If it wasn't Rollo, then it was someone who looked an awful lot like him.

He set out for where the boy stood talking with another youth. After a couple of steps, he glimpsed something that made him quicken his pace.

Blackwell, who was on duty at the marketplace, evidently noticed the boy, too, since the flaxen hair on the youth's head shone like a beacon in the late morning sun. He and three other soldiers in light armor and helmets advanced toward him, closing the distance between them with alarming speed.

For Kyle, it was like watching a nightmare unfold before him. He was too far away to catch up with the boy. All he could do was give chase as Blackwell and his cohorts bore down on their prey.

Someone shouted a warning to the boy just as Blackwell

reached out to grab him. He took off running like a scared rabbit, weaving his way through the crowd with the skill of long practice.

Blackwell and his companions dashed after the boy. Push carts parked in the aisles between the stalls hampered their forward progress. Local folk, most of whom held the English in contempt, made no effort to move out of their way.

The boy ran into the street and turned right. Blackwell and the soldiers followed on his heels.

Kyle reached the edge of the market grounds in time to see the boy duck into an alleyway between two houses farther up the street. Blackwell and the others plunged in after him.

Seconds later, Kyle turned into the alley, treading on litter and garbage as he hurried to catch up with them. He emerged at the far end and skidded to a halt.

The boy came up against a high wooden fence that enclosed a private yard at the end of the alleyway. When he turned to face his pursuers, there was no mistaking the fear in his eyes. He gazed wildly around him, like a cornered animal desperately seeking a way out.

A dark-haired woman washing clothes in a tub of water stopped to stare at those invading her rear yard. The sight of armed English soldiers brought her to her feet, her blue eyes immense with alarm. She snatched up the frightened toddler sitting on the ground beside her. With the wailing child clasped in her arms, she fled into the house and shut the door behind her.

The boy stood with his back against the fence, his chest heaving and his fair complexion blotched with red from exertion. There was nowhere to go, yet he slid sideways along the upright boards for a couple of yards before he quit moving.

Kyle got a good look at the boy's face in the sunlight. To his relief, it was not Rollo, although the resemblance was striking.

Anyone who glimpsed Rollo only once, like Blackwell and his men, might be fooled. That seemed to be the case, for they drew their swords and started toward him.

"Stand down," Kyle said in a commanding voice.

Blackwell and those with him paused to glance over their shoulders at Kyle, who stood several paces behind them.

The scrape of wood against wood brought their heads around in time to see the boy push aside a loose fence board and slip through the slender gap into the yard beyond. It was pointless to go after him, for by the time they scaled the sturdy fence, he would be long gone.

A snarled oath of frustration burst from Blackwell's lips. He slammed the butt end of his hilt into the nearest fence board, leaving a deep indentation in the wood. It was clear he really believed the boy was Rollo, as evidenced by his extreme anger over the boy's escape.

At that instant, Kyle saw the advantage of letting Blackwell go on thinking it was Rollo. The four soldiers knew the boy's testimony could expose them. In light of that, they might be induced to drop the charges against Macalister. If the boy stayed out of sight until after the hearing, which was likely since he looked pretty scared, he would no longer be in danger.

"Too bad he got away," Kyle said.

Blackwell swung around to face him. It was difficult to see his features clearly under the nosepiece of his Norman helmet. "My, my," he said. "What have we here? All alone, are you? Too bad that rebel will swing if you don't show up tomorrow. Aren't you worried that something might happen to you between now and then?"

"What could possibly happen to me?" Kyle said.

"Oh, I don't know," Blackwell said, gesturing with his sword. "An accident, maybe?"

"One that involves thirty inches of steel, I suppose."

"You're smarter than you look," Blackwell said with an unpleasant smile. He and his men started toward him, their blades poised for action.

Kyle drew his sword and went to meet them. As he approached, the four soldiers shuffled to a halt, uncertainty on their faces. Two of them even began to back up.

He knew he could be intimidating at times, yet he did wonder at their odd behavior, that is, until he caught a movement from the corner of his eye. He turned his head to see Hul and five of his tough-looking cohorts coming out of the alley to gather in the yard behind him. All six men carried spiked cudgels in their hands.

The cocky expression on Blackwell's face gave way to apprehension. "It was just a jibe," he said. "No harm done." His eyes shifted from Kyle to the ruffians and back again, as though weighing his chances of escaping unscathed. "I shall see you at the hearing, right?"

"Go," Kyle said, jerking his head at the alleyway.

Blackwell and his men nearly trampled each other in their haste to flee from the yard.

"Am I intruding?" Hul said after the soldiers left.

"Not at all," Kyle said with a grin. "How did you know I was here?"

It was Hul's turn to grin. "That lad ye chased is one of mine," he said. "I never send them out without watching over them."

The grin faded from Kyle's face. "Has the witness come forward?" he said.

"Not yet," Hul said. "It's barely midday. There is still time to find him."

"I don't think he'll do it," Kyle said, sheathing his sword. "His life would be worth less than dirt if he testified against Blackwell." He shook his head, a sage expression on his face. "There are some things money can't buy."

"I agree," Hul said.

Kyle cocked a skeptical eyebrow at him.

"It may sound strange coming from me, but what ye say is true. Money cannot buy friendship. Yer good advice the other day saved Gib's foot. Only a friend would do that."

"Glad I could help," Kyle said.

"Since I just saved yer arse from Blackwell and those louts with him," Hul said, "I'd say we were even."

"I would, too," Kyle said.

Hoprig spent most of the day stationed on the guard walk along the seaward side of the garrison wall. It was his duty to keep a lookout over the Firth of Clyde for seafaring marauders. Although the threat of such an attack was remote, it was still a possibility. At least, that is what the Castellan of Ayr Garrison claimed.

He also kept a sharp eye out for Blackwell, who was nowhere to be seen. He would bide his time, and when he did catch the man alone, he would warn him away from Isabel in the only language the man understood: with flailing fists.

The hours dragged by, for there was nothing to do but wait for his watch to end.

At last, the sun began to dip toward the western horizon. When the relief guards arrived, Hoprig descended the wooden stairs to the courtyard below and hurried over to the barracks. After shaving and changing from bull-hide armor into a clean shirt, he strode to the marketplace to keep his appointment with Isabel.

He stood on the verge on the river side of the street, out of the path of foot traffic and pony-drawn carts. From that location, he had a clear view of the market grounds.

As the shadows grew longer, the crowd began to dwindle. Men and women left with their children and their purchases.

Few people remained there by the time merchants and vendors started shifting their goods into wagons to haul them away for the night.

Before long, the marketplace was empty, except for stray dogs rooting through the rubbish for food.

Soon, red and orange streaked the sky in the afterglow of sunset. The pearly dusk that followed deepened slowly into twilight. Not a soul moved about the street. Even the dogs abandoned their labors and wandered away. The only sound that shattered the hush was the priory bell ringing in the hour of vespers.

Hoprig paced back and forth on the grassy verge. With each passing moment, his anxiety over Isabel's absence increased. He could not shake the feeling that something awful happened to her, for she would never forsake him without sending word.

Darkness settled around him, yet he refused to abandon hope that she would come.

A breeze blew in from the north, cooling the night air, a welcome relief after the heat of the day. The moon, large and yellow, rose above the tops of the houses to the east. The night sky was clear and full of stars.

He remained there on the verge, alert and vigilant, watching for any sign of her approach.

He was toying with the idea of riding out to Kilgate Manor to check on her welfare, when a cloaked figure emerged from the darkness and hastened toward him. The urgency of the light quick step on the cobblestones caused a flutter of apprehension in his stomach.

"Brian," Isabel said as she approached. There was a frantic note in her voice.

An iron fist closed around his heart as his mind spun with dreadful possibilities. "What's wrong?" he said.

He opened his arms, and she flung herself into his embrace.

"I couldn't go without saying goodbye," she said. Her words sounded muffled against his chest.

"But you just got here," he said. "Can you not stay a while?"

She edged back half a step to peer up at him. "Even as we speak," she said, "Edgar is loading my lady's possessions onto a ship in the harbor."

"A ship?" he said, curious but not yet alarmed.

"My lady told me tonight that she hired it early in the week and paid for it with a piece of her jewelry."

"Ah," he said, enlightened. "So that is what happened to the pearl."

"Aye. She dared not let on about it sooner, lest Captain Morhouse find out and try to interfere with her plans."

"What plans?" he said, puzzled.

"My lady is going back to Spain. She says Morhouse betrayed her in such a way that she can no longer tolerate the sight of him."

"I'm sorry to hear it," he said. He could not tear his gaze from her face. Her pale skin looked translucent in the moonlight. Something about her drew him like a magnet and held him in its thrall.

"That's not all. She wants to take Owen and me with her."

Her words knocked the breath from his lungs like a blow to the gut. "Are you going?" he said, trying to get his head around the notion that he might never see her again.

"My lady needs me now," she said. "I cannot let her down. She has been so good to my brother and me." Her eyes searched his face. "This doesn't have to be goodbye. Come with me. It will be a new start for us in a new land. Please say ye will."

He looked down at her, torn between love and loyalty. He could not, would not, choose between the two, for what good was one without the other? He did love her. Of that he was certain. On the other hand, he pledged his fealty to his king. To foreswear his word of honor was unthinkable.

"I am a soldier," he said, "bound by oath to serve England. It would be treasonous for me to desert my post. Besides that, I cannot leave tonight of all nights because of the hearing on the morrow, where an innocent man's life hangs in the balance." He lifted her hand to his lips and tenderly kissed it. "You are so dear to me. It pains my heart to refuse your offer, yet refuse it I must. I hope you understand."

"Ye are an honorable man, Brian Hoprig," she said. "And I love ye all the more because of it." She reclaimed her hand to draw her cloak around her shoulders against the rising wind. "I should go back now."

"Let me escort you there," he said.

At her nod, he slipped his arm under her elbow. Together, they crossed the empty market grounds and set out for the harbor. When they reached the end of the street, he pulled her into the shadows to kiss her. Her lips tasted of salt from the tears flowing down her face.

"I don't want to leave ye," she said, sniffling.

"I feel the same way, my love," he said. He wiped the moisture from her cheek with his thumb. "Now that I think on it, going with your mistress is a wise course. You and Owen will be safe in Spain. There is much discord between my countrymen and yours, and in the coming months, conditions will only get worse."

"What could be worse than losing someone ye love?" she said. Her eyes glistened with unshed tears. "Remember that crow on the manor gate the other day? I told ye it boded ill for someone. I just didn't think it would be me. It breaks my heart that I may never see yer face again."

"I will find a way to follow you," he said with fervor. "You have my word on that."

"I shall wait for ye, no matter how long it takes."

They kissed once again, clinging to each other with desperate devotion, neither willing to let the other go.

"Come," he said at last. "You mustn't be late." He frowned into the darkness. "This is one of those rare times that I regret the loss of my family's fortune. With sufficient funds, I could buy a proper release from serving in the army. Sir Percy would gladly accept my resignation, especially now that he needs the money."

They started forward, their hands clasped. As they turned the corner, they stepped from the quiet deserted street into a flurry of noisy activity under blazing lanterns on the waterfront.

A small army of workers trudged up a wooden ramp carrying boxes and crates and sacks of grain onto the deck of a massive ship docked against the wharf. Crewmen shouted to each other as they lowered the merchandise down into the hold with ropes to stow it for the voyage ahead.

The white letters of the vessel's name, *Ave Maria,* stood out against the dark wood of the bow. The central mast loomed high in the air over several rows of furled sails. The water that lapped against the underside of the wharf was extremely high, an unmistakable sign that the tide was about to turn. The wind was brisk and steady as it blew in from the east.

Lady Catherine sat in an open carriage parked near the wharf, perusing a letter spread out on a small escritoire propped on her skirted knees. She glanced up at Isabel's approach, at which time she folded the letter and put it in an envelope-like packet on the seat beside her.

Hoprig hung back as Isabel spoke with her mistress in a low voice for a long moment.

Lady Catherine removed a new sheet of vellum from under the lid of the portable desk on her lap and bent her head to the task of writing with the quill pen and ink taken from a narrow compartment along the top edge. After drying the ink with a sprinkle of fine sand, she placed that letter, too, into the packet.

"Master Hoprig," Lady Catherine said. When he drew near, she handed the stub of a candle to him. "Will you be so kind?"

He went over to the nearest lantern and touched the wick to the flame. On the way back to the carriage, he saw Lady Catherine slip a tiny item into the packet with the letters. She did it so quickly that he could not make out what it was.

Lady Catherine took the lighted candle from his hand and held the flame under a stick of red sealing wax. As it melted, she let it dribble across the flap until it formed a blob the size of a coin. She pressed her ring into the wax before it cooled and passed the sealed packet to him.

"Edgar refuses to set foot in an English garrison," she said. "Hence, I must prevail upon you to deliver this to Sir Percy." She set the escritoire aside. "Do it after the hearing tomorrow, if you please," she added, her expression grave.

"I am at your service, m'lady," he said with a slight bow. He tucked the packet into his shirt for safekeeping.

Edgar came down the ramp and walked over to the carriage. Without a word, he climbed into the high seat. Within minutes, he nodded off to sleep.

Hoprig stayed at Isabel's side until the first mate called out in a loud voice that it was time to board the vessel. He helped Lady Catherine down from the carriage and looked on as the two women walked up the ramp.

At the top, Isabel turned to wave at him.

He lifted his hand to her, a smile on his face despite the ache in his heart. Although he maintained an outward calm, he really felt like punching something, or somebody. Maybe later, he would go looking for Blackwell. God help the man if he caught him on his own.

Half a dozen dockside workers dragged the heavy ramp onto the wharf, while others cast off ropes as thick as a man's arm from around stout bitts to free the ship from its moorings. Agile crewmen scampered up knotted rope nets to stand on cross rigging, letting the canvas drop at the master's command. Those on deck heaved on taut lines to adjust the angle of the sails.

With the creak of wood and the clack of rigging, the *Ave Maria* eased away from the dock. Moonlight gleamed on the water churning up in her wake. Her sails billowed as she came about before heading out to sea.

Hoprig watched the ship until it vanished into the darkness, filled with a gnawing emptiness as a propitious wind and the outgoing tide carried away the only woman he'd ever loved.

CHAPTER 16

On Saturday morning, Kyle climbed the stairs to the third floor of the garrison castle and entered the room used for assizes and other judicial proceedings.

Burghers from town and soldiers from the garrison filled the rows of benches. Morhouse sat among them, smug and confident, as though anticipating a favorable ruling for his men. John Logan was also there in support of his friend and country-man, Macalister. Those who arrived too late to secure a seat stood at the rear.

There were at least eighty people in the room. Despite the two open windows on the outer wall, the air was warm and stuffy. The subdued voices of those present sounded like the hum of bees.

Kyle walked to the front and took a seat on the bench reserved for complainants and witnesses.

Blackwell and his men, all four of whom wore belted shirts and leggings, occupied the far end of the same bench. Three had bandages around their heads, evidently for effect since their superficial wounds must surely be healed by this time.

Hoprig and Vinewood ushered the blacksmith, shackled hand and foot, into the room. Chains clinked with every step he took. The murmur of voices grew louder as the three of them walked up the center aisle between the rows of benches.

The prisoner's brown tunic, torn earlier to expose his back to the lash, was now mended to make him presentable in court.

When they reached the front of the room, the two English soldiers helped the prisoner up onto a box with rails on three sides designed to expose him to view during the proceedings. They chained him to the railing before they retired to sit on the front bench.

"How do you feel?" Kyle said to Macalister, who was only six feet away.

"Nervous," Macalister said.

"Me, too," Kyle said.

The English marshal, a rotund man dressed in black leather from neck to toe, came through the doorway at the rear and stood off to the side. He thumped the staff in his hand on the wooden floor three times, drawing every eye in the room.

The drone of conversation ceased abruptly.

"Enter, Sir Henry de Percy, Eighth Baron Percy," the marshal said in a stentorian voice. "Castellan of Ayr and Warden of Galloway, appointed by His Majesty, Edward, King of England, and authorized by royal decree to sit in judgment."

Sir Percy, looking quite officious in a green velvet cotte edged with gold cord, marched up the aisle to the front of the room. He stepped onto the dais and sat in the judgment seat, which was nothing more than a large chair situated in the middle of a low platform.

Walter the clerk entered the room in a flowing black cloak with a black skullcap over his gray hair. In his arms, he carried a sheaf of vellum, a quill pen, and a corked jar of ink. When he drew near the dais, he placed the items on the small desk to Sir Percy's right and settled on the stool behind it.

The marshal made his way to the front, where he took up a position on Sir Percy's left. At the castellan's nod, he thumped the floor once with his staff. "This hearing is now in session," he said.

Sir Percy gazed down at the four complainants. "Come

forward and state your case," he said.

Blackwell and his men rose to their feet.

Kyle stood up at the same time. "May I interrupt, m'lord?" he said. Without waiting for permission, he continued: "Before we begin, I ask that three of these men be sent from the room while I question the one that remains. They will then return one at a time to be questioned separately in order to ascertain whether each of them tells the same tale."

Gasps of outrage rippled around the room.

Sir Percy stiffened in his chair. "The very suggestion insults the honor of these men," he said.

"On the contrary, m'lord," Kyle said. "It will only confirm that they are telling the truth."

"Have you ever heard of such a thing?" Sir Percy said to the marshal.

"Never," the marshal said emphatically.

Sir Percy turned to Walter. "What say you about it?" he said.

"It sounds like something the French would do," Walter said with a downward turn of his mouth.

"It is, actually," Kyle said. "That procedure is used in Philip the Fourth's court with great success."

Sir Percy made an impatient sound in his throat. "May I remind you, Master Shaw," he said, "that you are in an English court of law? Your request is denied. Now, let us get on with this hearing."

The four complainants approached the dais and stood at an angle so that both Sir Percy and those in attendance could see them, as well as hear them.

That was when Kyle noticed the condition of Blackwell's face. Besides the purple discoloration under both eyes from a broken nose, there were fresh cuts and contusions on the man's cheeks and jaw. His lips were swollen and bruised, especially the bottom one, which was split down the center and encrusted with dried blood.

He made no comment about Blackwell's appearance, for he was curious as to whether the man would try to claim that Macalister did that to him, too.

Blackwell leaned toward Kyle. "I don't see your witness anywhere in the room," he said with as close to a sneer as he could manage with bruised lips. "Without him, you've got nothing."

Kyle ignored him. "Tell Sir Percy about your encounter with the accused," he said, addressing the four of them.

"We rode south that day," Blackwell said, taking the lead. "We were patrolling the forest when we came across the prisoner fishing in a stream. Before we knew it, he sprang at us like a madman. We barely escaped with our lives."

The three others voiced their accord with Blackwell's story.

"So," Kyle said. "You were just riding along when the prisoner attacked you."

"That is true," Blackwell said, while the others nodded.

"Was he armed?" Kyle said.

"He used a quarterstaff on us," Blackwell said. He signaled to someone at the back of the room.

A man immediately came forward with a hickory staff in his hand. The thick rod was six feet long, stripped of bark and polished smooth, except for scars and grazes along the length that reflected prior use.

Kyle took the stick from the man. "This could be a dangerous weapon in skilled hands," he said. He examined every square inch of it before showing it to Macalister. "Does this belong to you?"

"Aye," Macalister said. "That is my mark there on the end. I didn't have it with me that day. They must have taken it from my shop."

Kyle presented the staff to Sir Percy for his inspection.

"Those men are fortunate they did not sustain worse injuries," Sir Percy said, handing it back. "That staff is sturdy enough to cave in a man's skull."

"I agree," Kyle said. To Blackwell, he said: "Where has this been for the past three days?"

"I hid it in the tack room," Blackwell said. "Nobody else knew it was there."

"Including them?" Kyle said, tilting his head at the other three complainants.

"Aye," Blackwell said.

"So, only you and the fellow who just brought it to me has handled it since the day of the incident. Is that correct?"

"That is correct," Blackwell said.

"When Macalister attacked you with this quarterstaff," Kyle said, "did he draw blood?"

"He did," Blackwell said.

The three others concurred, indicating the bandages on their heads.

"Blood leaves a stain on raw wood," Kyle said. He held out the staff for Blackwell and his men to see. "Why are there no such stains anywhere on this?"

"What are you implying?" Blackwell said.

"You took this quarterstaff from the prisoner's shop after the fact," Kyle said, "with the intention of further implicating him."

"That fellow," Blackwell said, jabbing an accusatory finger at Macalister, "attacked me and my men for no reason. We are lucky to be alive."

"M'lord," Kyle said to Sir Percy. "Perhaps it is time to let the prisoner give his account of the incident."

"Let him speak," Sir Percy said.

All eyes turned to the prisoner.

Macalister took a deep steadying breath, plainly aware that this was his only chance to exonerate himself before judgment was rendered.

"I rode out to Cragston Forest early on Tuesday morning," he said. "The fishing is so good out that way that I never take more than two traps with me. When I got to the stream, I cut some alder saplings to pin the traps under the water. By noon, I had a string full of perch. About then, those four Southrons rode up and demanded that I hand my entire catch over to them.

"When I refused to do it, that fellow," he said, pointing to Blackwell, "pulled out his sword and threatened to run me through. I threw the string of fish at him to slow him down so I could get away. That was when the other three drew steel and came at me from every side. I snatched up a fallen limb and fended them off. They all left shortly after that."

"Did you use your quarterstaff on them?" Kyle said.

"Nay," Macalister said. "All I had on me was a skinning knife, but I didn't pull it out. A blade that tiny is no match for a sword."

Kyle believed Macalister's version of the incident. Without a witness, though, it still came down to one man's word against another. In Macalister's case, it was one Scotsman's word against that of four English soldiers.

"You heard the prisoner, m'lord," Kyle said to Sir Percy. "There was no quarterstaff at the scene. If Blackwell lied about that, what else is he lying about?"

"What makes you think the accused is telling the truth?" Sir Percy said. "He has more to lose than his accusers."

"There is a witness who can settle this matter once and for all," Kyle said.

"Then bring him forward," Sir Percy said.

"I cannot locate him," Kyle said. "I must have more time to search for him."

"I am beginning to wonder if such a witness even exists," Sir

Percy said, skepticism evident in his tone.

Hoprig rose from the bench and approached the dais. "Such a witness does exist, m'lord," he said. He glanced from Sir Percy to Kyle and back again. "You are looking at him."

Kyle felt his own jaw drop in surprise.

Blackwell glared at Hoprig from under lowered brows "M'lord," he said, turning to Sir Percy. "That man was not there. I would have seen him."

"Well, I saw you," Hoprig said. "I also saw you chase that boy through the woods. Who do you think helped him get away from you?"

Blackwell thrust out his chin and started toward Hoprig with clenched fists.

Kyle stepped between the two men to avert a brawl in the courtroom. "Why did you not speak up sooner?" he said to Hoprig.

"I hoped this could be settled without my intervention," Hoprig said. "It is no small matter to testify against a fellow soldier." His upper lip curled in contempt. "In this case, however, it would be a pleasure."

Kyle shot a warning glance at Blackwell for him to keep his distance. "State your name for the record," he said to Hoprig. "Then tell us what happened that day."

"My name is Brian Hoprig," he said. "On Tuesday morning, I went out on patrol with the troop. Blackwell and his squad made a foray into the woods. They were gone so long, Captain Morhouse sent me to check on them. When I arrived on the scene, things took place exactly as the prisoner stated. Blackwell demanded the fish. The prisoner refused to give them up. Blackwell drew a sword on him."

"I wasn't going to hurt the man," Blackwell said, his tone defensive. "I was just having a bit of fun."

"He didn't know that, you fool," Hoprig said. "Especially

with you waving a blade in his face."

"I would have let him go," Blackwell said. "That is, until he struck me. He started trouble, and I meant to finish it."

"He hurled the fish at you to buy time to escape," Hoprig said. "When your men surrounded him, he had no recourse but to stand and fight. You brought that on yourself."

"I will have no bickering in my court," Sir Percy said in a thunderous voice. He frowned down at Hoprig. "Are you done?"

"Not quite, m'lord," Hoprig said. "While Blackwell and his men fled the scene, they flushed out a Scots boy who was watching them from behind a tree. When I saw they meant to trample him down, I helped him to get away from them. After that, I rode back to the troop and reported the incident to Captain Morhouse. He laughed at the notion that one unarmed man could take on four able-bodied soldiers and overcome them with a half-rotted pine bough."

Sir Percy's face held no trace of amusement. "Thank you, Master Hoprig," he said. "You may sit down."

"Lord Hoprig," Kyle said.

"I beg your pardon?" Sir Percy said.

"He is Lord Hoprig of Evesham," Kyle said. "His father fought in the last crusade."

"Oh, I see," Sir Percy said, impressed. "Why is he serving as a common soldier?"

"I will explain later, m'lord," Kyle said.

"Of course," Sir Percy said. "In the meantime, Master Shaw, it would greatly help the prisoner's cause if you could produce the Scots boy who saw the incident."

"I cannot, m'lord," Kyle said. "He and his family left town for personal reasons."

"That is unfortunate," Sir Percy said. He rubbed a thoughtful hand over his shaved chin. "The prisoner claims innocence. Yet, he accosted four English soldiers by his own admission, a fact confirmed by Lord Hoprig's testimony. Such conduct, if allowed to go unpunished, sets a dangerous precedent. Anyone so inclined thereafter might feel free to assault English troops without fear of reprisal."

Sir Percy's gaze strayed to his clerk, who was watching him intently. Uncertainty clouded his countenance, and he shifted in his chair, as though unnerved at being subjected to such close scrutiny by a mere hireling. "Walter," he said. "Do you have something to say before I render judgment?"

"It will keep until later, Sir Percy," Walter said, his steady gaze cool and calculating. His manner was not at all like that of a subordinate.

Sir Percy twisted the ring on his finger, his brows drawn in speculation. He seemed more concerned about his clerk's perplexing behavior than the matter at hand. After a brief moment, his expression cleared. He rose from the judgment seat and tugged on his green velvet cotte to straighten it.

Macalister tensed visibly, the sinews in his body drawn as tight as a bowstring. He gripped the rail in front of him with both hands, his knuckles white and his brown eyes fixed on the Castellan of Ayr—the man who possessed the power and authority to snuff out his life with a single word.

Sir Percy nodded at the marshal, who then thumped the floor three times with his staff. "I have reached a decision," he said in a loud voice. His gaze swept the faces of those gathered before him, including the prisoner.

"It is my opinion," he continued, "that the prisoner's actions made a bad situation worse. The four soldiers involved, however, must bear the blame for causing the prisoner to resort to violence. Since no lives were lost in this unfortunate encounter, and since the prisoner already received the requisite flogging for resisting arrest, I hereby rule that all charges against him be dropped. He is free to go."

Macalister's muscular body sagged with relief. A cheer went up from Kyle and the other Scotsmen in the room.

The burghers poured into the aisle and surged toward the railed box on which the blacksmith stood grinning.

Hoprig pushed through the crowd with the keys in his hand to release the newly acquitted man.

As the courtroom crowd moved toward the door, Walter the clerk got up from the stool and removed his black cloak to reveal the priestly garb beneath. A heavy gold necklace of flat chain links hung about his neck, with a medallion of the same precious metal suspended from it. He took off the skullcap, which exposed the tonsure on his head. "Forgive the ruse, Sir Percy," he said. "It was necessary while I conducted my investigation."

"What investigation?" Sir Percy said. He looked worried.

"A short time ago," Walter said, "a rumor of a serious nature reached His Royal Highness."

"What sort of rumor?" Sir Percy said with wary reserve.

"One that involves rendering frivolous decisions in civil and criminal matters," Walter said. "My lord the King fears that these Scots may be goaded into rebellion for biased and unfair treatment in an English court of law."

"How does this concern me?" Sir Percy said.

"The King wanted reassurance that you, a young man of twenty-four years, are handling the responsibilities of this office in a competent manner."

"How dare you check up on me!" Sir Percy said, incensed. "Who do you think you are?"

"I am John Walter Langton," he said. "Canon of Lincoln and Lord High Chancellor to the King of England."

The irritation on Sir Percy's face gave way to alarm, as though he realized how close he came to losing his exalted position as castellan.

"Rest easy, Sir Percy," Walter said. "Based on what I saw today, I would say that the rumor is completely unfounded. You seem to have a grasp of the importance of rendering fitting decisions in these volatile times."

"Under the circumstances," Sir Percy said, his manner ingratiating now that he knew his clerk's true identity, "I could come to no other conclusion in this case."

"Of course not," Walter said dryly. "By the way, you will need to hire a new clerk. I am leaving for London as soon as transportation can be arranged."

Kyle watched with approval as Hoprig removed the shackles from Macalister's wrists and ankles.

Hoprig was rising to his feet with the chains dangling from his fingers when Blackwell sidled up to him.

"I don't care who you are," Blackwell said in a menacing tone. "I'm not through with you yet."

"You don't scare me," Hoprig said. He turned to walk away, for that was neither the time nor the place to exchange blows. Blackwell grabbed his shoulder and spun him around.

Since the confrontation took place practically under Kyle's nose, he got a close look at Blackwell's left hand on the fabric of Hoprig's shirt. The sight of a joint missing from the man's little finger commanded his full attention.

"It was you," Kyle said, lifting his gaze to Blackwell's face. "You murdered Sir Peter Ryland."

Blackwell turned white, as though all the blood suddenly drained from his veins.

CHAPTER 17

Blackwell whirled and plunged into the crowd, shoving people out of his way as he headed for the open door. He made it halfway across the room before Kyle caught up with him.

"Not so fast," Kyle said, jerking him to a halt by the collar.

"It wasn't me," Blackwell said, with desperation in his voice. "I didn't do it."

People around them stopped and stared to see what was happening.

"Shackle him," Kyle said to Hoprig, who came on the scene a couple of seconds later.

"You've got to believe me," Blackwell said. He was so distraught, he held still while Hoprig clapped the manacles on his wrists.

"Take him to Sir Percy's office," Kyle said. "I will question him there while Sir Percy is still occupied here."

Vinewood joined Hoprig in hauling Blackwell, who protested his innocence with every step, from the room.

Kyle scanned those present until he spotted John Logan, whom he beckoned over to him. "I caught the killer," he said when the apothecary drew near.

"Who is it?" John said.

"Blackwell," Kyle said.

John whistled low at the news. "Did he say why he did it?" he said.

"Not yet," Kyle said. "I'm going talk to him now. Care to

come along?"

"I wouldn't miss it," John said.

The pair of them left the court room and descended the stairs to the second level. They went down the corridor and entered the large chamber at the far end.

The midmorning sun beamed through the unshuttered window overlooking the courtyard below. Blackwell sat on one of the two high-backed chairs in front of Sir Percy's marble-topped desk. Although he appeared calm and composed, his breathing was rapid and shallow, a telltale sign of high emotional distress. The bruises on his face stood out against the distinct pallor of his complexion.

Hoprig and Vinewood stationed themselves behind the prisoner, ready to spring into action, should it become necessary to subdue the man by force.

John leaned against the edge of the desk, while Kyle made himself comfortable on the other hard wooden chair.

"Why did you kill Sir Peter?" Kyle said to Blackwell. He watched the man closely, alert for any hint of deception in either expression or manner.

"I didn't," Blackwell said. "If I had done it, you would never find his body."

"I believe you," Kyle said. "However, I also believe that sooner or later every criminal makes a mistake that gives him away. Do you want to know what gave you away?"

Blackwell swallowed convulsively, but he remained silent.

"There were bruises from finger imprints on Sir Peter's neck," Kyle said. "All of them fit a specific pattern, except for the last one on the left side."

Kyle's words brought a look of apprehension to Blackwell's face. "I didn't kill him," he said.

"God's teeth, man," Kyle said with feeling. "You throttled him with both hands, and now he's dead. I know you did it because you left your mark on him with that stub of a finger."

"Why would I kill him?" Blackwell said. "He owed me money. It might not have been a large amount to him, but it was a lot to me."

"Is that what the two of you quarreled about in the stable that night?" Kyle said.

"It was more like a heated discussion," Blackwell said. "That is, until he started throwing punches."

"So you choked him?"

"He choked me first," Blackwell said. "Everything went black after that. I woke up with a splitting headache and there he was, swinging at the end of a rope."

"What did you do?" Kyle said.

"What do you think I did?" Blackwell said. "I got out of there. I wasn't about to take the blame for something I didn't do."

"Are you familiar with mistletoe?" Kyle said.

"Of course," Blackwell said. "I would never touch it. I heard it's deadly."

Kyle gazed at Blackwell for a long moment. The man was abrasive and obnoxious, and known to bend the truth when it suited him. His dubious testimony at the hearing was proof of that. He was also ruthless, which made him capable of anything, including murder. He appeared nervous when questioned, yet he exhibited none of the signs indicative of lying, like touching his ear or the back of his neck, giving evasive answers or nodding "yes" while saying "no."

"You don't believe me, do you?" Blackwell said.

"Give me one good reason why I should," Kyle said.

"Because it's the truth," Blackwell said.

"So you say," Kyle said. He glanced over at the two English soldiers. "Lock him up."

Raw fear flickered in the depths of Blackwell's eyes, for if convicted of Sir Peter's murder, punishment would be swift and sure. Chains rattled as he rose to his feet. He started for the doorway, his step reluctant and slow.

After Hoprig and Vinewood left with the prisoner, John settled on the vacant chair. "Ye have two reasons to celebrate today," he said. "Macalister won his freedom, which means ye won't end up in the dungeon, and ye caught the killer."

"I'm not so sure about the latter," Kyle said, frowning.

"Blackwell ran when you confronted him with his crime," John said. "Only a guilty man tries to flee from the law."

"Perhaps," Kyle said, unconvinced. "When I mentioned mistletoe, he had no idea what it meant."

"The fellow is an accomplished liar," John said. "Ye saw it for yerself at the hearing."

"He's right about the money, too," Kyle said. "Only a fool would kill a debtor before he paid the debt. Blackwell may be many things, but a fool he is not." He leaned back in the chair with a heavy sigh. "Everything points to him as the killer. He admitted he was in the stable at that late hour. He admitted he fought with Sir Peter. He even left his mark on Sir Peter's neck. Yet, my gut tells me there is more to this than meets the eye. I just wish I knew what it was."

"What about Sir Humphrey?" John said. "Ye didn't even mention him."

"There was no point in doing so," Kyle said. "Whoever killed Sir Humphrey intended for his body to be found. The mistletoe in his throat was placed there on purpose. The killer meant it as a veiled threat directed at someone in particular. It is also worthy of note that Sir Humphrey was struck from behind."

"Blackwell is quite capable of that," John said.

"He is," Kyle said. "However, subtlety is not his style. He's the kind of man who would look Sir Humphrey in the eye while he shoved a blade in his heart. Then, he would bury the body where no one would think to look for it, or else sink it in a bog. No body, no crime."

"Are ye going to let him go?"

"Not a chance," Kyle said. "He can stew in the dungeon until I figure out what really happened to those murdered men."

Kyle spent that afternoon following up with Blackwell's fellow complainants. The three men were understandably reluctant to open up to him about Blackwell's movements on Wednesday night. That was just as well, for he would not have believed them anyway. They made it clear that their loyalty lay with Blackwell. By the end of the inquiry, he knew no more than when he began.

Kyle rose on Sunday morning, saddled the gelding, and rode to St. John's to attend Mass. Throughout the service, his mind kept wandering back to the things Blackwell had told him during the interview.

It was hard to imagine that a couple of grown men who exchanged blows in an eight foot by ten foot horse stall left no sign of their presence there. When he initially inspected the confined area after finding Sir Peter's body, he did not recall seeing any new scratches in the wood or smears of blood on the walls that would suggest such a fight. He was not searching for evidence of that kind at the time, which is why he may have overlooked it.

Immediately after the benediction, he left the church and headed up Harbour Street, bound for the Bull and Bear Tavern to revisit the scene of the crime. The River Ayr on his left took on a brownish cast as saltwater from the incoming tide mingled with freshwater from the river.

On reaching the tavern, he went into the stable, where he noticed Hoprig's chestnut mare in one of the stalls. Morhouse's black was there, too, farther along the row. He tied the gelding to a post at the far end of the center aisle and pushed open the slatted half-door to enter the last stall.

Fresh manure in the straw indicated recent use. Light from the morning sun came through cracks in the outer wall, providing sufficient illumination for him to examine the interior. After a thorough search, he found no new gouges or stains to corroborate Blackwell's story. He even questioned the groom again, only to receive the same response as before.

Every thread he followed, it seemed, led back to Blackwell as the killer. The only thing that gave him pause was why the man would have done it.

Why did Blackwell not wait until after Sir Peter settled the debt? Why confess that he was even *in* the stable at the time of the murder? There were no witnesses to put him at the scene. As for the imprints on Sir Peter's neck, he could have denied they were his. He was not the only man in the shire with a maimed finger. If he'd stuck to his story, there was a good chance he could have gotten away with it.

It boggled Kyle's mind that a schemer like Blackwell failed to consider those options. His stomach growled as he walked out of the stall, so he left the gelding in the groom's keeping and headed for the tavern to break his fast.

He stepped inside the two-story wood building to the smell of old grease in the air and dirty straw on the plank floor. Oil lanterns hung on long chains from the rafters, casting a soft light upon a dozen trestle tables situated in no set order. There were about eighteen men in the large room, mostly soldiers who hunched over their food or nursed a mug of ale while they talked among themselves.

Morhouse and Hoprig, disheveled and red-eyed from a lack of sleep, sat at a table against the side wall. Each wore a day's growth of stubble on his chin. From the five empty pitchers lined up in front of them, it appeared they had been drinking steadily for hours.

Kyle walked over to their table and slid onto the bench beside Hoprig. "Have you been here all night?" he said.

"Pretty much," Hoprig said. He picked up an empty pitcher and held it aloft to signal the serving girl to bring another.

Morhouse focused his bleary eyes on Kyle. "Oh, it's you," he said. "Come to gloat over the outcome of the hearing, have you? Well, you're too late. I don't care about that anymore."

"You should," Kyle said. "Those men were under your command."

"I have more pressing concerns at present," Morhouse said. He produced from within his leather jerkin a crumpled sheet of vellum with crisp black lettering on it written in a bold hand. He laid it on the table and smoothed out the creases. "This, for instance. Sir Percy gave it to me last night from a packet he had just received."

"Oh?" Kyle said.

"The woman sent me a letter," Morhouse said.

"Who did?" Kyle said.

"My wife," Morhouse said, his lips drawn tight. He pounded the table with his fist, making the empty pitchers dance. "She should have told me to my face. I deserve that at least."

"Told you what?" Kyle said.

"That she is leaving," Morhouse said. The rancor on his face gave way to sadness. "She is going back to Salamanca, never to return."

Morhouse looked so forlorn that Kyle actually felt sorry for the man. "When?" he said.

"The day before yesterday," Morhouse said.

"Then go after her, man," Kyle said.

"What's the use?" Morhouse said, defeated. "Nothing can heal the breach between us. It is too wide, too deep, and has gone on for too long."

"Isabel left as well," Hoprig said, joining the conversation. His countenance settled into a resigned despondency as he related how Lady Catherine hired a merchant vessel a week ago, paid for it with the pearl that supposedly went missing, and took Isabel and Owen away with her.

"You knew this and you didn't tell me?" Morhouse said, turning on Hoprig.

"I only learned of it the night they embarked," Hoprig said.

About that time, a serving girl in her mid-teens approached to deposit a full pitcher of ale on the table. She also brought an extra mug for Kyle.

Morhouse took a small coin from the pouch at his side and dropped it into her waiting hand, after which she walked away to serve another table. He filled all three mugs and nudged one toward Kyle. "Remember how we used to share a jug in this very tavern?" he said, a nostalgic expression on his face. "Those were the good old days."

Kyle reached for the mug, attributing Morhouse's maudlin reminiscence to the ale. In the good old days that he recalled, the two of them had hated each other from the moment they met. They certainly never went out drinking together. If anything, they did their best to avoid each other's company. Whenever they did clash on occasion, his now-deceased wife always managed to intervene. Otherwise, one or the other of them would surely be dead by this time.

He lifted the mug to his lips, reflecting on the irony of sharing a friendly drink with an old enemy.

Morhouse opened his mouth to speak. Before he uttered a word, he toppled forward to crash head and shoulders onto the table, knocking over an empty pitcher on the way down. An instant later, he began to snore.

"Should we carry him back to the garrison?" Hoprig said.

Kyle eyed Morhouse's large frame slumped halfway across

the table. "I'm not sure we can pick him up," he said. "Let's just leave him here to sleep it off."

The two of them left Morhouse slumbering peacefully in the tavern while they went outside. They crossed the sunlit courtyard and entered the cool darkness of the stable.

The thump of their boots on the timber planks at the entryway brought the groom out of his room at the head of the stalls. He made a move to get their horses, but Kyle waved him away.

"I'm sorry to hear that Isabel left with Lady Catherine," Kyle said as he and Hoprig walked down the center aisle. "I know you were fond of her."

"More than fond," Hoprig said glumly. He drew in a deep breath and let it out with a long sigh. "You probably think I'm a fool for giving my affection so readily."

"Not really," Kyle said. "The first time I set eyes on Joneta, she took my breath away. From that moment on, my heart belonged to her."

Hoprig stopped in front of the stall where his chestnut mare stood looking out over the half-door. "I should never have fallen for her," he said.

Kyle clapped Hoprig on the shoulder. "When love comes for you, my friend," he said, "there is no escape."

"So it seems," Hoprig said, absently rubbing the mare's velvety nose. "We think of love as a gift, but it isn't really free. It is sold to us at the cost of the grief and sadness that comes later." He looked over at Kyle, his eyes haunted by inner pain. "I think I'll walk back to the garrison. I need time to clear my head."

"Of course," Kyle said. He watched as Hoprig led the mare up the aisle and out into the courtyard.

The melancholy atmosphere of lost love sparked in him an overwhelming desire to visit Joneta. He longed to see her face and hear her voice once again. It was high time he declared his love and presented the emerald ring to her as a pledge of his troth. She need not seek permission from an overlord to marry, for she was a widow as well as a landowner.

It occurred to him that she might refuse his offer. In that event, he would persist with his proposal, and over time, he hoped she would relent.

He tightened the girth on the saddle before he mounted the gelding. He tossed half a penny to the groom as he rode from the stable. He took Harbour Street all the way to the coastal road, where he turned south. With a nudge of his heels, the gelding broke into a steady lope that ate up the distance.

Soon, a rising wind started to blow in from the firth. Waves capped with froth washed onto the sandy beach. A bank of heavy black clouds scudded in from the west to veil the sun. Although not yet noon, the sky grew dark and sullen with the threat of rain.

Lightning flashed overhead, and thunder rolled in the distance. The gentle shower that followed swiftly escalated into a downpour.

By the time he reached Joneta's house in the meadow, he was soaked to the skin. He dismounted out front and knocked on the wooden jamb.

Joneta's niece, Meg, opened the door in her shift. Her face looked drawn, and there were smudges of weariness under her blue eyes.

"Oh," she said. She seemed disappointed. "Come in before ye catch yer death." She picked up a thin blanket and flung it around her shoulders for modesty.

"Thanks," he said. He stood just inside the doorway, dripping on the plank floor. "I came to see Joneta."

"She's not here," Meg said. "She went to town to fetch

Master John. The baby is sick. He cried all night. He finally fell asleep a little while ago."

"When did she leave?" he said.

"At first light," Meg said. "I thought it was her at the door."

"That was seven hours ago," he said, frowning.

"Dear me," Meg said, wringing her hands. "I must have dozed off."

"Where is Drew?"

"He's sick, too," Meg said. She put a hand to her forehead. "I don't feel so good myself."

"What about Joneta?" he said with concern. "Was she well when she left?" If she was ill, he feared that she might swoon somewhere along the way without anyone to help her.

"She looked all right," Meg said. "I mean, she didn't complain that she felt poorly." She brightened, as though a thought struck her. "Maybe she went to Cragston Castle so that Mistress Marjorie could take her to town in the wagon."

The notion that Joneta might have caught a ride with Marjorie consoled him somewhat. At the same time, it bothered him that he did not pass the wagon on the road, either coming or going. "Maybe I should go look for them," he said.

He tramped outside and mounted the gelding. As he made his way back up the track, the downpour slowed to a steady drizzle. Before long, it stopped completely, and the sun came out from behind the clouds. The grass on either side of the road looked green and lush, washed clean by the summer rain. Glassy pools of water gathered in the ruts, reflecting the sky above.

When he reached the firth, he followed the coastal road past the old ruins and around to Cragston Castle. He rode through the stone archway and entered the bailey in a clatter of hoofs on the rain-slicked cobblestones.

Arnald the groom came out of the stable to meet him. His brown hair gleamed with reddish highlights in the sunlight.

"Good morrow, Master Shaw," he said, taking hold of the gelding's bridle. "What brings ye out this way?"

"Is Mistress Marjorie here?" Kyle said.

"Not at the moment," Arnald said with a shake of his head.

"Did she take the wagon out today?" Kyle said.

"She did, as a matter of fact," Arnald said. "I hitched it up for her and Mistress Joneta. They sometimes go to market together."

"What time was that?" Kyle said.

"Early this morning," Arnald said. "Why do ye ask?" A furrow appeared between his eyebrows. "Is something wrong?"

"I'm not sure," Kyle said. He related what Meg told him about Joneta's errand. "It is not that far to town, and Mistress Joneta would never tarry there since the baby is ill. She and Mistress Marjorie should have gotten back hours ago."

"What will ye do now?" Arnald said.

"I'm going to check with John to see when they left his shop."

"Give me a minute to saddle the destrier," Arnald said. "I'm coming with ye."

"Sir Peter's horse is here?" Kyle said.

"Aye," Arnald said. "He wandered back on his own a couple of days ago." He glanced up at the stone tower. "Should I tell Mistress Ryland that her daughter may be missing?"

"Not until we know that for sure," Kyle said. "There is no need to upset her without cause." The suggestion that something dire happened to Marjorie placed a suffocating pressure around his heart, for if she fell victim to foul play, Joneta did, too.

CHAPTER 18

Kyle and Arnald made good time on the trip to town. They threaded their way through foot traffic on Tradesmen's Row and reined in before the whitewashed stone building that stood out from the wooden shops along the street. They dismounted and tied their horses to the rail out front.

Kyle led the way into the apothecary shop, where the fragrant scent of spice hung in the air like a spell. He called out a greeting to John, who sat at a table sorting through dried leaves of various shapes and sizes.

"What can I do for ye?" John said with a welcoming smile that made a dimple flash in his left cheek.

"I'm looking for Mistress Joneta," Kyle said.

"And Mistress Marjorie," Arnald interjected.

"Aye," Kyle said. "Mistress Marjorie, too. Did they come here this morning?"

"I haven't seen Mistress Joneta since she dined with us on Wednesday. As for Mistress Marjorie, she hasn't stopped by in a week or so."

A muscle twitched in Kyle's jaw at the news. Where could Joneta be? A frightening thought crept into the back of his mind, one that terrified him like no adversary on a field of battle ever could. What if the killer was still on the loose? What if he captured Marjorie to carry out the last step of the threefold death ritual? What if the same fate awaited Joneta because she happened to be in the wrong place at the wrong time?

He dared not dwell on that possibility. He must focus instead on finding her, and Marjorie, too, of course. It was imperative that the search for them begin at once.

He told John about the baby's illness, that Derek was bedridden and Meg might be next. "Can you go out to the house and attend to them?" he said.

"I shall leave right away," John said. He set about gathering bunches of herbs and phials of tonic to put into his medicament bag. "Should either of the ladies arrive while I am there, I will send word to ye."

"Thanks," Kyle said. "In the meantime, I'll hunt for them in town."

He and Arnald left John's shop and rode through a maze of lanes and alleyways until they wound up on a dead-end street in the poorer section of town. The last few houses faced each other across a tiny courtyard-like area, where weeds grew between the uneven stones. A couple of scruffy dogs basked in the sunshine on the cobbled paving.

Hul sat in front of his house on a bench in the shade of the overhang. He was eating from a wooden bowl, while his elderly mother stirred the contents of the black three-legged iron pot over an open fire.

The dogs scrambled to their feet to bark at the intruders. A sharp word from Hul sent them slinking away.

The old woman's face lit up when she saw Kyle. "Get ye down, ye and the lad with ye," she said. "Come and eat."

Without waiting for a reply, she picked up a bowl and ladled into it a thick stew full of sliced root vegetables and scraps of meat.

Kyle was about to claim a lack of appetite, when the tantalizing aroma made his stomach growl in protest. His last meal was sometime yesterday, and the ale he drank at the tavern this morning did little to satisfy his hunger.

"You are very kind, Mistress Abigail," he said as he swung down from the saddle. He took the bowl from her and started in on the stew. The turnips and onions melted in his mouth, and the meat was tasty, although he could not identify the animal from which it came. The gravy was rich and brown, with just enough bay leaves in it to enhance the flavor.

Abigail filled another bowl and handed it to Arnald, who received it with the gratitude of a starving man.

Hul gestured for Kyle and Arnald to join him on the bench. "Ye have the look of a lost puppy about ye today," he said to Kyle. "Is something amiss?"

Between bites, Kyle told him of Joneta and Marjorie's disappearance. "They could be anywhere," he said.

Hul fixed a knowing gaze on Kyle. "I think ye care very much for Mistress Joneta," he said.

"She means the world to me," Kyle said. It was easy for him to admit it aloud now that she was in peril. Yet barely a week ago, he could not say those words to her face.

"What can I do to help?" Hul said.

"Anything you can," Kyle said. "Someone must have seen them come into town this morning. I am willing to pay handsomely for information that leads to their safe return."

"That is the best way to get results," Hul said. "The day is half spent already, but I will see what I can do. The minute I come across anything of interest, I will let you know." He put the empty bowl on the bench beside him and wiped his mouth with the back of his hand. "By the way, I heard about the outcome of the hearing. Do ye think Blackwell had something to do with abducting the ladies ye seek?"

"Blackwell has been in the dungeon since the hearing," Kyle said. "His men, though, are another matter. He might well have put them up to such villainy."

"Can ye think of anybody else with a grudge against ye?" Hul said.

"The only person who comes to mind is Morhouse," Kyle said. "That goes back years, though, before I even met Joneta."

"Some men have a long memory," Hul said.

"You may have something there," Kyle said. "Morhouse is the kind of fellow who rarely forgives and never forgets. I wonder whether he is petty enough to take his quarrel with me out on my lady." He looked over at Hul, his expression grim. "If he harms her in any way, I will see that he pays dearly for it."

"Have a care, my friend," Hul said. "He is an officer in the King's army."

"And I am an officer of the law," Kyle retorted.

The thought of Joneta and Marjorie being held captive by Blackwell's men or even Morhouse troubled him, though not as much as the mental image of them burning at the stake.

When he and Arnald finished eating, they thanked Mistress Abigail again for her hospitality. After taking their leave, they mounted their horses and set out for the Bull and Bear Tavern, where Kyle hoped to find Morhouse.

"I don't know if ye heard about Mistress Eleanora yet," Arnald said as they wended their way back to Harbour Street. "She quit Cragston Castle for good."

"Oh?" Kyle said. "Where did she go?"

"Back to England," Arnald said. "They left on Saturday morning."

"They?" Kyle said.

"Sir Charles Ettwick called for her in a fancy carriage," Arnald said. "She seemed eager to go with him."

"I'll bet she was," Kyle said, recalling how Eleanora came alive at the mere mention of Ettwick's name. "I'm sure Marjorie is glad he is gone, and with him, the threat of an arranged marriage."

"She is, indeed," Arnald said. His smiling countenance clearly indicated that he shared the same sentiment.

Kyle turned into the tavern courtyard just as Morhouse walked out of the two-story wooden building.

"Wait here," Kyle said to Arnald. He dismounted and started toward Morhouse with a scowl on his face.

Morhouse's step faltered at the sight of Kyle advancing on him with lowered brows. "What do you want?" he said, squinting in the glare of the sun.

Kyle halted in front of Morhouse, who towered over him by half a head and carried double his weight. "Where is she?" he demanded, his fists clenched at his sides.

"Where is who?" Morhouse said. His befuddlement could have been from the ale, although he seemed quite sober at that moment.

"Mistress Joneta," Kyle said. "She was last seen leaving her house early this morning."

"Misplaced your lady, did you?" Morhouse said with a contemptuous laugh. "That was mighty careless of you. Not my problem. Now, get out of my way." He lifted a hand to sweep Kyle from his path.

Kyle grabbed Morhouse by the wrist and wrenched his arm up his back so quickly that he caught the man off guard. "Where is she?" he said, digging the fingers of his free hand into the man's beefy shoulder to keep him immobilized.

"I don't know," Morhouse said, gritting his teeth in pain.

Kyle applied pressure to the twisted limb until Morhouse grunted in agony. "Tell me where she is," he growled in the man's ear.

"All right!" Morhouse cried. "Enough!"

Kyle eased off slightly, but he held onto Morhouse's arm in case the man needed encouragement to talk. "What have you done with her?" he said.

"Nothing," Morhouse said. "I swear by the Virgin Mary and all the saints in heaven. They were going to put the fright into her to get back at you for showing them up at the hearing."

"Who?" Kyle said, nudging the man's arm a notch higher.

Morhouse drew in a sharp breath. "Blackwell's men," he said in a strained voice. "They didn't go near her. I promise."

"Why should I believe you?"

"Because they've been manning the garrison wall since dawn," Morhouse said. "When the officer of the watch heard what they planned to do, he assigned them to guard duty there so that he could keep an eye on them."

Kyle released Morhouse abruptly and stepped away. Although such violence was more than the man deserved, it served as a catharsis for his fear and frustration over Joneta's disappearance. "I must remember to thank the officer of the watch for doing that," he said. "In the meantime, I suggest you transfer those men to a garrison in some other shire. Otherwise, I will lodge a formal complaint against them and you."

"On what grounds?" Morhouse said, rubbing his sore shoulder.

"I'll think of something," Kyle said. "And trust me when I say that Sir Percy will be most displeased to hear the charges, especially now, with the Lord High Chancellor of England breathing down the back of his neck."

He should have been relieved that Joneta did not fall prey to Blackwell's men. It only served to scare him, though, because now he had no idea who was behind her abduction.

He started to walk over to where Arnald waited for him across the small courtyard, when Morhouse called out to him.

"Hold up a moment," Morhouse said.

Kyle paused to look behind him.

"I don't like you," Morhouse said. "I never did. Your lady, however, has nothing to do with the ill will between us." He shifted his weight from one foot to the other, as though uncomfortable with what he was about to say next. "She may truly be in danger. So, tell me what needs to be done to find her, and I will do it."

"I never liked you, either," Kyle said, turning to Morhouse. "Nevertheless, I appreciate your offer. If you really mean it, you can post a watch on the bridge to Newton and keep a sharp eye on the roads leading to the north. Check all wagons and carts leaving town, especially the ones with covered cargo."

"Shall I also conduct a door-to-door search for her here in town?" Morhouse said.

"I've got that covered," Kyle said. "Even as we speak, reliable people are combing every street and alleyway to look for them."

"Them?" Morhouse said. "Who else is missing?"

"Marjorie Ryland," Kyle said. "She and Joneta left Cragston Castle together earlier today. Neither of them has been seen since."

"I will dispatch a troop immediately," Morhouse said. "I will also notify Sir Percy about the missing ladies. He will want to know."

"If your men do find them," Kyle said, "send word to me immediately. Otherwise, meet me at the sheriff's office at sundown. In the meantime, I will be at the marketplace talking to anybody who comes forward with information as to their whereabouts."

The long-time rivals gazed at each other, bound by an uneasy truce to work together for a common purpose. How long that peace between them would last remained to be seen.

"One more thing," Kyle said. "I assumed that you had a hand in this foul deed, but I see now that I misjudged you."

"Is that your idea of an apology?" Morhouse said.

"That's as close to one as you're going to get," Kyle said.

Morhouse responded with a grunt, although he did look pleased. "Until sundown, then," he said. He made his way to the stable and vanished inside.

Kyle mounted the gelding, after which he and Arnald left the tavern courtyard to ride down Harbour Street.

When they arrived at the marketplace, Kyle sent Arnald on to the garrison with a message for both Hoprig and Vinewood. One was to take a handful of men to watch the southward roads that led out of town. The other was to do the same for the westward roads. Arnald was to stay with either group until the end of the day, at which time they would all report back to the sheriff's office, unless, of course, they found the women sooner.

The marketplace was more crowded than usual, for news of Marjorie Ryland's disappearance and the reward for her safe return had blown through town like leaves in the wind.

Kyle remained in the saddle so that people could see him from across the market grounds. Men and women came up to him all afternoon. Some imparted to him their advice on the best way to find the missing noblewoman, while others spoke of vague sightings in the hope of receiving payment for information supplied.

It was mid-afternoon when John Logan rode up on his mule to report on the baby's condition. "The wee bairn is sleeping better now," he said. "He should be back to good health in a day or so. Derek will, too. Meg is still on her feet, so she is able to take care of them until Joneta's return."

"Did you see anybody on the road that looked suspicious?" Kyle said.

"Not a soul," John said. "Don't worry. She will soon turn up, safe and sound. I feel sure of it."

"I wish I shared your confidence," Kyle said.

After John left, Kyle noticed a couple of Hul's boys in the crowd. They appeared to be loitering, yet their sharp eyes and ears missed nothing. They drifted away later in the day, as did everyone else at the marketplace, including the merchants and vendors.

The shadows grew longer as the sun dipped toward the western horizon. There was no longer any need to linger at the marketplace, for the grounds were now empty.

With a nudge of his heels to the gelding's belly, Kyle set out for the garrison just down the street. He was tired and frustrated. Despite all the claims and assertions he received that afternoon as to where to find the missing women, not a single one warranted serious consideration.

He rode through the garrison gates and on to the stable to feed and water the gelding. After giving the horse a good brushing, he walked over to the sheriff's office to await the arrival of the others involved in the hunt.

It wasn't long before Hoprig and his squad rode into the courtyard. He sent the three men with him on to the stable while he went over to report to Kyle.

"We searched every wagon that went south," he said as he dismounted.

"No luck, I suppose," Kyle said.

"Not at all," Hoprig said. "I left a couple of men behind to keep an eye on the comings and goings along the coastal road tonight."

"Good thinking," Kyle said.

Hoprig twisted the reins in his hands. "I'm sorry we didn't find her for you," he said. "I know what it's like to fear for the safety of someone dear to you."

"Perhaps we'll do better tomorrow," Kyle said with an optimism he did not feel.

"Of course, we will," Hoprig said.

Vinewood arrived a moment later with Arnald riding beside him. His account was much the same as Hoprig's, and he, too, posted men to watch the westward roads throughout the night.

"Well done," Kyle said.

Arnald swung down from the saddle. "I didn't think it would be this difficult to track Mistress Marjorie down," he said. "Where can she possibly be?"

"I don't know," Kyle said. "We shall keep looking until we find her."

"And Mistress Joneta," Arnald said with unexpected empathy.

"Aye," Kyle said softly. "Mistress Joneta, too." He shook off the despondency that threatened to engulf him. "By the way, where do you plan to sleep tonight?"

"At the tavern, I suppose," Arnald said.

"You can stay here if you like," Kyle said. "It's not fancy, but it is free. There are a number of empty stalls in the stable where you can leave your mount."

Arnald started toward the stable with the white warhorse in tow. Hoprig and Vinewood trailed behind him, leading their mounts in the same direction.

Shortly thereafter, Morhouse and his troop clattered into the garrison courtyard. Morhouse rode over to the sheriff's office, while the rest of his men continued on to the stable.

"Have you any news?" Kyle said.

"None," Morhouse said, reining in. "My men stopped several wagons that looked suspect, but there was no sign of either lady."

"Did you leave a night watch on the bridge?" Kyle said.

"I did," Morhouse said. "I will send out a squad to relieve them in the morning."

"Thanks," Kyle said. "Since there is nothing more to be done today, meet me here at first light to resume the search."

Morhouse looked like he was about to say something. He evidently changed his mind, for he laid the reins on his mount's neck and set out for the stable instead.

Kyle stood in the doorway of the sheriff's office as dusk

settled around him. The evening breeze brought with it the smell of the sea just beyond the western wall of the garrison. The red sky overhead portended fair weather for the next day, at which time the hunt would begin again.

The dull ache in his heart grew sharp now that he could ponder the matter of Joneta's disappearance without distraction. Disappointment over his failure to locate her became all the more acute, for he fully expected to meet with success long before the day drew to a close. How empty his world was, he reflected glumly, without her in it.

It occurred to him that ransom might be the reason for Marjorie's abduction. If that was the case, her life was not at risk. Otherwise, her abductors would never receive the money they sought. That, however, placed Joneta in grave danger, because her presence would neither be required nor desired.

On the other hand, if this was about completing the third phase of the druidic death ritual, the chance of survival for either Marjorie or Joneta became more remote with each hour that passed.

As twilight faded into darkness, disquieting thoughts of Joneta's fate churned in his mind. A knot of tension twisted in his belly, and his temples began to throb.

Perhaps he should go to bed, since it did no good to dwell on that which may never happen. After a good night's sleep, things might start to look up.

He laughed without humor at the absurdity of such a notion, for there was no way he was going to rest easy until he found Joneta. He hoped with all his heart that when he did find her, she would be alive and well.

CHAPTER 19

Kyle woke with a start on Monday morning to a cool gray dawn. After thrashing from one side of his pallet to the other for most of the night, he was grateful that he got any sleep at all.

Regrettably, yesterday's woes came rushing back into his conscious mind with a vengeance. Joneta had been missing for one full day now. He was beyond frantic over her safety and ready to go to any length to get her back. He, like Arnald, did not anticipate that it would be so difficult to track her down. Evidently, it was.

Arnald slept on the opposite side of the small chamber, sprawled across his pallet with the abandon of a child.

Kyle got up to gently nudge the young man with his bare foot. "Time to rise," he said.

He walked into the front room to wash his face and don his clothing. Since there was no telling what trouble the day might bring, he put his leather scale armor over his shirt and buckled on his sword belt. He picked up his short-handled battle axe and tested the blade with his thumb to make sure it was still sharp after the last time he used it.

A couple of minutes later, Arnald came into the front room, dressed and ready. He wore no weapon, except for the dagger at his waist.

Kyle owned an extra sword and belt, which he lent to the young man in case they ran into danger. With the axe in his hand, he opened the door of the sheriff's office and stepped outside to a thin mist that carpeted the ground.

There was much activity in the garrison courtyard at that early hour. Some of the soldiers were making their way toward the main hall for a bite to eat before going about their assigned duties. Others were leading their horses from the stable to join the swelling ranks of a troop that was forming near the gibbet platform in the center of the open area.

Kyle and Arnald joined Hoprig and Vinewood on their way to the stable to saddle their mounts.

"We are going to drop in on Sir Fulbert this morning," Kyle said.

"Do you think he had something to do with his daughter's disappearance?" Hoprig said.

"I have no reason to suspect him yet," Kyle said. "If Marjorie was taken for ransom, though, he should soon be receiving a demand for payment."

By the time the four of them rode from the stable, Morhouse, armed and armored, sat on his black horse at the head of a sizeable troop. "Where are you bound today?" he said when Kyle rode over to talk to him.

"I plan to go south," Kyle said. "You and your men can cover all the roads leading out of town. Post a watch on the harbor, too, just in case."

"And if we do not meet with success?" Morhouse said.

"Then I will see you back here this evening," Kyle said.

"I shall do my best to find your lady," Morhouse said, his gaze intent. "You have my word on that." He looked as though he actually meant it.

"I appreciate that," Kyle said. "I really do." He was touched by such ardent sincerity. At that moment, he felt an unaccustomed camaraderie for the man, which surprised him, considering their long-standing animosity for each other.

Morhouse turned away to bellow a command at his men, at

which time the entire troop set out by twos for the open gates in the curtain wall. Ground mist boiled up in their wake to mark their departure.

After the troop left the garrison, Kyle and those with him rode across the courtyard and passed under the metal teeth of the portcullis. That was when they came upon John on his brown mule waiting at the foot of the drawbridge. Macalister was there, too, astride his dappled gray. Simon, the druid acolyte, was perched on an old saddle strapped to the brown and white pony he ordinarily used to pull his cart.

"What is this?" Kyle said, reining in.

"We are here to help ye in the search for yer lady," Macalister said.

"I am grateful for it," Kyle said, glad of friends and acquaintances, and even Simon, who rallied to lend a hand when it was needed.

"Where are you headed?" John said.

"Cragston Castle," Kyle said.

"Then let us be on our way," John said.

The seven of them rode down Harbour Street to the wharf, where they turned south. When they started down the coastal road, they passed the squad that Morhouse had stationed there to replace Hoprig's night watch.

"We are looking for wagon tracks," Kyle said to the men with him. "Keep a sharp eye out on the inland side of the road for ruts in the mud. There may be some that yesterday's rain didn't wash away."

They spread out to cover a wide area, walking their horses so as not to miss any imprints that indicated a wagon turned off the road there.

The morning sun soon burned away the mist that settled in the hollows of the rolling pastureland to the east. On the seaward side, the outgoing tide exposed a large expanse of white sand that sloped gently down to the firth.

Farther down the coast, sandy beaches gave way to jagged rocks and high cliffs. Seagulls glided on updrafts, filling the air with piercing screams. The old ruins squatted at the edge of a precipice, its dilapidated state in sharp contrast to the stone tower of Cragston Castle looming in the distance.

Loose shale eventually replaced the grassy turf on either side of the road. They gave up looking for tracks and pressed on to Cragston Castle. As they approached the walled fortress, they left the coastal road to circle around to the causeway that led up to the entrance.

Before they reached the causeway, a swarthy man on a bay pony came out through the open gates and started down the stone ramp at a rapid pace. He raised an arm and flailed the air, not in greeting, but as though to head them off.

"That's Turval," Simon said, pointing to the lone rider hastening toward them.

Kyle reined in, signaling for the others to halt. "Master Turval," he said when the potter drew near enough to hear him. "What brings you out here?"

"A special order," Turval said. He opened one of the wrapped bundles suspended from either side of his saddle and pulled out a clay jug with an intricate design on it. "They are a matched pair. As you see, I am unable to make delivery. There is no one within to receive me." The front of his tunic was smudged and streaked with dried mud, as was common for someone in his trade.

"Mistress Ryland should be in residence," Kyle said. "Sir Fulbert, too. They rarely leave the place."

"It is completely deserted," Turval said. "I shouted for some minutes before I gave up and left."

Kyle frowned at the news. He wondered whether the absence of Sir Fulbert and his wife had anything to do with a ransom demand for their daughter.

Turval gave the other men a sweeping glance before his golden-brown eyes returned to Kyle. "Are you out hunting this morning?" he said.

"You could say that," Kyle said. "Mistress Marjorie and Mistress Joneta went missing yesterday. We are looking for them."

Lines appeared between Turval's dark eyebrows. "Mistress Marjorie is one of my best customers," he said. "I would like to join in the search, if I may."

"We could use another pair of eyes," Kyle said. "There is much territory to cover."

He started to divide the men into pairs to send them out in different directions, when Simon edged his pony up alongside the gelding.

"A private word, Master Deputy, if ye please," Simon said. At Kyle's nod, he leaned close to speak in a muted voice. "Have ye thought of bringing the matter to Master Rolf?"

"For what purpose?" Kyle said.

"He is a seer," Simon whispered. "As such, he may be able to tell ye where to find yer missing ladies."

"Are you not also capable of doing that?" Kyle said in a low tone, for it would not do to broadcast that Simon dabbled in the dark arts. Divination and other forms of devilry were censured by the church, as were those individuals who indulged in arcane practices.

"Not half as well as the Master," Simon murmured.

"At this point," Kyle said, "I am desperate enough to try anything." To the others he said: "Before we separate into groups, I wish to call upon a certain hermit who knows every trail and haunt in Cragston Forest better than anyone here. It could save us a lot of time if I talked with him first."

The others voiced their agreement, after which they all set

out for the woods beyond the stone ridges to the east. When they reached the trees, they picked up a deer trail that led them through twining vines and dense undergrowth for the next hour. The only sound that interrupted the hush around them was the sporadic twitter of a sparrow.

When they came to a stream that cut a crooked path through the forest, Kyle called a halt. "Wait here," he said. "I shall return shortly." He beckoned to Simon. "Come with me."

He and the druidic acolyte continued on, following the stream down to the secluded glade where Rolf lived.

The instant he rode into the shadowed clearing, the skin on the back of his neck prickled with apprehension. He glanced around to determine the cause of the disquiet.

All appeared as it did on his last visit, except Rolf was not there this time. Neither was there a fire in the small pit over which the old man cooked his food. In addition, the copper water bowl rested on its side, as though knocked over, and the carved staff lay on the ground, as if carelessly tossed aside.

He swung down from the saddle to look for any telltale sign in the vicinity that bespoke of violence. There were a few scuffs and gouges in the dirt, but nothing that required closer scrutiny.

"Simon," he said. "Check inside the croft."

Simon dismounted to do as he was bidden. A moment later, he came out and joined Kyle in the clearing. "Master Rolf is not in there," he said. He picked up the staff and wiped off the crusted mud with his fingers. "He never goes anywhere without this."

Kyle squatted to stand the copper water bowl upright. He was about to rise when his gaze fell on something in the underbrush on the far side of the open area. It looked like a bundle of brown cloth half-hidden in the bushes.

He went over to push aside the shrubbery, thus exposing the sandaled foot of a man lying on the ground. "By my faith!" he cried. "Not him, too."

He knew who it was without even seeing the man's face. There was no need to check for a pulse, for the visible skin had a grayish tinge to it.

Simon rushed forward to look at the body. Anguish clouded his features when he saw it. "Master," he said. His voice broke on that single word.

Kyle pursed his lips and whistled, a long shrill sound that brought the others into the clearing a few minutes later.

The riders dismounted and came over to peer at the dead man.

"Is that the hermit?" Macalister said.

"Aye," Kyle said with a nod of his head.

"Ye will get nothing from him now," Macalister said.

They converged on the old man's body to carry him into the clearing. They laid him down as they'd found him, on his back with his own dagger protruding from his chest. Dried blood stained the entire front of his tunic. Unlike the grimacing features of those who die a violent death, the expression on his lined face was serene, as though at peace with his fate.

They stood in a circle around the body to watch while John conducted his examination.

Simon wrung his hands as he looked on. "What am I going to do now?" he said. "He was a good master. Nay, he was more than that. He was like the father I never had."

"Are there others like him in the shire, besides Sir Fulbert?" Kyle said in a low voice for Simon's ears only.

"Only me," Simon said, his tone muted.

"I suppose Sir Fulbert will now take on the duties as master," Kyle said.

"That oaf is unfit for such an exalted office," Simon said with feeling. "He has brought nothing but reproach upon the Order."

"What prevents you from taking up the mantle of office

yourself?" Kyle said.

"I am but a lowly novice," Simon said. The seed, though, once planted, seemed to take root in his mind, for he squared his narrow shoulders and stood a little taller than before.

John climbed to his feet and wiped his hands on his tunic. "He has been dead for nearly a full day," he said.

"Would you say it happened around vespers yesterday evening?" Kyle said.

"Either then or close to it, in my opinion," John said.

"Cause of death?"

"A dagger through the heart, as ye see."

"Did you find any mistletoe in his mouth, like there was for Sir Humphrey?"

"Nay," John said.

"Were there any defensive wounds on his hands and arms?"

"None," John said.

"That means he knew his killer," Kyle said with a downward turn of his mouth. "There is a cold heart behind this one, for the murderer used his familiarity with the old man to get close enough to stab him to death. What is worse, he used the victim's own dagger to do the deed."

"Do ye think this murder and that of the Rylands was done by the same man?" John said.

"I doubt it," Kyle said. "This one does not fit the pattern of the others."

"I didn't think there was a pattern," John said.

"Of course, there is," Kyle said. "The common thread that links the first two murders is the Rylands themselves. As far as I know, Rolf was not even a distant relative. He was, though, more than a passing acquaintance to them."

"To my way of thinking," John said, "the fact that all three victims were members of a secret society constitutes a connection. And what about the killing thrust of the blade to the heart?

Does that not bring to mind the druidic method used to dispatch a sacrificial victim?"

"It does, indeed," Kyle said. "However, the difference here is that the killer murdered Rolf face to face, whereas both Sir Humphrey and Sir Peter were rendered unconscious before they died. The mode of death inflicted upon the Rylands involved much preparation and careful execution. The intent there was to convey a specific message designed to put fear into those who understood what it meant." He gazed down at the body lying on the ground. "This one has no such flair about it. I believe it was done for a singular purpose."

"And that was?" John said.

"To snuff out Rolf's life," Kyle said. "Whoever did this communed with him freely, which is how the killer could draw so near without any inkling of danger on the old man's part. Rolf was privy to many a fellow's dark deeds, so it was likely done to stop his mouth."

He walked over to where Simon stood apart from the others. "Have you any idea who did this?" he said.

"I do not," Simon said. "I wish I could give ye his name, so that he may be punished for this heinous crime." His eyes strayed to the old man's body before returning to Kyle. "I came along to help you find your lady because she has always been kind to me. Under the present circumstances, however, I wish to beg off from doing so. I must make preparation to bury the Master according to custom."

"A murder has been committed here," Kyle said. "What you suggest is most irregular."

"It would be a sacrilege to place the Master's earthly remains in the hands of the profane. Surely he deserves a proper burial, with the honor and dignity befitting his office. Would you deny him that?"

"What does such preparation involve?" Kyle said.

"His body will be wrapped in a shroud bedecked with evergreen fronds in symbol of the eternal circle of life. A vigil must be kept for him throughout the night. Then at the rising of the sun, he will be laid in the bosom of Mother Earth. Boughs of oak and sprays of mistletoe will be buried with him, along with his favorite staff for the journey to the netherworld. After I cover his grave with prayer stones, I will plant a tree beside it to perpetuate his memory."

"Master John already examined the body," Kyle said. "I have what I need to conduct an investigation, so I suppose there is no reason to delay interment. Can you dig the grave by yourself?"

"I was going to ask Turval to help me with that," Simon said.

"Why not do so?" Kyle said. "He is an able-bodied man."

"He isn't here," Simon said.

Kyle glanced around the clearing in a vain search for the potter. "How astute of you to notice," he said. "Did you also happen to see when he left?"

"He never arrived with the others," Simon said. "I know that because I looked for him at the time."

"Well, well," Kyle said, frowning. "I wonder what kept him away."

"I know what you are thinking," Simon said, "but you are wrong in this instance. Turval would never raise a hand against the Master."

"How can you be sure?" Kyle said.

"Because he wants to study the oral tradition of the Order under the Master's tutelage," Simon said. "He cannot do that if the Master is dead."

"Did Master Rolf approve of such an arrangement?" Kyle said.

"I never got the chance to discuss it with him," Simon said. "Turval reveres our beliefs, though. I am sure of it. Every time we get together, he questions me at length about our customs and rites."

Kyle took a moment to reflect on Simon's words, for they added another piece to the puzzle. Unfortunately, the components were still so random that none of them as yet fell into place.

Take the first two murders, for instance. Such meticulous planning revealed that the killer possessed knowledge of druidic rituals. Now, according to Simon, it seemed that Turval knew a lot about that subject, too. But then, so did Sir Fulbert and Simon himself. Blackwell claimed ignorance of such practices, although he could have been lying, as he was inclined to do.

That odd smudge on Turval's tunic, half-hidden among the streaks of dried mud, might be the phosphorescent substance from Sir Peter's cotte. Yet, it was possible that it came to be there merely as a result of the potter's handling of moist clay.

Turval's hasty exit from Cragston Castle effectively stopped them from going inside. Was there something within those stone walls the potter wanted to keep hidden, or was he telling the truth about the unsuccessful delivery of the clay pots? Did Sir Fulbert's absence from the castle have anything to do with his daughter's abduction, or was it for a more sinister reason, like hiding out after stabbing Rolf to death?

Turval did not enter the clearing with the others. Was it because he knew Rolf was already dead? Was he the one who killed the old man? Did he also kill Sir Humphrey and Sir Peter? Or did Sir Fulbert do it, or even Blackwell? What drove them to commit murder? And finally, which one was responsible for Marjorie and Joneta's disappearance?

Such conjecture made Kyle's head spin. There was but one thing to do if he wanted the right answers. He must put the questions to the right person. Now, all he had to do was figure out who that was.

CHAPTER 20

After Kyle committed Rolf's body into Simon's keeping, he and the others started back up the trail. A canopy of leafy branches along the way provided shade from the mid-morning sun. It did little, though, to relieve the escalating heat of the summer day.

All too soon, they left the cool shadows of the forest to cross the sunlit stretch of open ground past the edge of the trees. When they reached the coastal road, they came to a halt.

"The pair of you can go on to Cragston Castle," Kyle said to Hoprig and Vinewood. "Wait there for Sir Fulbert to return. See if you can bring him in for questioning. Being an English nobleman, he may not mind an escort to town by English soldiers. If he refuses to go with you, stay put to make sure he doesn't leave again. I will try to join you there later today."

To John and Macalister, he said, "You two can make inquiries about the missing ladies in the villages north of the River Doon, starting with Alloway. Be sure to mention the reward. If anybody knows anything, they will have to go to the sheriff's office to tell me. Arnald and I will cover the villages on this side of the river."

Hoprig and Vinewood went south, while the rest of them rode north. When they reached the first inland track that met the coastal road, Kyle and Arnald turned aside onto it. Macalister and John continued on their northward course.

On the way up the track, Kyle wondered what Prior Drumlay would say if he ever found out that the ancient Order of Druids was actively practicing their rites and rituals in the shire. He would not be the one who informed the prior, though. Based on what he gleaned thus far about that secret society, its members were neither as bloodthirsty nor as menacing as folks made them out to be.

As for Simon, it was remarkable that such a timid man like him should assume the role of Master Druid. Perhaps it was not so surprising after all, since he served as an acolyte under Rolf who, before his death, was more than just a powerful mystic. The old man treated those who came to him with compassion, in addition to taking the responsibilities of his office seriously.

On reaching the end of the track, Kyle and Arnald approached a tiny settlement consisting of two modest wooden houses separated by a large garden plot.

A stocky man with silver streaks in his ginger beard sat on the shady side of the first house, sharpening the metal edge of a hoe with a whetting stone. He paused in his labors to exchange a friendly greeting with the visitors.

The sound of their voices brought a woman of middle years out of the house. Her gray homespun tunic had a dusting of flour on the front of it.

Kyle identified himself and Arnald, after which he told them of the search for Joneta and Marjorie.

"Oh, aye," the woman said, walking over to stand beside the man in the shade. "I heard about it at the market." She turned to him. "Don't ye remember me telling ye about it?"

The man lifted his shoulders in a noncommittal shrug.

"We went to town yesterday," she said to Kyle by way of explanation. "My husband drove us there in the pony cart."

"What time was that?" Kyle said.

"Sometime in the morning," she said.

"Did you happen to notice the ladies on the road," Kyle said. "Either on the way to town or on the way back?"

The woman shook her head, as did the man.

"Sorry we can't help ye," she said.

Kyle tilted his head toward the other house. "Who lives there?" he said.

"Our daughter," she said. "She is heavy with child just now. That's why she didn't go to market with us."

"And her husband?" Kyle said.

"He won't leave her side, God bless him," she said. "He does his chores, but the dear boy goes right back to her when he's done."

"Well, thank you for your time," Kyle said with a cordial nod.

He and Arnald turned their mounts and headed back to the coastal road to look for the next track that would take them to another inland village.

They found just such a one within sight of the old ruins and followed it across open land to the hillock beyond. Clumps of wild purple and yellow pansies grew in profusion among the clover beside the beaten path.

In a short while, they approached a village on the near side of a shallow stream in a sunlit dale. Half a dozen houses lined the dirt lane that ended abruptly at the water's edge. The weathered thatch on the roofs of the dwellings was as gray as the stones from which they were built.

Across the way, a shirtless man walked behind a team of oxen plowing neat furrows in the turf. Some distance from the plowman, a teenage boy tended a sizeable flock of sheep.

Three women and an adolescent girl sat on a bench in front of one of the houses. The youngest of the women and the girl were shelling peas into a wooden bowl. The stout middle-aged woman was spinning sheep's wool with a drop spindle, while the eldest, a thin woman with wiry gray hair, was busy plucking feathers from the carcass of a dead goose.

The women appeared to be related because of their resemblance to one another. They all stopped to stare as Kyle and Arnald drew near to them.

The man left the plow and the oxen in the field to hurry over to join the women. He was built like a bull, with sturdy legs and a head set low in his shoulders. The bulging muscles on his arms and chest gleamed with sweat. His ruddy complexion stood out against his black beard.

"Good morrow," Kyle said as he reined in before them. "I am Kyle Shaw, Deputy to the Sheriff of Ayrshire," He waved a hand at his companion. "This is Arnald, groom to Sir Fulbert of Cragston Castle. We are searching for the two ladies who went missing. They were last seen yesterday in a one-horse wagon on the coastal road."

"And ye think I took them?" the man said. He snorted with contempt. "There are already too many mouths around here to feed as it is." He spoke with the pronounced burr of a northerner.

"There is a reward for information that leads to their whereabouts," Kyle said.

"Even so, they're not here," the man said.

"How much is the reward?" the thin elderly woman said, intruding into the conversation.

"Two pennies in the king's silver," Kyle said. "There will be another two when the ladies are found." In truth, he was willing to give much more than that for Joneta's safe return.

"That's a fair sum," she said. "We were out and about yesterday morning. There wasn't anybody on the road but us." She glanced at the other women for confirmation, which they gave by nodding their heads. "Sorry," she added, gazing up at him.

"Thanks anyway," Kyle said.

He was about to turn away when the adolescent girl leaned down to gather another handful of pea pods from the wicker basket on the ground. His heart skipped a beat at the sight of the delicate gold ribbon binding the dark hair at the nape of her neck.

The ribbon looked just like the one he purchased in Glasgow for Joneta, the one she'd worn in her hair the day he dined with her at John and Colina's house.

Of course, it was possible that the delicate silky streamer might actually belong to the girl. It looked out of place on her, though, considering her frayed homespun tunic and dirty bare feet.

He could not leave without first ascertaining how the girl came by the ribbon. His query must be worded carefully. Otherwise, her parents would think that he, as a man of law, was making an accusation against her, in which case he would never find out if it was given to her or whether she'd found it. And if so, where and when?

On the way to Cragston Castle, Hoprig reflected on what he could say to convince Sir Fulbert to submit to further questioning at the sheriff's office concerning the untimely demise of the man's brother, son, and now Rolf the hermit. There were simply no words to make such interrogation sound appealing.

He dared not bring Sir Fulbert in at sword point, lest Sir Percy clap him—Hoprig—in irons for the coercion of an English knight favored by the King. A more expedient course would be to use tact and persuasion, even though he knew that would prove ineffective, given Sir Fulbert's obstinate and surly nature.

His thoughts strayed to Isabel, as they did so often since she left. Was that only two days ago? It seemed like an eternity to him. He wondered if she was keeping well and whether she missed him, like he missed her. He longed to see her and hold her in his arms. Deep down, though, he knew that such a thing would never come to pass. She was young and pretty and would likely forget all about him in a month or two, whereas he would cherish for the rest of his life the brief time he'd spent with her.

He snapped out of his reverie to urge his chestnut mare up the causeway leading to the castle entryway. The ring of shod hooves on stone announced his and Vinewood's presence long before the two of them rode under the stone arch into the bailey.

In light of Turval the potter's earlier claim that the castle was deserted, the sight of Mistress Ryland in the courtyard surprised him. She stood before a mound of straw near the pigpen. Her back was to him, yet he recognized her immediately. He thought it odd that she should be there, since there were no pigs in the pen.

When she turned to look in his direction, he caught a glimpse of the lighted torch in her hand. That, too, was when he saw Sir Fulbert bound with chains to the corner post of the empty sty, with a gag in his mouth and straw packed around his body up to his waist.

Both soldiers hauled back on the reins, bringing their mounts to an abrupt halt on the cobbled paving.

Hoprig dismounted and started toward Mistress Ryland, swiftly closing the short distance between them. When he drew within twelve feet of her, he stopped, for his presence served only to agitate her. He was near enough to smell pine resin tainted with sulfur emanating from the oily-looking straw that cover the lower half of Sir Fulbert's body.

"Mistress Ryland," he said. "Do you remember me? I came here to see you the other day." He spoke in a calm voice so as not to distress her further.

Sir Fulbert began to spout unintelligible gibberish around the strip of linen that cut across his open mouth. Although the words were unclear, his demeaning tone was unmistakable. The brunt of his insulting diatribe was directed at Mistress Ryland.

She seemed frightened and confused as she turned from Sir

Fulbert to Hoprig and back again.

Hoprig noticed that the torch in her hand was not the usual solid wooden shaft with flammable pitch on the end. This one was made from a bundle of reeds bound tightly together, which when set alight, was designed to burn slowly down the entire length of it, like the wick of a candle. This kind of torch, however, was much more difficult to snuff out.

He crept ever closer in the hope of snatching the torch from her hand. The moment she turned her head toward Sir Fulbert, he lunged at her.

Then, and only then, did he see the metal holder positioned at the foot of the mound, placed there for the purpose of keeping the lighted reed torch upright until it burned low enough to ignite the straw. He realized too late that Mistress Ryland was not trying to set her husband on fire. She was the one who had removed the torch from the stand in an effort to save him.

The scrape of Hoprig's boots on the cobblestones brought her head around. His sudden approach caused her to stumble back. The torch slipped from her grasp and hit the ground at her feet. In the next instant, the hem of her skirt caught fire and began to burn.

The fallen torch ignited the loose tinder at the edge of the mound. The oily straw immediately burst into flames.

Gold and red blazons devoured the straw with frightening speed. Sir Fulbert let out a wailing cry, his face contorted and his eyes wide with fear. Cobalt blue flames licked at his clothing. He struggled violently against the binding chains. Billows of thick yellowish smoke swirled around him, enfolding him in a suffocating embrace. Noxious fumes filled the air. In a matter of seconds, he slumped over, now silent and unmoving against the sturdy post.

Mistress Ryland just stood there, screaming hysterically while the dry cloth of her skirts went up in flames. She seemed frozen in shock, unable to help herself or even move back from the blaze.

Vinewood rushed forward to drag her away from the fiery inferno. He beat the smoldering fabric of her skirts with his hands to put it out. She hardly noticed that he rendered such assistance, for her entire focus was on her husband, at whom she stared in stunned disbelief.

Hoprig got as near as he could to stomp on the burning straw to keep the fire from spreading. Before he made any real headway, the tremendous heat drove him back. The skin of his face and hands was scorched red from exposure to the flames.

Streamers of fire ran along the weathered rails of the pigpen. Within half a minute, the whole roofless structure went up in a gush of crimson flames. Particles of gray ash swirled high in the air. Red embers soared into the midmorning sky.

Hoprig huddled together with Mistress Ryland and Vinewood in the courtyard, grateful for the comfort of other living souls. His eyes stung from the smoke. The sulfurous stench of brimstone choked him with every indrawn breath. The fire burned out of control, and there was no means at hand to extinguish it. He, like his companions, watched in helpless horror as the leaping flames consumed the body of Sir Fulbert Ryland, the ill-fated Master of Cragston Castle.

Kyle rode down the track at a gallop, bound for the coastal road. Arnald followed close behind him on the white destrier.

With much diplomacy and a lot of restraint, he'd managed to winkle the information he wanted from the adolescent girl. Her biggest concern, it seemed, was giving up the ribbon. After he assured her that she could keep it and after he paid her mother the sum promised, she told him exactly where she found it in the grass at the head of the track that led to her village. She'd seen it there early yesterday, before the rain came. Otherwise, it would have been covered with mud, and she never would have spotted it.

If the girl was telling the truth, and he dearly hoped she was, it meant that whatever happened to Joneta and Marjorie occurred where this particular track intersected with the coastal road. The question was, where did they go from there? Was the ribbon torn from Joneta's hair, or did she remove it and let it drop to the ground to mark the location?

When he reached the coastal road, he reined in. He ignored the thin column of white smoke ascending from Cragston Castle a mile to the left. At that moment, he was more concerned with his own troubles. Sir Fulbert's problems would have to wait until later.

The old ruins lay a quarter of a mile to the right, perched on a rise at the edge of a cliff. There was no other place in the vicinity to hide. He wondered how he passed it by earlier without stopping to search it.

"This way," he said to Arnald. He turned to the right and urged the gelding into a lope.

On approaching the ruins, he slowed his mount to a walk. At first glance, the old fortress looked like a moldering heap of stones. Over the centuries, the outer wall had crumbled into random heaps of loose gray stone. The parts of the wall that remained intact looked like jagged teeth protruding from the ground, four feet thick and twelve feet high, with huge gaps between them. Within the bailey, a single tower of mortared gray stone jutted skyward. The cylindrical structure appeared to be undamaged, except for the roof, part of which was missing. Slotted windows in the side of the tower provided a clear view in every direction.

Kyle and Arnald rode through a breach in the outer wall. They paused in the open bailey to look for any signs of life. Nothing around them moved, not a snake or a rabbit or a bird.

Even the screech of seagulls beyond the cliff's edge sounded far away.

Kyle nudged the gelding in the belly with his heels. On drawing close to the tower, his horse lifted its head, its ears pricked and its nostrils dilated. The destrier beside him reacted in the same manner.

"There is something inside," he said, reining in. "I think we should take a look." He removed the battle axe from the loop on his saddle before he dismounted.

Arnald slid to the ground and followed Kyle through the arched opening, where in former days an oak door blocked entry to a sizeable chamber that served as a storeroom. Rusted sockets set in stone on one side of the doorway marked where the iron hinges had been attached.

Kyle cast a measuring glance around the large circular chamber. The air within was cool and had a musty smell to it. The floor was littered with shards of stone and ancient detritus. The timber beams overhead supported the floor of the second level and appeared to be intact, except for rotted places in the timber planking, where light from the hole in the roof shone through.

It was unnaturally quiet inside the storeroom. Birds frequently inhabited such abandoned structures where they could nest undisturbed. The abundance of droppings was evidence of their occupancy. Yet, there was no sudden flutter of wings by feathered denizens being startled into abrupt flight by the two men who invaded their domain.

That could only mean that something or someone already scared the birds away.

"Stay here while I see what's up there," Kyle said. He started toward the inner doorway that led to the stone steps ascending to the second level. He held the axe ready in case he encountered that something or someone while he was on the way up.

Arnald drew his sword and waited as bidden at the foot of the steps.

The enclosed stairway was steep and narrow. It curved to the right by design in order to give a right-handed defender the advantage over a right-handed invader climbing the stairs.

Kyle slowly mounted each step with the axe poised for action, alert for whatever man or beast might be just around the bend. In his opinion, a beast was the least dangerous of the two.

Sufficient light came through a slotted window set high in the outer wall to dispel the gloom in the circular stairwell. He was about halfway to the top when the glitter of steel suddenly flashed in his face.

Chapter 21

Kyle jerked his head back in time to avoid the jab of a halberd. The clang of steel echoed in the empty stairwell as he raised his axe to block the next deadly thrust.

Arnald shouted something from the foot of the stairs just as Kyle thwarted another quick stab from the fifteen-inch hatchet-like blade. The ring of metal against metal drowned out the young man's words.

Someone on the steps above was clearly determined to stop him. It soon became apparent that his battle axe was no match for the long-handled halberd. In spite of that, he held his ground. Evidently, his foe meant to do the same.

He could not see the man, for the jabbing thrusts came from around the bend and kept him at a respectful distance. He was sure it was a man, because the halberd needed a man's strength to wield it effectively, especially in such close quarters. It was an ungainly weapon, with most of the weight on the bladed end.

His options were either to back down or continue to exchange blows without the hope of forward progress. As things now stood, they were stalled where they were. The only way to break the impasse was for one of them to give in to the other.

He was not about to stand down. There was only one reason his adversary would fight so hard to keep him from ascending any farther, and that was because there was something of value up there in the tower room.

His guess was that it was Joneta and Marjorie. The knowledge that they were being held captive on the second level was bad enough. The fact that neither one had cried out for help made him fear that they might already be dead. A knot of tension grew in his belly as he brooded on that disturbing thought.

"This is the only way out," he shouted up the stairwell. "You must come down sooner or later. Save us both a lot of trouble and make it sooner. Throw down and give up."

He waited for a response that never came. In the silence that followed, he heard the scuffle of shoes on the stairs above him.

He mounted the remaining steps with caution. At the top, he eased onto the landing, fully expecting the halberdier to jump out from behind the door jamb to strike at him. When nothing happened, he leaned forward to peer inside the circular tower room. His relief at seeing Joneta instantly gave way to anger.

Joneta and Marjorie stood on the far side of the chamber, clearly visible in the sunlight coming through the hole in the roof. Their mouths were gagged, and they were bound to each other with their backs together. Although their legs were free, their mobility was limited by the hemp rope hanging down on either side of an overhead beam. One end of the rope was tied around Joneta's neck, with the other end around Marjorie's neck. Their hair fell in disarray around their shoulders, and their tunics were begrimed and wrinkled. Otherwise, they appeared to be in decent condition.

Turval stood behind them, using their bodies as a shield. He held the halberd under Joneta's chin in such a way that if he shoved her forward, the sharp point would puncture her throat.

Prior to seeing the potter in the tower room, there was no reason to connect him to the murders. Now that he tipped his hand, the odd pieces of the puzzle began to come together in Kyle's mind.

The meticulous attention to detail evident in the killing of Sir Humphrey and Sir Peter was also manifest in Turval's pottery creations, which customers prized for that very reason. As for his knowledge of druidic rites, that likely came from Simon's efforts to convert him to the Order. His friendly interaction with Marjorie at the marketplace allowed him to get close enough to take her unawares, possibly on an isolated stretch of the coastal road. In addition, he could come and go anywhere in the shire under the ruse of delivering his custom-made clayware.

The answers to all the questions that perplexed Kyle earlier came to him in a split second. All, but one, that is. "Why?" he said.

"I have my reasons," Turval said.

Arnald came bounding up the steps, undoubtedly drawn by the exchange of voices. He paused on the landing to gaze with incredulity at the scene in the tower room.

"Lay down your arms or she dies," Turval said. He pressed the steel tip of the halberd deeper into Joneta's throat to prove he meant it. The finely honed point did not break her skin, but her eyes grew wider.

Arnald pushed past Kyle with his brows lowered and his sword raised. "I'll kill ye," he roared at Turval.

Kyle grabbed the young man's arm. Though he could barely contain his own fury, it was more prudent at that moment to comply with Turval's demand. "Do as he says," he commanded. He let the axe fall from his hand.

Arnald hesitated for several heartbeats before he threw down the sword with a hollow clank. He stood there glaring at the potter with his fists clenched.

Kyle mentally calculated how long it would take him to dash across the twenty-foot room. He dismissed the notion as swiftly as it came to him, for he could never reach Joneta in time to save her.

"And your sword," Turval said to Kyle, who drew the weapon and dropped it beside the axe. "That's better." He eased back on the halberd against Joneta's neck now that the intruders no longer presented an immediate threat. "I know you will not believe this, but I came here to release these ladies. Had you not shown up, they would be on their way home by now."

"You're right," Kyle said. "I don't believe you." He watched the potter like a hawk, waiting for an opportunity to overpower the man.

"It is true," Turval said. With his free hand, he began to work on the knot at Marjorie's throat.

"Why did you do it?" Kyle said.

"You would not understand," Turval said.

"Try me," Kyle said.

Turval gazed at Kyle for a long moment, as though trying to make up his mind. "I did it for my mother and my sister," he said at last.

"What happened to them?" Kyle said.

"They were raped and murdered when the infidel invaded my homeland to march on Jerusalem," Turval said bitterly. He did not seem like a foreigner, since he spoke with hardly any accent at all. Yet, he was a Saracen by his own admission, with the swarthy skin, black hair, and scimitar-like nose common to his countrymen.

"In any conflict," Kyle said, "there are always casualties of war. Some are innocent and some are not. You must not take it personal."

"Oh, but this was personal," Turval said. "The others in the village were slaughtered, but my mother and my sister were spared for the pleasure of the Rylands. When they finished abusing my kinswomen, they dispatched them, coldly and cruelly." His golden-brown eyes glittered with hatred. "I tracked them to Cragston Castle and bided my time to take revenge. It was one of your acquaintances who gave me the idea of how to go about it."

"Simon?" Kyle said.

"Aye, Simon. He told me all about the holy man in the forest, the sacred ceremonies, and other such nonsense. I did not particularly like using him because he was my friend. However, it suited my purpose to do so. I had come too far in my quest for justice to turn back."

"It is a dangerous thing," Kyle said, "to confuse vengeance with justice."

"Do not presume to judge me," Turval said, scowling fiercely. "Where was justice when Christian soldiers beat old men to death with cudgels? Where was justice when those same Christians abused our women or used our babies for target practice or threw them into the fire just to watch them roast?" His Syrian spirit burned with righteous indignation. "Tell me that."

Turval's words had the ring of truth about them, especially in light of the elder Lord Hoprig's account about the last crusade. Yet, there was a limit as to how far and on whom revenge should be taken. "These ladies had nothing to do with that," he said. "They are innocent of those crimes."

"My family was innocent, too," Turval said. "That did not keep them safe when the Rylands beset them. I am sorry about taking your lady along when I abducted Sir Fulbert's daughter. I only needed Mistress Marjorie to lure Sir Fulbert to the ruins. He was too much of a coward, however, to put himself at risk to rescue his own daughter."

"What do you mean 'was'?" Kyle said, frowning.

"Sir Fulbert should be dead by now," Turval said grimly. "Since he would not come to me, I went to him." In a matter-of-fact voice, he recounted how he tricked Sir Fulbert into going down to the courtyard, how he chained him to the post with straw laced with sulfur and oil packed around his legs, and how he set the torch in front of him to burn down within the hour. "I wanted to give him time to think about his sins." He laughed without humor. "You nearly spoiled everything when you showed up there this morning."

"Were you not concerned that someone might find Sir Fulbert and release him, like Arnald or even Mistress Ryland?"

"I was sure Arnald would not return as long as Mistress Marjorie was missing. I saw the way those two looked at each other. As for Mistress Ryland, I doubt she would lift a finger to help her husband after his despicable treatment of her over the years."

"Are you hashshashin, then?" Kyle said. "Is that what this is about?"

"Do not insult me," Turval said. He spat on the dusty floor. "The hashshashin kill for money. They smoke drugs to dull their senses, as well as their conscience. The hashshashin are known for their ruthlessness. Christians on crusade in my country, though, were much worse than them. Christian soldiers called themselves Knights of Christ, yet they spilled innocent blood in the name of their God."

"He is your God, too."

"Allah would never approve of what Christian soldiers did to Saracen women and children. I wanted Sir Fulbert to suffer the loss of his family, just like I suffered the loss of mine." He gave Kyle a tight smile. "Did you know the Rylands were cursed with ill luck as long as they resided at Cragston Castle?"

"I heard about it," Kyle said.

"At first, I thought I might use that to dispose of them."

"Are you the one who poisoned the feed?" Kyle said.

"I am," Turval said. "That did not seem to faze them. They just took their trade elsewhere. I had to come up with something unique to get their attention. The idea came to me when Simon told me about the threefold death ritual. The Rylands were familiar with it, too, which meant each of them would know that, sooner or later, he would be next."

"Very clever," Kyle said.

"It was brilliant," Turval said with pride.

"So you killed Sir Humphrey first," Kyle said.

"He was easy," Turval said, not in the least contrite. "In fact, he even turned his back to me, as though he knew what was coming."

"And Sir Peter?" Kyle said.

"He was a tough one. I could never catch him alone. Only by chance did I see him on one of his rare visits to the tavern. I followed him into the stable, but an English soldier by the name of Blackwell was waiting for him there. He and Sir Peter got into an argument that came to blows. They ended up choking each other. While Sir Peter was still dazed, I slipped a linen noose around his neck. I had to knock Blackwell on the head to keep him insensible, so that by the time he awoke, the deed was done."

"Well, well," Kyle said. "I guess Blackwell was telling the truth for once in his life." His hope that the phosphorescent substance would lead to the killer did not work out, for it seemed that neither Turval nor Blackwell came in contact with the smudge of it on Sir Peter's cotte. Even so, there was still one question that needed to be addressed. "What about Rolf?" he said, looking the potter straight in the eyes. "Did you kill him, too?"

Turval tugged the rope free from Marjorie's neck. "Of course not," he said. "I had nothing against the fellow. Why do you ask?"

"Never mind," Kyle said.

Turval moved Joneta and Marjorie several shuffling paces to the left, after which he leaned the halberd against the stone wall behind him. Before any of them realized his purpose, he gave the women a mighty shove onto a section of the floor where the wood was badly rotted.

The decayed timber planks gave way beneath Joneta and Marjorie's combined weight. Joneta screamed as she dropped through the rotten flooring up to her waist, dragging Marjorie along with her. The only thing that kept the two of them from falling through was a thick timber beam under the floor that had not quite rotted all the way across. While Joneta dangled in midair, Marjorie lay with her rigid legs braced against the crumbling beam. Neither of them moved a muscle for fear of plunging eighteen feet to the stone floor below.

With his heart in his throat, Kyle leaped forward half a step ahead of Arnald to render assistance. Neither paid any heed to Turval, who bolted across the room toward the stairwell.

Kyle assessed the situation in the blink of an eye. The rope on the overhead beam was still tied around Joneta's neck. If he tried to pull on the loose end to haul her aloft, he would strangle her in the process. The only other way was to climb out on the half-rotted floor beam to get to them. He was too heavy to risk it, for the beam looked unsound. Should it break under his weight, he would fall to his death, taking Joneta and Marjorie with him.

His gaze flicked to Arnald, who was smaller and lighter than he was and thus more suited to the job. He picked up the halberd and laid the butt end on the solid part of the flooring to make a slender but sturdy bridge to the damaged beam.

"Arnald," he said. "Lean on this to get as close as you can to Joneta. Untie the rope from her neck, and then re-tie it to the one binding her and Marjorie together. Make sure the knot is secure before you come away."

He held his breath as he watched Arnald crawl forward on hands and knees to get to Joneta. After completing the task at hand, the young man backed slowly onto the sturdy flooring behind him.

Kyle shifted the rope into position on the overhead beam to

avoid dragging Joneta sideways, for that would scrape her body across the jagged edges of the splintered wood.

When all was ready, he and Arnald slowly hauled on the rope until they lifted Joneta clear of the gaping hole. Marjorie helped by pushing against the rotted beam with her feet.

Kyle kept steady pressure on the rope while Arnald swung them clear of the damaged area. After letting them down with care onto the solid part of the floor, he drew his dirk and hurried over to help Arnald cut them loose.

"My baby is sick," Joneta said the instant her gag was removed. "I must see to him."

"Bruce should be just fine by now," he said. "John went out there yesterday to tend to him. Meg and Derek are doing well, too."

"Oh, thank God," she said. Her face crumpled as she gave way to tears. She flung her arms around Kyle's neck and sobbed into his chest. "I was so worried," she said, her voice muffled against his leather scale armor.

"I've been searching for you for two days," he said, enfolding her in his arms. His heart swelled with joy now that he found her at last. His happiness was short-lived, though, for it gave way to a rush of genuine concern for her welfare. "Are you injured? Did he hurt you?"

She shook her head, clearly unwilling to move out of his embrace.

"I am sorry this happened to you," he said. "It must have been awful." He held her at arm's length to assess the damage from the fall through the wooden floor.

Her face was ashen beneath the streaks of dust and grime. Her hands shook, which was understandable after her trying experience. There were superficial scrapes and scratches on her legs below the hem of her tunic, but none that appeared to be critical.

He turned to look at Marjorie to gauge the extent of her injuries. There were no visible wounds on her that he could see. He did notice, however, that she welcomed Arnald's attentions, which made him wonder whether the young man was more to her than just the hired help.

"How did ye find us?" Joneta said. "Was it because of the ribbon?"

"Aye," Kyle said.

"It was all I could think to do at the time," she said.

"I am glad you did," he said. "That is what led me here."

She put a hand up to smooth the tangle of hair on her head, as though suddenly aware of her disheveled state. "I must look a fright," she said.

"You look beautiful," he said with fervor.

"That is very kind of ye to say so. Nonetheless, I think the ribbon would help. I'll take it now, if ye don't mind."

"I don't have it," he said. He told her how he'd chanced upon the young girl who picked it up on the road, and how he'd had to promise that she could keep the ribbon before she would tell him where she found it.

"Oh," she said.

In his experience, that simple word, when used by a female, could mean any number of things. Depending on the inflection, it may indicate enlightenment, curiosity, or disappointment. He, like most males in a similar situation, had no clue which of those she meant to convey. Since her gold ribbon was now gone forever and he was the cause of it, albeit unintentionally, he could only conclude that it was most likely an expression of disappointment.

"I shall buy you another ribbon," he said. "Better still, I shall buy you as many as you want."

She rewarded him with a luminescent smile. "I'd like that," she said.

Gratified that he read the signs right this time, he gazed into her hazel eyes. "I feel like I let you down," he said. "What could I have done to prevent this from befalling to you?"

"The fault was mine and Marjorie's," she said. "We were on the way to fetch Master John for the baby when we found the potter lying there in the middle of the road. We didn't know if he was dead or what. The minute we stopped to help him, he accosted Marjorie with a knife. He threatened to kill her unless I went along with him."

"It's over now," he said. "You are safe."

"Did those things really happen?" she said, holding his gaze. "During the crusade, I mean."

"I never went on crusade, so I cannot say. On the other hand, some who did go to the Holy Land came back with tales of the savage and wanton behavior of Christian soldiers there."

"How dreadful," she said.

"Come along," he said. He gathered up his sword and his axe. "It is time we left this sad place."

"Indeed," she said. "It seems like forever since I felt a cool breeze on my face."

"Are you able to make it down on your own?" he said. "Do you want me to carry you?"

"That would be mighty gallant," she said, obviously pleased with his offer. "It isn't necessary, though. I can walk."

"Of course, you can walk," he said with a mischievous grin.

He sheathed his sword and handed the axe to her. Before she could protest, he scooped her up in his arms. It did his heart good to hear her laugh once again as he carried her over to the stairwell. She clung to his neck as he descended the circular steps to the storeroom below. When he walked out into the bailey, he felt the tension drain from her body now that she was no longer confined in the makeshift tower prison.

"I must leave you now," he said, setting her down gently.

"Turval is getting farther away every minute I tarry here."

She frowned as her feet touched the ground. "Was he not justified in what he did?" she said as she handed the axe to him.

"Possibly," he said. "But not in the way he went about it."

He went to look for the gelding, which he found dozing in the shade around the side of the tower. The white warhorse was nowhere in sight. He slipped the axe handle through the leather loop on the saddle before he led his mount around to the front.

At that moment, Arnald and Marjorie stepped through the tower doorway, their hands joined and their eyes on each other. She looked tired and worn, although she seemed to perk up in the fresh air outside.

"Turval took the destrier," Kyle said to Arnald. "I need to go after him. Watch over the ladies while I'm gone." To Joneta, he said. "Will you be all right?" He took her hand and kissed the back of it. "I can take you home right now, if you prefer."

"Are ye certain Bruce is well?" she said.

"John assured me of the baby's full recovery," he said.

"In that case, I'll be fine," she said.

He swung up into the saddle and, with a parting glance at her, he turned the gelding's head to the south.

He rode at a steady lope along the coastal road, headed for Cragston Castle, where he figured Turval would go to make sure that Sir Fulbert was dead. He did not expect to capture the man there. He only hoped the pause in the potter's flight would buy him a little time to catch up.

Before long, he topped the rise that led up to the castle. The taint of smoke hung in the air, although the white column he'd seen earlier no longer rose from within the surrounding walls. The land to the south spread out before him, a vast wasteland of scrub bushes and rock formations, windswept and desolate, unfit for habitation except by the hardiest of wild creatures.

He was about to turn onto the causeway to approach the

castle when he spotted the destrier some distance ahead of him. The bright white of its coat in the early afternoon sun stood out against the brown shrubs that clung to life on the open heath.

He estimated that Turval had a two-mile lead on him. His only hope of catching up was if the man stayed on the southward road, which followed the coastline in a sweeping curve along the cliffs.

He urged the gelding down the hill at a gallop. Instead of taking the road, he cut across the rough terrain at an angle to shorten the distance between him and the potter.

With the furious pounding of hooves in his ears, he rapidly closed the intervening gap. The grueling pace soon took a toll on the gelding, for lather began to slick its neck and flanks. White foam gathered around the bit and flew from its mouth.

Turval glanced behind him, only to see Kyle bearing down on him. He kicked his mount's belly to quicken its pace. As the deputy came alongside of him, he leaned to the right to avoid being pulled from the saddle.

The destrier, trained to respond to the pressure of its rider's knees, veered to the right.

The sudden change of direction took Turval out of Kyle's reach. He turned the gelding to the right, urging his horse to greater speed to recover lost ground. As he drew near, the destrier swerved away once again.

Since the two of them could continue the game of cat-and-mouse until both horses dropped from exhaustion, it was time to employ a different strategy. Each time Turval altered his course, Kyle maneuvered the gelding so as to stay on the inland side. His goal was to herd the destrier ever closer to the cliff's edge until there was nowhere else to go.

Turval soon noticed that he was being cornered. He drove his heels into the destrier's flanks, intent on running Kyle over in a desperate bid for freedom. The great warhorse took off like a shot, thundering straight toward the gelding.

Kyle kicked his mount's sides while pulling back on the reins to make the horse rear up. The destrier instinctively shied away from the gelding's flailing hooves, slowing its pace in the process.

While Turval struggled to bring the warhorse under control, Kyle launched himself from the saddle to drag the man to the ground. The pair of them rolled together on the rocks and thistles, coming to a stop in a prickly shrub that scratched their faces and hands. Both men scrambled to their feet.

Turval pulled out his dagger and went into a crouch, ready to strike. "Stay back," he said. "I do not want to hurt you."

Kyle drew his sword and leveled the blade at Turval's chest. "I admire your optimism, misplaced though it is," he said. He took a step forward, forcing the man back a pace. "I ought to run you through for what you did to my lady."

"She came to no harm," Turval said.

"No thanks to you," Kyle said. "If you spoke the truth about what the Rylands did to your family, your grievance has merit in the eyes of the law. It would have been on your side, had you challenged each of the Rylands to a fair fight in front of witnesses. Instead, you chose to pursue a course outside the law. Because of that, you must face the consequences of your actions. Now, throw down and give over."

"Look at me," Turval said, indicating his modest stature. "Do you really think I could prevail in single combat against seasoned warriors like the Rylands?"

"The law allows those who cannot defend themselves to enlist a champion to do battle for them. As things now stand by your own admission, you took the lives of Sir Humphrey and Sir Peter in a malicious and covert manner. If Sir Fulbert did in fact die by your design, then you are accountable for his death, too. In addition, you are guilty of kidnapping, along with the willful destruction of valuable livestock. I have no other choice but to place you under arrest to stand trial for your criminal deeds. Drop your weapon, and come with me."

"Nay," Turval said, shaking his head. "I will not endure the shame of hanging from the gallows for doing what was just and fair to avenge my family." He swung around and ran toward the cliff. When he reached the edge, he trotted along the rim, as though looking for a way to escape.

Kyle hurried after Turval, trying to intercept the man before he found one of the paths that smugglers used to carry contraband down the face of the cliff to the caves below. If anyone knew where those pathways were, the potter would, since he and Simon had been smuggling goods into the shire for quite some time now.

"One of the men you killed was innocent, you know," Kyle said in a loud voice.

Turval paused in his flight. "You are mistaken," he said, turning to face Kyle. "All three Rylands got what they deserved."

"Sir Humphrey was not a party to the abuse and murder of your kinswomen," Kyle said, coming to a halt. He was so close to the edge that he could hear the surf pounding against the rocks far below.

"How can you be certain?" Turval said. "You were not there at the time."

"So says an eyewitness who was with Sir Humphrey in the Holy Land."

"Sir Humphrey took part in the crusade. That makes him as guilty as Sir Peter and Sir Fulbert."

"I do not deny that," Kyle said. "However, he did not harm your mother or your sister. And there is something else you should know about Sir Humphrey. He was a true penitent. If Allah can show mercy to a repentant sinner, should you not also?"

"How do I know what you say is true?" Turval said.

"After we pulled Sir Humphrey from the river, we discovered that he wore a hair shirt under his clothing. For a Christian, it is a form of penance. I saw it on him myself. Later, Rolf told me that Sir Humphrey came to him seeking absolution for sins committed during the crusade."

"You lie," Turval said, his upper lip curled in contempt.

"Why should I?" Kyle said. "I have nothing to gain from doing so."

Turval appeared to contemplate the matter. "I did not know that about Sir Humphrey," he said with a note of regret in his voice. He looked down at the dagger in his hand. After a brief moment, he slipped it into the sheath on his belt.

The remorse on Turval's face prompted Kyle to walk toward him. Perhaps now the man would come along quietly.

Turval took a step back. He was already so close to the edge of the precipice that the loose shale there crumbled under his feet. Down he went, clawing at the sloping face of the cliff with both hands to slow his descent.

Kyle sprang forward, covering the distance between them in four bounding steps. He reached the rim just as Turval's head disappeared below ground level. He fell to his knees and leaned over with his hand thrust downward.

Turval lifted an arm at full stretch to latch onto the proffered hand. The movement, although slight, dislodged his toehold from his precarious perch on the rock face. His legs swung free, sending a hail of stones and dirt down to the surging water of the incoming tide far below him.

The sudden tug of Turval's weight on Kyle's arm pulled him forward. He flopped onto his stomach, dropping his sword to dig his fingers and the toes of his boots into the earth to keep from being dragged over the edge.

The thud of his own heart deafened him to the incessant crash of the waves. He lay flat on the ground, with his head and one shoulder protruding over the void, his hand clasped around Turval's in a desperate handshake. With each second that passed, the man seemed to grow heavier. He gritted his teeth as he attempted to haul up the dead weight on the end of his arm.

He managed to raise Turval several inches before his grip on the potter's sweaty palm began to slip.

Turval evidently felt it, too, for his eyes flared with fear. "May Allah forgive me," he said, holding Kyle's gaze.

Kyle tried to lift Turval still higher, even as his fingers slowly slid through the man's grasp. He did what he could to hold on, but to no avail. "I'm sorry," he said as the potter's hand finally slipped out of his own.

Turval skidded backward on loose shale down the steep incline, which ended in a sheer drop. He plummeted over the edge in a shower of rocks toward certain death on the granite stones at the base of the cliff.

A surging mass of water came crashing in a split second before the potter smashed onto the rocks. The frenzied surf enveloped his body and swept him away.

Kyle watched the man disappear beneath the waves, unsure whether he felt relief or outrage that his quarry slipped the figurative noose. He climbed to his feet, his eyes trained on the restless sea shimmering in the sunlight as he waited for the body to reappear.

After a moment, Turval's head broke the surface. He bobbed around like a piece of flotsam, treading water until the current swept him out of sight around an outcrop of land to the south.

Kyle stood there with the breeze ruffling his tawny hair, looking out over the firth in astonishment, for what he witnessed was nothing short of a miracle.

It was still possible, though, that Turval was spared one dire fate, only to suffer another by drowning. Then again, he might wash up on shore farther along the coast, alive and well and free to start over somewhere else, now that his loved ones had been avenged.

Kyle turned away from the edge of the cliff, aware that he would never know if Turval's God did indeed forgive him or whether the man simply possessed the devil's own luck.

CHAPTER 22
EPILOGUE

Kyle returned his sword to the sheath at his hip and mounted the gelding. He tried to catch the destrier, but his attempts to grasp the trailing reins spooked the skittish creature and sent it running across the heath in the direction of Cragston Castle.

He followed at a slower pace, keeping to the road where the ground was smoother. Since the destrier would likely head for the castle stable, he would retrieve it and bring it to the ruins for Arnald and Marjorie. After that, he would be free to take Joneta home. Then, he would be able to finish what he set out to do yesterday.

On the way to Cragston Castle, he turned his mind to the matters at hand. Now that the identity of the man who killed the Rylands was known, Blackwell could be released from the dungeon. Still, all was not well just yet, for Rolf's murder remained unsolved. The potter appeared to be innocent of that particular crime, mostly because there was no reason for the man to lie about that, while admitting to everything else.

Based on the evidence found at the scene, Rolf was undoubtedly killed by someone who knew him well. Simon could have disposed of the old man in order to assume the coveted role of Master Druid. However, the acolyte's grief at Rolf's passing appeared to be genuine. More than likely, it was somebody who feared the old man, or better still, who entrusted the old man with an incriminating secret, only to regret doing so later.

When he reached the rise, he rode up the causeway leading

to the castle drawbridge. On entering the courtyard, the stench of burnt flesh assaulted his nostrils. The smell evidently unsettled the destrier, for the nervous animal led Arnald, who was trying to catch its bridle, on a merry chase around the cobbled yard.

Across the way, Joneta stood beside Marjorie in front of the blackened wreck of the pigpen. The two of them appeared to be consoling Mistress Ryland, who looked rather haggard, even from several yards away. Hoprig and Vinewood were there, too, standing slightly apart from the women.

Kyle rode across the courtyard to where the small group was gathered. As he drew near, the charred form of a body became discernable against the blackened stump of the sty's corner post, a silent witness as to the truth of Turval's claim.

Joneta greeted him as he climbed down from the saddle.

"We decided to walk here," she said. "It wasn't that far." She searched his face, as though looking for the answer to an unasked question. "He got away, didn't he?"

"Not exactly," Kyle said. He told her how the potter fell off the cliff, only to be swept away in the surf. He then turned to Mistress Ryland, who leaned on her daughter's arm for support. "My condolence on your husband's passing."

"Thank you," Mistress Ryland said. She retained her poise, despite the smudges of soot on her face and the fire damage to her skirts. "He was a hard man to live with, but he did not deserve to die like that."

"I'm not so sure," Marjorie said, her lips compressed in anger.

"Marjorie!" Mistress Ryland said, appalled. "You must not say such things about your father."

"He can't hurt me now, Mother," Marjorie said. "He can't hurt you, either. Go ahead and tell the deputy what you told me."

Mistress Ryland bowed her head, as though from shame. Her

silence prompted Marjorie to speak in her stead.

"Mother said that Father came into the main hall yesterday evening with blood all over his clothing. When she asked him where it came from, he refused to answer. What is more, he burned the stained garments in the fireplace, as though he did not want them found."

"Did Sir Fulbert seem agitated at the time?" Kyle said.

"Very much so," Mistress Ryland said.

"What time did he go out earlier?" Kyle said.

"About mid-afternoon," Mistress Ryland said. "He had been drinking heavily all morning. By the time he left, he was in a black mood."

"Could he have gone hunting?" Kyle said. "Field dressing an animal would account for the blood on his clothes."

"There was more blood than would come from gutting a rabbit in the forest," Mistress Ryland said. "Besides, he was in no fit state to hunt. On those rare occasions when he did go, he took the game he killed directly to the kitchen for Arnald or his mother to clean and dress."

"So, where do you think the blood came from?" Kyle said.

"Master Rolf was murdered yesterday," Mistress Ryland said. "I fear that my husband might have done it."

"I do not doubt that Sir Fulbert was capable of murder," Kyle said. "But why Rolf? I thought they were friends."

"My husband had many secrets," Mistress Ryland said. "Master Rolf knew them all. Is that not reason enough?"

"Did Sir Fulbert fear that Rolf would expose him as a druid?" Kyle said. "Rolf would never do that since he himself was one."

"My husband did many things in that role," Mistress Ryland said. "I am ashamed to say that my son did them, too."

"What sorts of things?" Kyle said.

"Terrible things," Mistress Ryland said. "Twice a year, they met late at night. There is an oak grove deep in Cragston Forest where they gathered to hold their ceremonies."

"Rolf told me they met there at certain times of the year to harvest mistletoe."

"Did Rolf tell you what else they did during those ceremonies, particularly to the lone woodsman or roving tinker whom they abducted? They preyed on that sort of man because his disappearance would go unnoticed. They disposed of the body afterward in such a way that no one would ever find him."

Kyle blinked at Mistress Ryland, trying to take it in. "Human sacrifice?" he said, stunned. "Are you sure?"

"Absolutely," Mistress Ryland said, nodding her head.

"Why did you not tell me this sooner?" Kyle said.

"My husband threatened to kill me if I breathed a word of it to anyone," Mistress Ryland said.

"What about Rolf?" Kyle said. "Did he not try to intervene?"

"Rolf conducted those rituals," Mistress Ryland said. "Humphrey was the only one who opposed them. He disapproved of what they did, yet he would never turn them over to the law. The ties of brotherhood were too strong among them."

"And Simon?" Kyle said. "Was he also a party to it?"

"Of course, he was," Mistress Ryland said. "He learned the druidic arts at Rolf's knee."

"At least he won't get away," Kyle said. "I know where he will be until dawn."

"Simon will be long gone by then," Mistress Ryland said. "Too many people are privy to his secrets. It would be risky for him to remain in the shire now."

"You may be right," Kyle said. "Prior Drumlay was, too, about the druids, that is. Rolf had me completely fooled. Too bad there will be no retribution against any of them for their deeds. With the exception of Simon, they are all now far beyond the reach of English law. The only good to come out of this is that Cragston Forest is no longer haunted." He glanced over at the rigid corpse before his gaze returned to Mistress Ryland. "I hate to intrude upon your grief. However, I will need a wagon to transport the body to the priory. Do you have one you can spare?"

"Of course," Mistress Ryland said. "Arnald will hitch it up for you."

Arnald, who caught the destrier and put it in the stable by that time, walked over to stand beside Marjorie.

"The minute we bury our dead," Marjorie said to her mother, "let us pack up and depart from this accursed place. Those Scots can have their ancestral home back. It was wrong to take it from them in the first place. Good riddance, I say."

"Oh, dear," Mistress Ryland said with a worried frown on her round face. "We ought not to travel all the way to England on our own. The roads are so dangerous these days."

Marjorie and Arnald exchanged a knowing look. "We won't be alone, Mother," she said. "Arnald can come with us for protection. What do you say to that?"

Mistress Ryland cast a dubious glance at the groom. "What about his mother?" she said. "He can't just abandon her here to fend for herself."

"She can come, too," Marjorie said.

"I suppose it will be all right, then," Mistress Ryland said. She scrubbed a hand across tired eyelids.

"Come, Mother," Marjorie said. "You look weary. Let us go inside. There is no need for you to fret anymore. It's over."

"Aye," Mistress Ryland said, her gaze on the charred remains of her husband. Grim satisfaction flashed in her hazel eyes for an instant. "It is now."

Hoprig parked the wagon in front of the mortuary chapel on the priory grounds. He climbed down from the high seat and approached Prior Drumlay, who waited for him near the arched doorway.

"Who is it this time?" the prior said.

"Sir Fulbert Ryland," Hoprig said.

"Dead?" the prior said.

"Very," Hoprig said. He walked around to the wagon bed and drew back a length of cloth to reveal the soot-blackened corpse beneath.

The mouth gaped open in the rictus of a scream, showing a full set of teeth. There were bits of metal here and there that stuck to the burnt flesh shriveled against the bones. The only way to tell it was a male was from the breadth of the shoulders and length of the body. Although stiff and brittle, it was still in one piece from head to toe.

The prior gazed upon the charred remains. "Not a pretty sight," he said, wrinkling his nose at the foul smell. "I've rarely seen worse."

"I was there when it happened," Hoprig said.

"Oh?" the prior said, looking at him with keen interest.

Hoprig went on to relate in detail everything that led up to Sir Fulbert's death at Cragston Castle.

"Who would do a thing like that?" the prior said.

Hoprig told him about Turval the potter's retribution against the Rylands.

The prior whistled long and low. "Ye just never know about folks these days," he said. "How is the widow holding up?"

"She seems to be doing well," Hoprig said. "She and her daughter are going back to England directly after the funeral."

"That is a wise decision," the prior said. "Nothing good can come from staying at Cragston Castle."

"There's more to tell," Hoprig said. He reported what he heard about druidic ceremonies being conducted in the forest.

"How dare they infest my precinct," the prior said, burning

with vengeful zeal. "I'll root them out, every one of them." He glanced down at the burnt corpse. "That reminds me. Sir Fulbert cannot be buried in consecrated ground. Neither can Sir Peter."

"What shall I do with the body?" Hoprig said.

"Leave it here," the prior said. "I will dispose of it as I see fit."

Hoprig unhitched his chestnut mare from the wagon and rode down Harbour Street to the garrison, glad to get back to the peace and quiet of his mundane existence. Perhaps he would apply for a transfer to a garrison in some other shire, partly because he could use a change of scenery and partly because there were too many things around here that reminded him of Isabel.

The minute he entered the courtyard, the officer of the watch came out to meet him.

"Sir Percy wants to see you," the officer said, squinting against the afternoon sun.

"Very well," Hoprig said. He went on to the stable to feed and water his horse. He took off his bull-hide armor and left it in the stall before he went out to the well in the courtyard to wash the grime from his face and hands. After that, he crossed over to the main hall.

He climbed the stairs to the second level and went down the long corridor to the open doorway at the end. He cut through the small anteroom and knocked on the door jamb of the office beyond.

Sir Percy sat at his desk in a midnight blue cotte with his back to the window.

John Walter Langton, the castellan's former clerk, occupied one of the two chairs in front of the marble-topped desk. He wore the long black robe of his priestly office of Canon of Lincoln and Lord High Chancellor to the King of England.

Too late, Hoprig wished he had taken the time to shave the stubble from his chin and to change out of his dusty shirt and leggings into more suitable clothing.

"Ah, Lord Hoprig," Sir Percy said, turning his head toward the entryway. "Come in." He gestured for Hoprig to sit in the chair beside Walter. "I've been expecting you."

Hoprig did as he was bidden under the assumption that he was summoned to report on the day's events. He waited politely for the cue to begin. The subject of Sir Percy's conversation took him completely by surprise.

"I heard about your father's reversal of fortune after the last crusade," Sir Percy said.

"He went broke and died friendless because of it," Hoprig said with a bitter edge to his voice. "There is no other way to put it."

Sir Percy cleared his throat, as though uncomfortable at hearing such plain speech. "Well," he said. "It seems you no longer share that misfortune."

"Which misfortune is that, m'lord?" Hoprig said. "Being broke or friendless?"

"Both, I suppose," Sir Percy said.

"How is that?" Hoprig said.

"You have a patroness," Sir Percy said.

Although his face remained expressionless, Hoprig was completely taken aback by the news. "Who might that be?" he said.

"Lady Catherine de Salamanca," Sir Percy said. "I received a letter from her the other day. In fact, it came in the packet you delivered to me after the trial on Saturday." He gave Hoprig a bland smile. "Forgive me for not revealing the contents to you sooner, but organizing the hunt for Mistress Marjorie Ryland and the other lady took most of my time. I am sure you understand."

300

Hoprig did not recall Sir Percy being involved in the search at all. He thought it prudent, however, not to contradict the man at that particular moment. "Did Lady Catherine disclose why I was chosen to be the recipient of her good will?" he said.

"It is more than good will," Sir Percy said. He unfolded the sheet of vellum and removed a piece of jewelry. "She bequeathed this to you." He held up a fine silver chain from which hung a pendant studded with diamonds. The polished surface of each precious gem sent splinters of light dancing around the room.

Hoprig stared at the pendant. Such a tiny thing, yet so much hinged upon it. His mind raced with possibilities. The diamonds alone would fetch a good price. Set as they were in the silver frame, the piece was worth a small fortune. The money from the sale could easily fund a one-way voyage to Spain.

"What do you plan to do with it?" Sir Percy said.

"I'll think of something," Hoprig said. He was not about to bare his soul to a stranger.

Walter spoke up for the first time since Hoprig entered the room. "That pendant is quite valuable," he said. "You could purchase many things with it, including a release from the king's service."

A sense of foreboding came over Hoprig, for he feared that Sir Percy and the Lord High Chancellor invited him there to put him to the test. "Why would I buy a release?" he said. "I am an English soldier, loyal to the King's cause."

"Perhaps you should speak to the young lady," Walter said. "She can be very persuasive." He got up and left the room.

"What young lady?" Hoprig said, puzzled.

"You'll see," Sir Percy said.

Hoprig shifted in the wooden chair, for he found it difficult to relax under Sir Percy's speculative gaze.

A moment later, Walter came back into the room with Isabel. She wore the belted yellow linen tunic she had made herself, the one with white embroidery at the neck.

Hoprig rose abruptly to his feet, his jaw slack in wonder, at once shocked and thrilled to see her.

She flew into his arms and clung to him.

He crushed her in his embrace, gratified to the very depths of his soul that what was lost to him was now restored. In that instant, his despair and loneliness changed to hope and joy. "You came back," he whispered in her hair. He swallowed hard to dislodge the lump that formed in his throat. "I missed you so."

"I missed you, too," she said. The last word ended in a sob.

He leaned back slightly to look into her face. "How did you get here?" he said

"When we left on Friday night," she said with a sniffle, "we sailed a day's journey down the coast before my lady had enough of my constant weeping over you. She instructed the ship's master to turn around and go back to Ayr. We arrived this morning. I went looking for you, but you were out on patrol. This kind man,"—here she indicated Walter—"arranged for me to wait in a room down the hall until you returned."

"Don't go back to the ship," he said with fervor. "Stay here with me. I will provide for you and Owen."

"In her letter," Sir Percy said, intruding into the conversation, "Lady Catherine tenders an offer worth considering."

Hoprig stepped back from Isabel. He held onto her hand, for he was unwilling to let go of her completely, even for a moment. "What is the offer?" he said.

"Lady Catherine wants to employ you as an armed escort," Sir Percy said. "One who will ensure her safety and that of her traveling companions throughout the voyage and during the overland journey afterward. The shipmaster was to dock at Weymouth to await your arrival there. The arduous trek to the southern coast of England is no longer necessary now that the ship is here in our harbor."

Hoprig frowned as he considered Lady Catherine's proposal. It sounded like a viable solution, for that way, he and Isabel could stay together. Even so, that only took care of the travel arrangements. There was still one more obstacle in his path. "What will it cost to obtain a release from the King's army?" he said.

Sir Percy's eyes strayed to the diamond pendant before returning to its new owner.

"I see," Hoprig said.

The price was unreasonably high, and Sir Percy knew it. At that moment, though, Hoprig was willing to pay any amount to be with the woman he loved. Sir Percy knew that, too. In fact, he counted on it.

"As you wish, then," Hoprig said. "Consider it yours."

An expression of immense satisfaction came over Sir Percy's face as his hand closed possessively over the pendant.

"Well, Lord Hoprig," Walter said. "How did it feel to be rich again, even if it was for but a moment?"

"No different from being poor, actually," Hoprig said.

Walter gazed with approval upon Isabel, who remained at Hoprig's side in supportive silence the whole time. "At least you are not friendless, too." He turned to Sir Percy. "Have your clerk draw up a document attesting to the legality of Lord Hoprig's resignation."

"I no longer have a clerk," Sir Percy said dryly. "Remember?"

"Not to worry," Walter said. "I shall draw it up myself." To Hoprig, he said: "Come back in half an hour. The document should be ready for your signature by then."

An hour later, Hoprig walked across the garrison drawbridge with Isabel beside him and his chestnut mare on a lead rope behind him. All of his worldly possessions, which consisted of a change of clothes, his armor, his tack, and his gear, were tied to the saddle. It felt good to be free from servitude as an English soldier, with back wages in his coin purse and good prospects for employment ahead.

As they headed down the street toward the harbor, Macalister the blacksmith rounded the corner on his dappled gray. The minute he saw them, he rode purposefully in their direction.

When he drew near, he reined in before them. After giving Isabel a cordial nod, he turned to Hoprig. "I never did thank ye for speaking up for me at the trial," he said. "I want ye to know that I really appreciate what ye did.

"I could not do otherwise for a man I knew to be innocent," Hoprig said.

"If I can ever return the favor," Macalister said, "just let me know."

"No need for that," Hoprig said. "I was glad to do it."

Macalister looked down at Hoprig with a thoughtful expression on his bearded face. "For a Southron," he said, "ye are not such a bad fellow after all."

"Neither are you," Hoprig said, returning his gaze. "For a Scotsman."

They said their good-byes and parted ways.

Hoprig and Isabel continued on to the waterfront, where they would board the ship that would take them far from this troubled land. No matter what the future held for them, from now on, they would face it together.

On the way to Joneta's house, Kyle kept the gelding to a walk to give himself time to think. He had much to say to her and a short time in which to do it. Once she was reunited with her family, he would be hard pressed to find a private moment with her, and rightly so.

She sat behind him on the gelding's rump. He liked the way

her arms felt around his waist. He would like it even better without the leather scale armor covering his chest and back. That, unfortunately, was a necessary part of life in that day and age.

On entering the woodland, he reined in. "I would like to talk to you," he said, looking at her over his shoulder.

"Go ahead," she said from her perch behind him. "I can hear ye just fine."

"May I speak to you face to face?" he said.

"As ye wish," she said.

He grasped her arm to help her slide to the ground. He swung down from the saddle and captured her hand in both of his. "That's better," he said.

They stood gazing at each other there in the cool shade of the trees. A blue jay squawked overhead. The iron rings on the bridle jingled as the gelding chewed on tender foliage protruding into the pathway. The earthy scent of green moss and decayed leaves hung in the air.

"I love you," he said.

"I love ye, too," she said. "Is that what ye wanted to tell me?"

"Not quite," he said. He brought her hand to his lips to kiss her open palm. "While you were missing, I had a lot of time to think."

"Me, too," she said, caressing his cheek with the hand he just kissed.

He drew in a deep breath to steady the shaking of his knees. "For a while," he said, "I thought you might be gone forever. That reminded me of how short life can be. It is far too precious to waste a minute of it. Times are hard, and getting by each day is even harder. Yet there are moments of joy between the difficult ones that make it all worthwhile." His heart began to thud in his chest as he gazed into her hazel eyes. "I want to share those precious moments with you, and all the other ones for the rest of my life, if you'll have me."

"Kyle Shaw," she said, visibly pleased. "Are ye proposing marriage to me?"

"I am," he said. Now that he spoke the words, he could breathe again.

He removed the tiny box from his pouch and opened it to present the emerald ring to her. The polished green stone glittered even in the muted light under the trees.

"Oh, that is so exquisite," she said, staring at the ring. "If it were me alone, I would accept yer offer in a heartbeat." She let out her breath in a heavy sigh. "As it is, I have a son to rear and property to manage."

"Let me share that burden with you," he said. "Bruce needs a father. I could never take the place of his real father, but I could teach him the things a boy needs to know."

She lowered her gaze to avoid his pale blue eyes. "I have a confession to make," she said.

He placed his bent index finger under her chin to lift her head. "I don't care what it is," he said. "It won't make any difference to me."

"It's not that kind of confession," she said. "Ever since I first laid eyes on ye, I've wanted ye for my own. I still do."

"But?" he said in anguished anticipation of a negative response.

"No 'but,' " she said with a smile. "I'll take ye as husband, and gladly, too." She plucked the ring from the box and slipped it on the heart finger of her left hand.

"You are a little vixen for keeping me in suspense," he said. He swept her up in his arms and swung her around in a complete circle before putting her down. He held her against his heart and kissed her soundly.

Nothing could spoil his happiness, neither yesterday's regrets nor tomorrow's troubles. He was with the woman he loved and who loved him in return. At that moment, that was all that mattered.

ABOUT THE AUTHOR

E.R. Dillon was born in New Orleans and still lives in Louisiana, although she now resides on the north shore of Lake Pontchartrain. Her acquaintance with certain aspects of the law comes from working for civil and criminal attorneys for many years. As a medieval history buff and a fan of mysteries, she likes to incorporate both elements into her stories. Her current work in progress is a third novel in her historical mystery series set in thirteenth-century Scotland featuring Deputy Sheriff Kyle Shaw.